THE ROAD TO SELF- ACCEPTANCE

RENIER NIENABER

CONTENTS

Sometimes when you look at yourself in the mirror, you ask yourself what you see, or what you want to see, but somehow you know that you will never be able to be that person. Many questions arise in your mind about who you are, but you are unable to answer them.

This is something every teenager has to deal with, whether they want to or not. It's just one of those things, like the air we breathe, the food we eat or the people we have to deal with every day of our lives.

CHAPTER 1

What a beautiful morning it had been. The yellow sun hung high in the sky. The sky was without clouds; it looked like a field of turquoise without any ripples. Birds sung their beautiful lullabies atop the green trees that surrounded them.

It was a Saturday morning, around seven o'clock. A ray of yellow sunshine crept through the shut curtains and made its way through the room.

The purple duvet cover that enfolded Cameron Williamson's unconscious body was sprawled up into an absolute mess. He had never been able to sleep like perfect Snow White and more so resembled the beast from Beauty and the Beast.

"Cameron, my dear, are you up yet? You know you have to get ready a little earlier today, don't you remember?"

It was his mother's voice that woke him from his so called "Beauty Sleep", but that was certainly not the case. It was as if the birds could sense a beast awaking from its long sleep, because once Cameron's brown eyes glared out the window, all the birds stopped singing at once.

Sometimes Cameron wished that he could have been Snow White, not for the way she woke up, but for the fact that she had eaten the poisoned apple and fell victim to a state of everlasting sleep. He wished he could have eaten the apple and slept through eternity.

His mother had once sworn that sleeping was one of his worst qualities, but he had expressed his amusement and excused himself to take a power nap.

"Yes, mom, I am up," Cameron replied out from beneath the purple duvet cover. He rolled his eyes and decided to close them again.

If his mother's knowledge on him had been a super power, she would have been one of the strongest superheroes out in the comic book world. She knew better than that and knocked on the dark oak door of Cameron's room.

"Come on, Honey, we don't want to be late for church now, do we?"

Cameron muttered something under his breath, but his mother couldn't hear anything.

"Honey, if you don't get out of bed right at this moment, I will be forced to show everyone in the church choir last Christmas's *fun* photos..."

"Ugh, fine. Jeez, why do you always have to blackmail me with that god darned photo?"

"That's no way to speak, young man. Are you going to get out of bed now, or what?"

Cameron felt the need to cuss, but to himself, not his mother. How stupid hadn't he been to let his mother take that photo? He didn't realize she would use it against him for many years to come.

Cameron pulled the duvet off his body, annoyed that he couldn't find a reason for him not being able to go to church.

Although it was blisteringly hot outside, the cool air inside the room sent his arms into a state of gooseflesh as the cold air mixed with his fairly hot skin.

"I thought I told you to get up," Cameron's mother said as she entered the room.

Once inside, she saw that he had already gotten out of bed and was now pulling the duvet cover over the bed.

"Oh, goodness, can't you put on a pair of pants first?"

"I have pants on, Mom," Cameron said and looked at the red boxers he had been wearing. "They are called boxers, and they are very comfortable to wear when it's summer."

Cameron's mother sighed in disagreement, turned around, and left the room.

He ran a hand through his dark brown hair and yawned for so long that he was certain that he would pass out from a lack of oxygen.

As he moved to make up the bed, every bone in his body seemed to unwind at the sudden movements. Bones were crunching, fingers were popping, and pins and needles were jabbing at the soles of his feet.

Once the bed was made to absolute perfection, he left the room and made a left turn. He continued along the hall and made another left turn into the bathroom.

The bathroom's white tiles glinted like tiny little diamonds. The whiteness made him want to vomit, because he had always been a guy of colour.

Cameron found himself staring at his reflection in the mirror. Almost at once he wanted to shout at the top of his lungs until his throat was sore and the mirror shattered into shards.

His face was covered with pimples as white as the tiles on the floor. *One, two, three...Oh my God! Why am I being punished like this? What the hell did I do wrong to deserve this?*

He found himself asking the question every teenager asked themselves in the mirror: *Who am I, am I desirable, will I ever be as hot as xyz, what will the people think of me?*

It seemed to him that he did have answers, but none of the answers were what he wanted them to be.

He opened the hot water tap, waited for it to turn hot, and looked in the mirror once more. A thin stream of steam rose from the tap and began overtaking the mirror. His reflection in the mirror faded quickly.

Good, he thought and shook his head. *Something should cover up the face of Frankenstein's monster.*

He opened the cold water tap as well and balanced the water until it was mellow enough to splash over his face. The warmth of the water against his cold skin felt wonderful.

He opened the medicine cabinet without having to look at himself in the mirror again. Scanning through the cabinet, he spotted his anti-anxiety medication. He grabbed the bottle of pills, removed two, and swallowed them, gulping water from the tap.

That was one of the things he grew so fond of while living at the beach with his cousin: the water was crystal clear and could be drank right from the tap. Back at home when you did that, you would have probably had to get your stomach pumped out in a hospital.

There was a low knock on the bathroom door. It was unmistakeably his mother's.

"Hon, are you ready to go to church?"

"Jeez, Mom, I am almost done. Just stop nagging me," Cameron sighed. "It's not like God is going to disappear, is it?" This made him grin for the first time that Saturday morning.

"Oh my, Cameron Williamson, you open that bathroom door right away and apologize for being so rude!"

"I wasn't being rude, Mom, I was just being brutally honest with you."

Before long, the bathroom door swayed open and hit the wall, "Don't you dare use that *sarcastic* tone with me again, do you understand me?"

This made Cameron's grin grow even bigger. He frowned at his mother and made his best impression of the sweet baby boy he had been years back, "I am so sorry, Mommy, could you *ever* forgive me?"

Cameron's mother seemed to regard this for a moment or two before she sighed and said, "Was that sarcasm?"

"*Of course not,* Mom," he replied and grinned whilst white toothpaste foam ran down his chin and collected beneath it. "*I would never be sarcastic with you,* Mom."

"Well, if you say so. Now quit being so darned childish and wash your mouth. It looks like you are convulsing," she said in a fun and mocking tone. "We have to leave in ten minutes, okay?"

"Yes, Mom," he said and turned back to the sink. He spit the last bit of toothpaste foam out and took a sip of water, splashing it around inside his mouth and then spitting it out again.

No more than five minutes had passed. He pulled on a pair of black jeans, a white shirt, black shoes, and a black tie. It seemed as if there was going to be a funeral with the way he dressed for church. His mother never complained, so he didn't say anything, not a *single* word.

"Hon, it's time to go now," his mother said and walked into the bedroom he was sleeping in. "I don't want to be late again. Do you remember what happened last week when we were late?"

Cameron nodded and said, "Yeah, I remember, Mom. I am ready to go, but I would have liked to drink a cup of coffee before we went."

"Oh, Cameron, you can drink a cup of coffee at the church when the ceremony is over, okay? We really ought to get going now if we don't want to be late."

Cameron sighed in disappointment, because he didn't like the way the church coffee tasted. It seemed so, earthy, almost dirt-like, and he didn't have the acquired taste for it.

An awkward silence filled the van. The van wasn't getting any younger. Noises like neither of them has ever heard came from within the hood. The dirt-brownish paint started to peel off, yet his mother didn't want to buy a new vehicle.

Cameron was the icebreaker, because he couldn't keep his mouth shut any longer.

"Mom, we really ought to get a new car," he said. "I mean, it's not like we aren't able to afford a new one."

Miss Williamson inhaled loudly and exhaled even louder. "How many times have I told you that the van is still in good shape? We don't need a new car. What would a seventeen year old boy know about our finances anyway?"

Cameron could feel the irritation building up inside him, waiting to plume out like lava in a volcano, but he decided to shove those feelings back to where they originated.

"Nothing, Mom, I know nothing. Why don't we just forget about it?"

Miss Williamson sensed that the conversation was going to take a turn for the worst if she pushed him, so she decided to sweep it back under the rug.

"We have been here for almost a week now, Cam," she said and looked at him for a second before focusing on the road again, "Have you made a friend?"

It was as if Cameron didn't hear her, because he chose to stare out the window. Whether he was ignoring her or daydreaming, she wasn't sure.

A couple of seconds of awkward silence once again filled the car. This time the silence was broken by Miss Williamson. "You have to make friends, or at least a friend, Cameron. What good is summer vacation if you have no one to talk to, to joke around with, or do activities with?"

Cameron sensed that his mother was not going to let this one slide, so he said, "Mom, I really don't need friends. I don't want to have any friends. I am more than satisfied with being by myself."

Before Miss Williamson could say something else, the car stood still in front of the church. He jumped out of the car and slammed the door shut.

Sometimes I wish you could be here to talk some sense into him, she thought. *He would have never been so distant to me if you had been here.*

Once Cameron entered the church, he was hit by a wave of elderly cologne. He couldn't quiet explain the smell, but it was always associated with old people.

The reverend was at his podium, just like the statue of liberty, always on one spot. There was something different about the reverend though.

It took Cameron a moment to realize what it had been. Since their previous church visit the week before, the reverend had cut his hair off. He was almost bald. The sunshine streaming through the tinted windows made a rainbow sparkle off the top of his head. This made Cameron snicker.

Before long, his mother was standing behind him. She tapped him on the shoulder and said, "This is a church, Cam, not one of your comedy movies. Please show some respect."

Cameron sighed and made a left turn into the row of wooden seats all the way in the back, away from the reverend. There had only been one churchgoer in that row.

She hadn't really worn church clothes. She wore black jeans that were torn and barely hanging on a thread at the knees, revealing ever smooth legs that he couldn't stop admiring. Her beautiful silk blond hair was made into two braids, pulled back; the two braids were tied together, making a braid ponytail. It seemed as if though she was wearing make-up to church as well.

He didn't realize that both his mother and the girl were staring at him. His mother faked a cough and waved at him, "Come sit in the front with me, Cam."

Cameron nodded his head, smiling. He knew that his mother was going to have a fit, but he also knew for a fact that she wouldn't dare take it out on him whilst they were in church.

Miss Williamson seemed to regard this for a moment before turning around and walking away dissatisfied.

This made him chuckle.

Once everyone was inside the church, the reverend commenced the day's ceremony. Without having to say anything, the people in the church showed their respect for the reverend by standing up, but the girl didn't stand up and neither did he.

This made Cameron feel as if maybe he wasn't the only one in the world that felt it was unnecessary to stand up.

When the reverend said, "Let's bow our heads in prayer," everyone sat down and bowed their heads.

Once again the girl didn't bow her head or shut her eyes. Cameron was unsure whether he should try to scope another look at her. He decided that he would, so he turned his head and looked at her intently.

Before he could try to dodge a bullet, she looked back at him. At that moment he wished that the church floor would break open and consume his miserable life, but that didn't happen.

He dared not look at her again, because he was certain that she was still staring at him, trying to burn a hole in his worthless skull.

He wondered what colour her eyes were. He didn't quiet see them the first time he looked at her, because he was more interested in her legs.

Cameron decided that it would be best if he *excused* himself from the church early, and when he squeezed past her, he would be able to exchange looks and see her eyes.

He was absolutely sure that it would work. He felt fairly confident enough to look this strange yet satisfyingly beautiful girl in the eyes.

At last he worked up enough courage to stand up from the chair. He walked without any nuisance. How glad hadn't he been that there was only the other girl in the row with him?

Just as he reached the girl that pricked his interest, the reverend said, "Amen!" and everyone's eyes opened.

He exchanged an apprehensive look with the girl, but he didn't have time to look her straight into her eyes, because all of the sudden gravity plucked him down.

Cameron fell onto the church floor with a loud banging noise. He was sure that his head had cracked open. Everyone's eyes darted back to see him stumble to get back on his feet.

When he looked away from the crowd, the girl had a wicked grin plastered unto her face. She shook her leg, as if to give him a sign.

He immediately recognized the irony, which made him shake with amusement. Once again the people in the church nearly broke their necks to look at the boy who dared to laugh in a church.

The girl turned her head the other way and snickered. It was the most sincere sound he had heard in a while.

Cameron stood there for a minute or two before deciding that it was best if he would just sit down again. He squeezed past the mysterious girl and sat four seats away from her.

He knew that she would stare at him eventually. He would sneak a peek and see what color her eyes were.

Before long, the girl rose from the chair and headed for the church door. She didn't feel any fear or shame, Cameron was certain, because she ripped the church doors open as if they were having a catfight.

Cameron was uncertain whether he should run after her and wanted to respect boundaries. He didn't want her to think that he was an eerie prowler.

He got up from the chair and ran out of the church; he didn't feel self-conscious at all, as he usually would be.

Once he was outside, he was hit by a wave of excruciatingly frosty wind. He looked around to see where the mystery girl had disappeared to, but she was long gone...

CHAPTER 2

C ameron sighed in utter disappointment. He really wanted to see her eyes. His father always said that true beauty could be seen within a person's eyes if you looked deep enough.

He knew his mother was going to be fuming, steam coming out of her ears and tiny nostrils. He would probably get grounded for months, if not years.

The sun hid behind the darkening clouds, making the day feel morbid. Deep within the dark purple clouds, thunder flashed restlessly. There was for surely going to be a thunder storm later that night.

Cameron decided not to agitate the people of the church any longer, so he sat outside. Luckily for him, the sun was no longer a peril to him, or else he would burn to a crisp in no more than ten minutes.

The time just didn't fly by fast enough. It was as if he was experiencing his life in slow motion. He couldn't help that all he had had on his mind, was the mystery girl.

Before long, the church doors opened and people were leaving the church; some of them were holding each other's hands, others were holding their wives or husbands around the waists, and then there was Miss Williamson.

Her arms didn't move as she walked; they stayed at her side as if she was an android. Cameron immediately realized she was past the point of being furious; she was now filled with rage, maybe even hate.

"Get in the car, now," Miss Williamson ordered once she walked past him.

He didn't really want to get up from the steps, because his bum was just getting warm from sitting on the cobblestoned steps.

At last he had a change of heart as Miss Williamson suddenly stopped to give him the death stare. If looks could kill, Miss Williamson would have gotten arrested right on the spot.

Cameron got up and hurried to get to his mother's side. He was almost sure that she was going to repeatedly hit him over the head with her purse.

Miss Williamson rummaged through her black worn out leather purse, found the car keys and unlocked the driver's door. She got into the car, unlocked the passenger door and waited patiently for Cameron to get in.

Cameron continued to stand outside the car next to the door. He really didn't want to go home with his mother, but what choice did he have?

He worked up enough courage to get into the car, closing the door as softly as he possibly could.

It was as if she was giving him the silent treatment, because not a word came out of her, for a while anyway.

"What was going on with you in that church today?"

Her voice was serene, which was very odd considering the events. *I knew it was going to be too good to be true that she was going to keep quiet!* He sighed.

"I am so sorry for my behaviour today, Mom. I have absolutely no idea what came over me, but I know for a fact that it would never happen again. I promise you, Mom, cross my heart and *hope* to *die*."

"You better hope it does not happen again," she replied and felt as tears formed in her brown eyes; they stung terribly. She wiped them away with the back of her left hand before speaking again. "You would never have had a go at me like today if your father was still here."

This actually made Cameron's eyes tear up as well, not because she was right, but because he yearned for his father's love.

Awkward silence once again filled the car.

Suddenly Cameron was hit by a wave of nostalgia that made him surrender to the tears that welled up inside his eye sockets. He felt a shiver as a cold tear ran down his left cheek, thinking back to one night his mother and he had fought.

Hail, the size of golf balls, struck the roof and shattered into tiny shards of ice. The sun hid behind the dark purple clouds.

The Williamson family sat at the dinner table. Miss Williamson had prepared a marvellous Sunday roast, even though it was Saturday: golden brown roasted chicken, vegetables ranging from broccoli, cauliflower, peas, carrots and potatoes.

"Let us say prayer," Miss Williamson insisted.

This made Cameron smile as if though he just found out that he had won a million bucks. He revealed white teeth. One front tooth was a little askew, but nobody seemed to mind.

Cameron said, "Let's bow our heads in prayer," and took his sister's hand in his and his mother's hand in the other.

"Our father, we thank you for the food we are about to receive and we thank you for our blessings, amen!"

This seemed to satisfy his mother greatly, because she rose from the dark oak wooden chair and said, "Thank you, Cameron. Let's eat."

As she said those last words, she picked up a carving knife and carved the chicken into thin slices as if she were an expert at it.

Meanwhile, Mr Williamson passed on several bowls of vegetables.

"So," Mr Williamson said and looked around the table, "tell me all about your busy week, Honey."

This seemed to confuse Miss Williamson and her daughter, because Mr Williamson called them both "Honey".

Miss Williamson and Cat (a pet name Cameron came up with for her) exchanged a brief look and turned to face Mr Williamson.

"Cat, dear, I was talking to you," he said and took a bite of a potato that was stuck on his fork; a piece of potato fell back into his plate.

Cat smiled, revealing the tiniest of teeth, a few of them missing. She had come to the critical point of losing her baby teeth, but she feared the tooth fairy to the point where she would hide her teeth elsewhere.

She rolled her eyes and put her tiny index finger on her lip, the so called "thinking" sign characters from her favourite cartoons always *did.*

"Well, the other day my friend and me talked about the big, scary Mister Bogeyman," she started, but was soon interrupted.

"Cat, dear, you have to say 'My friend and I', not 'My friend and me', okay?"

Cat frowned and nodded her head in acceptance. "Anyway, my friend and me, sorry, my friend and I were talking about the big, scary Mister Bogeyman."

This made Cameron sigh in frustration. He hated it more than anything in the entire world when his sister repeated herself.

"Well, she asked me if I was afraid of him, so I said yes, because I is very scared of him," she said, but was once again interrupted by Miss Williamson.

"You have to say 'I am', not 'I is', okay?" she said and turned her face to look at Mister Williamson. "What are they teaching the kids at that school?"

Mister Williamson shook his head and said, "Honey, there is no need for her to speak as if though she has a degree in English; just let her finish her story."

Miss Williamson didn't seem to like that at all, because she folded her arms in frustration and frowned, deep lines forming on her pale forehead.

"Well, she just laughed at me, so I asked her if she was, but she only said, 'Fuck the Bogeyman, I ain't scared of that ugly son of a bitch!'."

Cameron was then sipping some of the water from his icy cold glass. He spit the water out as he guffawed at what his sister said. Once he received a look of utter disapproval from his mother, he put his right hand in front of his mouth, but giggles sill escaped.

Miss Williamson's eyes nearly bulged out of their sockets. "That is no way to talk at the dinner table, actually, that is no way to talk at all. Go get the cayenne pepper from the cabinet this instant!"

This seemed to bamboozle Cat, because she only stared at her mother with an open mouth (a fly almost flew in there) and widened, glassy blue eyes.

"Oh, come on, Darling. I am certain she doesn't even know what she did wrong. I mean, those words are the ordinary language of every citizen I have to deal with every day of my entire life."

"I did not ask for your opinion," she replied with a disgusted look, which revealed even more lines across the entirety of her face. She pushed forty, but the lines appearing on her face made it look like though she was a seventy year old woman with burnt granadilla skin.

"Just leave her alone," Mister Williamson ordered, but his wife was persistent.

"I ordered you to get the cayenne pepper, Cat, didn't I?"

At last more tears stung Cat's eyes. A frown appeared on her face and her mouth turned down into a sad face emoji.

"I'm sorry, Mommy," she uttered before tears spilled down her cheeks in streams, much like the rain that was then pouring outside.

"Just leave her the hell alone, Mom," Cameron said before he could register and filter, "I mean, she has no idea what she has done wrong."

"I agree with, Cameron, Darling," Mr Williamson replied.

It was just one of those things he missed so dearly about his father: the way he always stood up for Cameron. His father had always been the understanding one, the so called 'Good Cop' in the marriage.

Cameron brushed a couple of tears off his cheeks.

When the wave of utter nostalgia finally dissolved from his mind, he noticed that his mother was currently driving into a parking lot.

"What are we doing here?" he enquired.

This seemed to bring out a little bit of impatience from his mother, who also began frowning.

"Haven't you been listening to a word I have been saying to you?" she asked and in a moment stopped frowning. "Of course not. I said we were going to stop at the grocer before we go home."

Cameron rolled his eyes in disappointment, because he knew that they weren't going 'home' anytime soon. Once his mother was inside the grocery store, it was as if her mind and soul were trapped inside.

He sighed and said, "Can't I just stay in the car and listen to some ACDC?"

This seemed to bring a look of utter disapproval from his mother, which he took great pleasure in. He didn't really listen to ACDC, but he was willing to do anything his mother disapproved of.

Even though he knew she knew what he was saying, he said, "You know, After Christ, Devil Comes?"

His mother scoffed and turned around. Feeling that there was no way that she could win the fight that was slowly brooding between them, she got out of the car and slammed the door.

Cameron smiled victoriously, because he had won, but he felt a wave of defeat when she turned around and said, "You better get out of that car, or else I'll come around and pluck you out of there."

Defeated, agitated, and disappointed, he got out of the car and heard the little *beep-beep* sound the van's alarm made as she pressed the lock button.

The air inside the grocery store was scorching compared to rain and thunder outside. Cameron didn't mind, but Miss Williamson pulled off the brown coat she had on.

Miss Williamson went to the aisle where the trolleys were stacked behind each other in neat and narrow lines, removed a large one, and continued along to the first aisle that was numbered with a large sign.

She muttered a list of items she needed softly to herself. This always made Cameron feel as if though she were talking to herself and being crazy. It was better than having a list scribbled on a piece of paper, he according to her.

Over the speakers in the store, John Legend was pouring his heart out, stating that he gives his all to someone.

Cameron had no interest in the helping her with the shopping, but as he looked ahead into the aisle where his mother was grabbing things off the shelves, his eyes caught a glimpse of himself in a little round mirror that was mounted unto one of the shelves on the right. He shut his eyes, and when he opened them again, he saw someone behind him in the mirror.

He jumped around as fast and swiftly as he could, but his feet nearly caused him to slip and fall on his face. When he recovered, he noticed that the person behind him was already gone, but there was a sneaker on the floor.

Cameron appreciated the irony and mystery of the shoe. It made him feel like a prince, reminding him of Cinderella's story. As he walked closer to where the shoe was, the smile on his face disappeared. What if it was a homeless guy's shoe? He decided to pick it up though, even though he didn't have a clue to whom it belonged.

The entire time it felt as if he was being watched. He couldn't help but get the feeling that somewhere out there, a sex prowler was following him.

Just before he stood up from his half sitting position, he glanced around and saw something that made him want to rip in half with laughter: in the next aisle was someone wearing only one shoe. The shoeless foot was clad only in a black sock. The other sneaker matched the one Cameron held in his right hand: white, with thin lines of brown dirt smeared unto them.

Quickly he rose from the half sitting position and sprinted ahead, turning left and then left again to get into the next aisle.

He stopped dead in his tracks when he saw that the person that was standing there not a minute ago was already gone. At the far end of the aisle, somebody was running away from something for dear life. The person was running away from him, he soon realized.

Cameron decided to run after the mysterious shoeless stranger.

Cameron's own black sneakers squeaked as he ran along the smooth white tiles of the store. His heart was in his throat, because any form of physical activity was not on his do-to-list; luckily for him his length was a sure way of keeping him thin.

As he ran into the next aisle, confident that he would catch up with the mystery person, he could only see a glimpse of ever smooth blonde hair that fluttered behind her back. She had a pair of black jeans on, and one of her white sneakers was missing...

"Hey, you," Cameron called out, but it was visible that the mystery girl had no interest in retrieving her sneaker.

She glanced back at Cameron for a brief moment; in that time he caught up with her just in time to get a hold of her arm, which he grabbed and held tightly.

"I am sorry, but you seemed to have lost your sneaker," Cameron said, but was interrupted by someone shouting from within the store.

Cameron turned his head to see where the commotion was coming from, never releasing his grip on the girl's arm.

"Stop that girl!" the security guard was shouting and pointing at the girl he was grabbing. "Stop that girl! She's shoplifting!"

Cameron frowned in utter astonishment and turned around to face the mystery girl, finally getting a good look at her: she was facing him with her back turned to him. She wore a brownish shirt. Her smooth blonde hair hung down her back.

"Stop that girl!" the security guard bellowed once more. This brought Cameron's attention back to the guard. He noticed that the security guard had come much closer.

Cameron felt a sharp and sudden pain shoot through his left foot; immediately he let the grip on the girl's arm go. Just as fast as the Flash, the girl ran away, her blond hair fluttering behind her once more.

The security guard finally reached Cameron, panting like a race-horse. He was in his black uniform, wearing a utility belt, from which hung a flashlight (even though it was brought daylight) and a keychain with a minimum of 20 silver keys on that continued swaying even though he stopped running.

Sweat trickled down the brownish skin of the man's face. His brown hair, recognizably the same tone of his skin, was wet with sweat, making his hair shine.

"Didn't you hear me, man?" the guard bellowed out of breath. "That girl just shoplifted."

"I am so sorry," Cameron replied.

"Did you get a good look at her?"

"No," Cameron replied.

It was in that moment that he realized that he might have seen a glimpse of her before: it was the girl from the church.

I never get a good look at her, Cameron thought as he stared at the white sneaker in his hand.

CHAPTER 3

After five minutes, even though it seemed to last longer than that to Cameron, the security guard left and went back to his position, which was situated at a small marble counter in the front of the store.

"How much fun was it to let a criminal escape?" Miss Williamson asked; Cameron immediately snapped out of the daze he was in.

Cameron was bamboozled, not because his mother was being sarcastic, but for the fact that she had a smile (whether it was real or not, he couldn't tell) plastered onto her thin red lips.

"Oh, Cam, I was just kidding around, you know?"

It looked good on her, he had to admit. It was something he hadn't seen on her face in a long time, yet it instantly made her seem more youthful. He stared at her for a moment longer before she snapped him out of it.

"Oh, mind coming back down to earth, space cadet?"

"I'm sorry," Cameron replied, "Are you ready to go?"

"Yes, I am," she said and continued to push the trolley forward; the wheels of the trolley were making the most ear deafening screeching sounds, sending Cameron's arms into a state of gooseflesh.

Once they left the store, they continued along the side of the road. Cameron was annoyed about his sneakers getting wet with brown water and mud from the rain.

He was still clutching the mystery girl's shoe.

There was a moment of utter silence between them, but was broken by his mother saying, "Oh, Cam, where on earth did you get that awfully dirty sneaker?"

Miss Williamson pointed at the sneaker still clutched in his hand. Cameron looked down and realized that he had held onto the sneaker even though he had no idea where he could find its owner.

"Uh, nowhere," Cameron replied and tossed the sneaker into the back of the van.

Miss Williamson scrounged up her nose in disgust and said, "You ought to throw that sneaker away when we get home."

A sigh escaped through Cameron's barred teeth as he said, "Home is far away from this place."

His mother sighed in utter disappointment. Her facial expression turned into one of which Cameron liked to call a "life is always good" one.

"You know, if you just give this place a chance, Cameron. I mean, we are only here for summer break, that's all."

Cameron murmured something under his breath. His mother only sighed and smiled a little. "You know, you really are anti-social. If it wasn't for your cousin, you would be a total recluse."

A sarcastic smile formed on Cameron's face. His mother shook her head and as he said, "I am just socially selective," she mouthed the words with him.

He had said those exact words to her so many times before. Cameron just wasn't a social person, which was odd in an obscure way, seeing that all teenagers were very talkative, especially when it came to their problems and needs.

"You still haven't made any friends?" she asked him, touching his left shoulder with her scrawny right hand. He pulled away reluctantly, letting her arm drop back to her side.

Cameron felt as if his mother was drilling a hole in the back of his skull as he turned around and got into the passenger seat of the van.

Oh Lord, just help him to make a new friend, Miss Williamson thought as she pulled on the driver's door, but it didn't give way.

In the back of her mind, she realized that Cameron was not always wrong. This was one of the things he did know: they really had to get a new car.

She tried pulling on the door again, but it did not give way. As the anger began boiling within her pale skin, she softly tapped on the window.

Cameron turned to face his mother, smiling. He knew exactly what he needed to do. He got a hold of the handle on the inside and pulled it open. The door popped open.

His mother got into the car and without saying anything else, she said, "Yeah, I know."

Cameron immediately understood what she had meant by it. He couldn't feel less satisfied with himself. They both knew that it was time for a new car. He smiled victoriously.

"Hey, Cam," Ira said as she entered the guestroom where he slept.

Cameron was sitting on the window seat, reading a paperback.

"So, uh, am I interrupting anything important?"

Cameron's eyes peered up from the paperback novel he stuck his nose in; it was Stephen and Owen King's Sleeping Beauties.

"No, not at all," Cameron replied as sarcastically as he could manage. "Come on in, make yourself at *home.*"

It took his cousin, Ira, a moment to realize what he had meant with the pun. At last she realized that it was her home, so she only giggled in high pitched sounds that were unnerving to the ear.

"Anyway, cousin, I was wondering if you'd like to go out with my friends and me later tonight."

Cameron smiled and said, "I believe the correct way of saying that sentence is my friends and I."

That didn't seem to amuse Ira as much as it did Cameron, because she only stared at him with her light blue eyes, almost setting him on fire.

"Whatever," Ira said and shook her head. "Your mom said that you have to go with me, so, uh, be ready to go at seven tonight, okay?"

Cameron opened his mouth to protest, but Ira shut him up quickly, knowing exactly what he was going to say.

"I don't want to hear your protests. It was your mother's order," she said and put her thin-fingered hands on her hip. "Anyway, I think it would be nice to have a sober chauffeur for the night."

This time Cameron was the one that was not amused at all. He could have killed Ira with his death glare.

Ira, sensing the tension building between them, said, "Oh, Cam, I was only kidding about the chauffeur part. Just wear something cool and nice, okay?"

"Yeah, sure," Cameron replied and rolled his eyes, "Why don't I just go naked?"

Ira grinned, revealing teeth that were lightly nicotine stained, "Sure, if you are *that* confident with yourself, you can."

Without further ado she left the room; her hips swaying back and forth with her hands still on her hips.

Cameron felt absolutely disappointed, astonished even, that his mother had organised that ridiculous party thing for him to go to. He rolled his eyes and continued to read his paperback.

The digital clock inside the bathroom read 18:17 pm. The nerves were starting to creep their way through Cameron's body.

He found himself standing in front of the hateful mirror, staring at the weirdo that looked him in the eye.

Cameron lifted his right arm into the air, smelling his arm pit. The smell was rancid; he was certain that he could use it as acid. He showed all signs of stress, and he could feel an anxiety attack on the horizon.

At last he came to a conclusion that would help him solve a problem or two: take a shower.

Cameron's body swayed into the shower. With his left hand he opened the hot water tap. He despised waiting for the water from the hot tap to actually turn hot.

As he waited for the water to turn hot, he removed his clothes. By the time he had done that, steam clouded the inside of the shower.

He adjusted the water to his liking and felt as the first drops of hot water tinge his pale skin, turning his skin red on impact.

It took him no more than 10 minutes to finish showering. When he was finished he wrapped a beige coloured towel around his scrawny body.

He then walked over to the mirror again but couldn't see anyone looking back at him, because the mirror was covered in a thick layer of steam. He used his right hand to wipe it away.

He was left to stare at someone he didn't love, nor hate. This person's hair was a dark colour still wet with water. His eyes were dark brown. His skin, which was still fairly hot, was still a pale colour, with a few reddish spots on his face. This guy's nostrils were oval shaped. This guy was Cameron Williamson.

Looking at himself always made him feel like he's ugly. Not ugly, but really ugly. He knew exactly what he wanted to look like, but life was never fair. Pretty people have a privilege mere mortals can only dream of.

He understood that the next task was one of utter extremity: his outfit for the night.

The closer he got to the time of attending the party, the more anxious he began feeling. He was sure that he would die from the knotted intestines inside his belly.

Even though he just showered, he could already feel the moistness of his armpits. His hands were sticky with sweat. Sweat lines began forming on his forehead.

Soon, he realized, patches of the stress rash he so often acquired would creep up his left arm.

He found himself standing in front of the closet door. It was painted a purple colour. He pulled the closet open and peered inside.

Cameron picked his favourite jeans: pitch black with two pockets on either side. He also picked his favourite shirt: red. It wasn't very surprising that the pair of sneakers he chose was also red.

There was a knock on the door. Cameron guessed who it was, but once his mother stepped into the guestroom, he understood that he had been wrong.

"Oh, Honey," his mother said utter with distaste. "Don't you wear anything that is not either black or red?"

A smile formed on Cameron's faded pink lips as he said, "No, I love those colors."

His mother only scoffed and said, "Well, I know you probably want to peel an onion and an apple with me, but just listen to me before you go off on me."

She waited for Cameron to nod his head or reply using words, but when she saw that he wasn't going to answer any time soon, she sighed.

"I want you to go out tonight and try to make a new friend. Or if you just want to go out and not make friends, that would be okay too. I just want you to go out tonight and have as much fun as you can."

"I don't need friends or parties to enjoy myself. All I need is a paperback in hand and time to read it. I swear I'll meet my soulmate in a library one day."

Miss Williamson walked over to where Cameron was standing, hugged him fiercely (one might have guessed that she would never see him again), and kissed him on his left cheek.

It was at that exact moment that Ira also entered the room. Cameron was astonished by the way she had dressed for the occasion: her hair had been loose, hanging down to her bosom. Her black hair came in contrast with the white T-shirt she had on.

Her cheeks were rosy; dark eye-liner made her light blue eyes pop with utter beauty.

Her cheekbones sat high on her cheeks, looking as if though she was a model from Vogue.

"Wow," Miss Williamson said aloud. "You look fabulous!"

Cameron was sure that if Ira hadn't put on as much blush as she did, that she would have rosy cheeks.

"Thanks, Auntie," Ira said and turned her head to take a good look at Cameron. "Wow, Cam, I didn't know you could look that good."

He just shook his head and grinned.

"Oh, you kids go on now and have some fun," Miss Williamson said and smiled. "Remember: I want pictures!"

In no time at all, the two of them were sitting inside Ira's car. They were on their merry way.

It took them about forty minutes to get to the location of the party. All around them people were talking, sipping alcohol. The worst part about it was that the two of them were still in the car, parked outside. Cameron didn't even want to think about how it looked inside the house.

"Okay, listen," Ira said, her voice changing from the sweet one to one of serious note. "I have a reputation to upkeep here. You see, I am the popular girl in this town. I don't want you to embarrass me tonight, okay?"

Cameron knew that it was going to happen sooner or the later. He was sure that she would confront him much earlier than she had.

"Oh, I am so sorry. I didn't mean it the way it came out," Ira babbled. "It's just..."

"I totally get it," Cameron replied. "I'll do my best not to do anything stupid."

"Oh, Cam, I have to warn you though."

Cameron was afraid of what was to come. Usually those sorts of sentences never ended well for him.

"My friends aren't as smart or classy as you are, so please don't judge them or constantly correct them when they speak, okay?"

This made Cameron smile. He hadn't expected her to say that. He was sure that she would say something like, "Stay the hell away from me" or "I don't even want to see you", but luckily she hadn't.

"I'll try my best not to confuse them with my intellectual mind."

"Exactly. Sentences like those would confuse the shit out of them."

The two of them exchanged a look before bursting into laughter.

"Let's get this party started," Ira said and opened the driver's door. She got out of the car, almost slipping on the slippery grass with her black stilettos. "Are you coming?"

"Yeah," Cameron replied. He got out of the car as well and made his way to her side.

"Hey, Baby Girl," a girl from behind them called.

Ira turned around and screeched at the top of her lungs. She scurried over to the girl.

The other girl's white hair was made into a bun atop her head. Her face shone with glitter in the moonlight. Her red dress hugged her body to perfection, all the curves in the right places, like an hour glass figure.

"Cam, get over here," Ira said. "Amy, meet Cameron. Cameron, meet Amy."

"It's a pleasure to meet you, Cameron." Amy said. Her voice was strong and resonant, not what you would expect from a seventeen year old teenage girl. "I've heard so much about you."

"The pleasure's all mine," Cameron said as he approached the girls. "Hopefully my cousin only told you all the good stuff."

"You can count on it," Ira replied, her attention still on Amy. "Where is Bruce?"

"Oh, yeah, you know how guys are," Amy replied. "They had to go get a tank of beer for the party."

"Oh my," Ira said. "Boys will be boys, am I right?"

"You said it, girlfriend," Amy replied.

Cameron had no idea of what to say to either of them, so he just stood there in utter uncomfortable silence.

"Hey, Cam," Amy said. "Let's go meet some sexy girls, huh?"

This made Ira snicker. Amy turned her head and looked intently at Ira, her eyes demanding an explanation.

"Cam," Ira said. "Well, he's not really one of *those* guys."

"Oh, do you have a special someone?"

Cameron hadn't realized that Amy was talking to him, because he was distracted by the glitter that was in contrast with Amy's dark brown skin.

Ira snapped her thumb and index finger together in front of Cameron's face, trying to snap him out of his daze.

"Oh, I'm sorry," Cameron said apologetically. 'Did you say something, Amy?"

"Yeah, I asked if you have a girlfriend."

"No," Cameron said swallowed and gulped down a mouthful of spit down his dry throat.

"Oh."

"Yeah," Ira replied.

There was a moment of awkward silence between the three of them, but it was broken by the arrival of three boys.

Two of them appeared to be carrying a gigantic beer tank, their muscles bulging beneath their sleeves.

One of them wore a green tank top, revealing more layers of rock hard muscle beneath. He also wore a green short with matching green sneakers.

The other boy had the same shade of brownish skin that Amy had. He wore a plain black T-shirt with faded and ripped blue jeans with black sneakers.

"I hope we didn't miss the party, girls," the tank topped boy said.

"Bruce," Ira said aloud in a manner which showed she had loved him very well. If there had been emojis above them, the one with the heart shaped eyes would fit perfectly.

"Hey, Baby," the other boy said.

"What took you so long?" Amy enquired.

"Oh, Baby, if you only knew what we had to do to get this beer…"

Amy walked over to where he was standing, crossing her arms.

"Whatever, Jaleel," she said in a mocking way.

"Who's that weird Norman Bates looking guy staring at us?" Bruce asked no one in particular.

"Bruce!" Ira said in a shocked manner. "That's my cousin, Cameron, you idiot."

CHAPTER 4

There was a moment's worth of utter silence between the party goers.

Bruce smiled apologetically as he said, "Hey, man, you know I was just goofing around, don't you?"

Cameron hadn't the faintest idea of what to reply. He could be sarcastic and risk a beating, or he could be friendly and just let it go.

"Yeah," Cameron replied. "Are we going to stand out here all night, or are we going to party or what?"

Bruce looked at Ira for a moment. His eyes shined with utter excitement as he said, "I like this guy already, Ira."

Nobody protested; at last they were on their way to the real party. Ahead of the group, Bruce and Ira walked hand-in-hand. Behind them walked Amy and Jaleel. Cameron was all by his lonesome, walking behind the others.

The house in front of Cameron's eyes made him ache with jealousy. It was the biggest house he had ever seen in his entire life; to him it looked more like a hotel.

It was hard to tell the exact color of the house at night, but to him it seemed white or beige. There were lots of gigantic windows; not a lot of privacy, Cameron guessed.

The path they were walking on had been paved beautifully. Little stones ran along the sides of the narrow pathway.

"Hey, Cam," Amy called aloud. "You're getting behind. Come on."

Cameron couldn't help but feel ashamed. His mother had always taught him not to feel jealous of someone else's things, but he couldn't stop feeling envious.

At last Cameron realized that he had stopped dead in his tracks, staring with widened eyes at the house. He said, "Oh, yeah, I am on way."

The rest of them continued along the pathway. Not a minute later, he had caught up with the others, taking a few seconds to catch his breath.

Their group was getting closer to the front door. This made Cameron feel anxious. He knew that there was going to be a lot of people inside the house. His breaths were ragged. His palms were sticky with sweat. Little droplets of sweat formed on his brow.

"Welcome, Ira and co." the door man said as they stood still on the archway of the front door. "Uh, I am sorry, but you can't come in."

Cameron hadn't even realized that the door man was talking to him, because he was staring at this guy's so called 'outfit'.

The door man didn't have a shirt on. His hard abs stuck out like hard rocks. His arms bulged with veins that would surely erupt some-day. Hard biceps stood out, even though the man did not make any attempt to flex them. His perfectly tanned legs stood as straight as the base of a tree. The man's pitch black hair was wet with sweat, making it shine in the moonlight.

"Oh, no," Ira said as she handed the man something that looked like twenty bucks. "He's with us."

The door man nodded in approval, but as Ira entered the house, he slipped the cash into the back pocket of her jeans.

Cameron smiled, not having the slightest idea of what was happening. He understood that the only reason he had gotten into the house, was because he was with Ira. It suddenly came to him with a gobsmacking sound: Ira really was the queen of this place.

"Thanks," Cameron said to the door man as he entered the house.

Cameron briefly made eye contact with the man. He noticed that it hadn't been a door 'man', but a guy of his age group. Excitement glinted in the guy's blue eyes.

"What's your name?" the guy asked him.

Behind Cameron a row of patient party goers were lining up. It seemed as if though they didn't have a care in the world, because they were all participating in unison conversation.

It felt to Cameron as if though his tongue was frozen solid, because when he spoke, he could barely hear himself.

Cameron cleared his throat and said, "Cameron, nice meeting you."

"Eric," he said and smiled without revealing any teeth. "And I believe the *pleasure's* all *mine*."

Cameron felt a river of blood flowing into his cheeks. He was bamboozled, since a guy was actually hitting on him.

"Oh, here you are," Amy said as she took Cameron's arm. Her cold skin against his hot skin sent shivers down his spine. "I thought we lost you again."

This time Cameron smiled apologetically to Eric and said, "I have to go now."

Eric winked his right eye at Cameron and said, "I'll find you later, if that's okay."

Cameron nodded his head and turned around, walking beside Amy.

When they were finally a couple of feet away from Eric, Amy giggled in high pitched sounds that nearly exploded Cameron's ear drums.

"OH MY GOD!" Amy said. "That guy was totally checking you out. Is it just me, or did you just get some colour in your face?" She lightly pinched his cheek, but he pulled away quickly.

Cameron muttered something Amy couldn't hear. He tried swallowing, but there was nothing to swallow. His mouth and throat were as dry as a desert.

"Okay," Amy said and continued along the long halls of the house. "We don't have to talk about it then."

"Hey, Cam," Ira said. "Can I ask you a favour?"

"Sure," Cameron replied and looked intently at his cousin.

"Just keep up with us, okay? I mean, I don't want Amy to be your watcher all night long."

Cameron nodded his head. "Deal."

Just before one of them broke the silence that brooded between their little groups, someone spoke over an intercom of some sort.

"Testing," the girl's voice said. The volume of the intercom was almost deafening. Cameron cupped his hands to his ears to protect his ears from the sound.

"Welcome to my party!" the girl bawled. The crowd cheered, roared, and some actually shouted.

Ira and Bruce exchanged glances; if there was a picture of puppy love in the dictionary, it would surely be of them.

"Thank you all for coming. The DJ will get this party started for us with some great tunes!"

Just as she said the last word of the sentence, music jammed over the speakers. It was not something he could recognize, but at least the music wasn't as loud as the girl's voice had been.

Cameron should have known that it was too good to be true, because suddenly the music turned louder; Cameron could barely hear himself think.

Before long the little group scattered. Bruce and Ira were off together (probably to scout for a good making-out spot), and Amy and Jaleel were also gone (Cameron doubted that they were looking for the same thing as Ira; there was something off about the two of them).

Cameron was left to stand there all by himself. His head throbbed because of the loud music. He decided to find an exit to the back yard. He was sure that it would be much quieter outside.

The only problem was that he hadn't the faintest idea where he could exit. He only knew where the front door was, but he couldn't remember how to get there; geography and direction had never been his strong suit.

Just when he lost all hope of getting out of the house, someone looped their right arm into his left arm. Cameron almost jumped through the roof, even though the roof was high above his head.

"Hey, it's getting a little loud in here," Amy said and smiled. "Want to get out of here and go someplace quiet?"

Cameron and Amy shook their heads in unison. She pulled on his arm and dragged him along the white halls of the house, scurrying past crowds of teens.

No more than four minutes had passed. They went through a glass sliding door that was located in the pool table room.

Once they were outside, Cameron breathed in a gulp of fresh air. He was sure he could feel his head get cleared of the alcohol and cigarette smell that stunk up the house.

"Thanks," he said to Amy, unlocking his arm from hers.

They sat down next to the pool. There were two people in the pool; they splashed around and made waves of blue water rush against the sides. The moonlight reflected off the water, making little diamond shapes.

Other than the two of them, there were about ten people outside. The air outside was fresh and crisp, but chilly as well. The smell of rain was pleasant to the nose.

"You are very welcome," Amy said and turned her head to look at the water from the pool. "It's so beautiful."

"Yeah, it is," he replied and looked at the water as well. "So, where's your boyfriend?"

Amy looked away from the water and looked straight into Cameron's dark brown eyes. "My boyfriend is probably making out with his boyfriend."

Cameron immediately understood why something about their relationship seemed off to him. He frowned and said, "Oh, what do you mean?"

"You know, Jaleel is one of the most famous and sexy guys in school. As you could have guessed, he's not that into me. He's gay, but he has to keep up his reputation. I agreed to be his supposed girlfriend because I wanted to get popular as well, you know."

"Oh," Cameron said. "I am certain you know this by now, but you deserve someone that loves you to the moon and back. Life is too short and precious to be wasted with improper intentions. Why don't you tell him how you feel?"

Tears formed in Amy's eyes, stinging terribly. "I want to, you know, but I just can't seem to find a way."

Just before Cameron could reply, Amy moved closer to him. She put her hand on his inner thigh, brought her face closer to his, and tried to land a kiss on his lips.

Cameron pulled away reluctantly. He took the hand that was on his inner thigh and held it in his left hand.

The two of them looked at each. Sorrow, anger, hurt and disbelief were buried behind her eyes.

"I'm sorry," Cameron replied, releasing her hand. "I just can't."

For the first time that night she smiled for real. "Oh, I get it."

"You are a very pretty girl, don't get me wrong, but I am just not interested, that's all."

Amy kept smiling. The tears that welled up in her eyes had dried away.

"You know what, Cameron?" she asked him. Once she had his full attention, she said, "You really are a good guy."

This made Cameron blush a little. "What do you mean by that?"

Amy scoffed, her entire body shaking with laughter. "Any normal teenage guy would have had me on my back already, trying to get into me. But you, Cameron, are different. Any girl would be lucky to be able to call you their boyfriend."

"You know, this really isn't my type of gig. I think I am going to get out of here. It's been nice talking to you though."

"Thanks," Amy said and watched as Cameron stood up and left. She had to admit she was yearning to feel his lips press tightly against hers.

Cameron hadn't the faintest idea of where he was going to go. He decided that walking was his best option. Where he was going to walk to, he hadn't known yet.

The night was not getting any hotter. The streets were empty, except for the occasional car passing by or fellow pedestrian crossing the street.

The street lamps burned brighter than the ones where Cameron's home was. The streets weren't full of litter, which was another one of those things he grew so fond of.

Cameron felt anxious walking on the pavement all by his lonesome. Luckily for him, though unlucky for his potential attacker, he had a pocket knife and some pepper spray with him.

As he walked with his hands in his pockets (both of them clenching either the pepper spray or the knife), he saw the grocery store to the left.

The entire time he couldn't help but hope for another pedestrian on the sidewalks, because it seemed that he was the only one there.

It was at that exact moment that his wishes came true, but just not in a way he had hoped.

Ahead of him a hooded person stood by the entrance of the grocery store. This person was not very tall though, just about the same height as he was.

The person packed stuff out of the bag: a hair-dryer, a curling iron and a lot of other hair accessories.

The hooded person turned around and walked towards Cameron. Surely they would pass each other in a moment or two.

As the person came closer to intersecting with him, he grabbed the steel pocket knife; the steel would have cut him if he pressed a little harder. He was ready for anything.

Just when the person was at his side, he quickly glanced at the person's face. It was unmistakeably a girl's face. Little strands of blonde hair hung over her eyes.

It was at that exact moment that she glanced at him, not noticing that a brick was missing from the sidewalk. Her foot got sucked into it and before long gravity was plucking her down to the tar road.

Cameron's eyes widened at the sight. He jumped after her and caught her just in time; both of them fell into the street. Cameron hit the tarred street with his back first. The girl fell on top of him, still clutching him wherever she could find a spot.

In that moment Cameron realized that it was the mystery girl he had so often seen. It explained why she had put a lot of stuff at the entrance of the grocery store. She had returned the items she shoplifted.

He understood that in that moment he had to see her eyes, if not then, he was sure that he would never see them. It was as if some force didn't want him to see her eyes, because he couldn't see her eyes in the dark.

The two of them lied in that position for about another minute or so before they awoke from the daze they were in.

"Get out of the road!" someone shouted form somewhere, but neither of them could see where.

There was one thing both of them could see straight away: lights bearing down on them. They could also hear the roar of the truck's engine.

"TRUCK!" that voice shouted again.

The mystery girl got off Cameron, but gravity immediately took her in its wing. She fell back onto him. Cameron groaned as her elbow made contact with his stomach; he was certain that he would throw up.

It felt as if the events that unfolded then were playing out in fast forward. Before he knew exactly what he was doing, he was up on his feet. His right arm hooked under her legs. His left arm hooked under her left arm. He picked her up and started walking with her as fast as he could. Just when he put her on the sidewalk, his foot slipped on a giant rock. He plummeted down next to her.

As the truck continued along the road, its horn blared at the two of them.

In the distance they could hear the trucker screaming, "Bloody fools!"

Cameron felt as his own breathing was ragged, but he could clearly hear the mystery girl gasping for air too.

Somehow during their near death experience her hood had gotten off her head.

Cameron stared at her beautiful and silky blonde hair. The street light above them made her hair shine like rivers of liquid gold.

"Are you two okay?" the man asked as he approached the two of them. "Man, I was really worried that you were going to be splattered to juice by that truck." He snorted like Sandra Bullock in Miss Congeniality.

"Yeah," Cameron said. "I think I am okay. I maybe almost wet myself there, but I think I will be fine."

Cameron turned his face so that he could see the mystery girl's face.

"Are you okay?" he asked her.

The mystery girl sighed and sat up straight. "Yeah, I am okay, thanks to you."

The man snorted a couple of times again and said, "Wow, you kids really had me worried there. I think we ought to take both of you to the hospital just to make sure that you are okay."

Both of them protested the man's suggestions, but both of them had had a different reason for doing so.

"I am seriously fine," Cameron said, but felt a sharp tinge in his left wrist. "I think I just sprained my wrist a little."

Cameron turned his face one more time to look at the girl. At last he saw the one thing that had bothered him so much: her eyes.

The street lamp above them made her eyes shine like miniature emeralds. Her eyes were a beautiful emerald green colour that complemented her white blonde hair.

"Yes, thank you," both of them said in unison and with that the man left the two of them alone.

"Hi, my name is Cameron."

The not-so-mysterious girl held her hand out to him and said, "Hi, I'm Tamara."

CHAPTER 5

The two of them made eye contact again; there was a moment's worth of silence between the two of them, but it was not an awkward silence, but very well one of admiration. From which side the admiration came, neither of them could tell.

Cameron was the first to break their gaze, because he pushed himself off the ground by pushing his hands on the bricked sidewalk.

As he did so, he grunted in utter pain. He shook his left wrist and felt a sharp tinge pain shoot through him.

"Ah," Cameron said in utter disbelief and anger. "I think I sprained my wrist."

Tamara came closer to him. Once she was in front of him, she reluctantly took his left hand and examined it.

"Yeah," she said and frowned. "It's been pretty badly sprained. I think you ought to come with me to the clinic."

Cameron tried to protest, but he hadn't been a match to her.

"You better not try to protest," she said and smiled at him. "Follow me."

And with that they quickly left the scene where they had almost been roadkill.

Cameron continued to walk ahead, never realizing that Tamara quickly shot one more look at the spot where they had fallen unto the road. Just thinking about the near death experience she had just been through, shivers spiralled down her spine.

"Are you coming or what?" Cameron called back to her. "I mean, without you I'll never find the clinic, and without a clinic, I'll probably lose the hand."

Tamara headed back to where Cameron was standing and said, "Don't be so dramatic."

With that said, they both broke out in laughter. Tamara clutched her stomach from utter pain.

"Oh, by the way, do you wear sneakers?"

This question seemed to make her think. Her beautifully sculptured ears turned redder than a tomato.

"You do, don't you? Well, anyway, I was wondering if maybe you would like," he said, but was interrupted by her.

"Yes, I know, and yes, I would like my sneaker back," she replied, but she never once looked at Cameron.

Cameron guffawed at that. She didn't look embarrassed, but she surely didn't look amused.

"Oh, come on," Cameron said. "It is really funny. What was the other day about anyway?"

At last he got some reaction out of her, because she looked straight into his dark brown eyes and said, "That...that was just a...a misunderstanding, you know. Surely you have had some of those before, haven't you?"

Cameron realized that if he spoke his mind that things might turn awkward between them, but the poor fool never learned how to keep his thoughts to himself.

"Of course I have had some of those before, but I never had a situation where a guard was yelling stuff about shoplifting."

With that said, Tamara's entire face turned the color of a tomato. When she spoke, her voice was low, "I can explain that. I didn't..."

Cameron interrupted her before she could say anything else. "You know you really don't have to justify yourself to me."

He could see the expression on her face. He understood that she would soon explode, babbling on and on about what had happened that day.

"I kind of think it was cool," Cameron said in a low tone. This time he felt ashamed, because he looked down at his lightly mudded shoes.

Tamara smiled nervously and said, "What do you mean by that?"

"Oh, I just," but he was lost in thought. "I think it's cool that you did that. I mean, I never do exciting and heart-pounding stuff, that's all."

Some of the red color on her face started to fade away. She smiled but did not reveal any teeth.

"Here we are," Tamara said as they approached the front entrance of a pharmacy. On the glass window there were multiple posters: one poster said that you could get pregnancy tests there. Another stated that flu shots were available at the end of every season.

"Here we go," Cameron said and laughed nervously. When he saw that she was looking at him, he said, "Are we breaking and entering now? You know it's called a felony, right?"

Tamara made a phony surprised expression, lifting her hand up to her lips as she said, "Oh, my, really? I had *no* idea."

Both of them again burst into laughter. It was a sound Cameron hadn't really ever heard coming from him, but in this short period of time, he had grown to accept it as a natural thing.

Tamara rummaged through her right jeans' pocket and found a set of keys. She used the little black remote control to turn off the alarm inside. Next she picked out a key and slid it into the slot.

Not a moment longer, the lock popped open. Tamara pushed the door open and waited for Cameron to enter the pharmacy before shutting and locking the door again.

"Welcome to Kellerman's Pharmacy, sir. What can I help you with today?"

"Oh, I would like some tinned dog food and a beer to wash it down with," Cameron replied sarcastically. The level of cringe he felt was exhausting.

"Does this pharmacy belong to someone you know, or do you just work here?"

Tamara led him to the back of the pharmacy while she said, "Oh, a little bit of both I guess. I work here during vacation. My mother owns the place."

"Oh," Cameron said and sat down where she had appointed him to. "So, how bad is it sprained?"

Tamara left him for a moment and returned with a white medical kit clutched underneath her left armpit. She examined his wrist once more. She sighed deeply and finally said, "Those blue marks beneath your skin is most definitely an indication that your wrist is sprained, perhaps even broken, in a lot of regions."

"Oh, all this doctor talk is making me crazily sleepy."

Tamara filched a roll of medical tape from the medical kit. She plucked it and started unrolling it.

"I have to put this on as tightly as I possibly can," she said and frowned. "If it hurts at all, just let me know."

She started rolling the white tape around his sprained wrist as carefully as she could have.

"Ouch!" Cameron yelled aloud. Immediately she stopped rolling the tape and examined his face.

"Oh, you asshole, stop doing that," she said and smiled.

"Thanks," he said as she finished off. "I really appreciate it."

"Fortunately, you won't be losing the hand," she said as she looked down at his bandaged hand. "I hope, I have no idea what I was doing!"

"NOT AT ALL?" Cameron replied.

She nodded approvingly; that glamorous smile reappeared on her face. "Then you probably need to get back to wherever you were going, huh?"

"No," Cameron said and scoffed. "There's no way that I am going back to that darned party any time soon. I guess I'll just go home or whatever."

Tamara wondered if she had to make the offer. She just met him and she wasn't sure whether she should or shouldn't, but she did it anyway.

"You are welcome to hang around with me for a while," she said and touched his left shoulder. "I mean, if you want to."

"I wouldn't be invading or anything, would I?"

Tamara shook her head a couple of times and said, "No! Not at all, I mean, you did save me from getting splattered onto the road."

"Oh, come on," he replied and smiled. "You would have done the same thing for me."

I'm not so sure I would have, Cameron, she thought as she stood up from the couch they sat on.

"Would you like anything to drink or to eat?"

"No, I'm fine, thanks."

"Don't be like that, Cameron," she said and put her hands on her hips. "Would you like some juice, coffee, coke or anything else?"

"I'd have some coffee, if you wouldn't mind making some."

"Oh, no, we don't make our own coffee here. We just have these iced coffee or coffee shakes. Which would you prefer?"

"Iced coffee sounds great."

With that, she left him once more. Cameron looked at his covered left hand. She had done a pretty great job. She obviously had some experience with it, or was he being delusional and blinded by her charm?

Not a minute later she returned with the iced coffee bottles in her hands.

She handed Cameron an iced coffee with milk and coffee. He thanked her and sipped his coffee.

"Oh, that's great," Cameron said and sipped another mouthful of it. "We don't get this product at home."

Tamara put her iced coffee down and looked intently at him. To Cameron it felt as if she was somehow admiring or studying him.

"I really want to, uh, thank you for before."

Cameron was sure that he could see the gratefulness in her eyes. He swallowed the last of the iced coffee and put down the empty bottle.

"Oh," Cameron said and coughed a little. "It was nothing, really. As I said before, anyone would have done it."

There was another moment of silence between them, but it was also not an awkward silence. It was the type of silence that could only be found in romantic movies. The tension, the chemistry, the urge and necessity of being close, took over their hormonal bodies.

Before Cameron could guess her next move, she advanced toward his face, pursing her lips. He pulled away just in time before she landed the kiss.

Tamara looked baffled. She shook her head in disbelief and sighed of frustration.

"Oh, I'm sorry," Cameron pleaded, but was interrupted by Ruelle singing that there were monsters inside her head. How had he not heard the music before? This girl was too enchanting.

Cameron looked at her apologetically and filched his cell phone from his pocket. He looked at the device's screen and immediately answered.

"Hey, Ira," Cameron said and frowned. "What's wrong?"

"Oh, Cam, I should ask you the same question. We want to go home now, but we started looking for you, but when we couldn't find you, I started worrying about you."

"I'm sorry," Cameron said and smiled without thinking about it. "I got...*distracted* and left the party."

"Oh, well, we want to go home now, but we can't, because our driver is gone, doing god knows what. Get your skinny butt over here."

Ira hung up on the other end of the line. Cameron stared at the cell phone in disbelief. He didn't really want to go, but he didn't have a choice either.

"I guess you have to go chauffeur your guests now, don't you?"

"Yeah," Cameron said disappointed and sighed. "I'm really sorry, Tamara. I want to stay a little while longer, but I guess I'll have to get going now."

"Goodbye then," Tamara said and hugged him fiercely as if though they had known each other for years and years.

Reluctantly he said, "Can you just promise me one thing, please?"

Tamara frowned in confusion. She bit her lip, almost tearing it open. In her experience, when someone wanted a promise from her, it was usually just trouble.

"Yes," she mouthed softly.

"Promise me that we'll see each other again soon."

Tamara's anxiety disappeared. She smiled, revealing ever-white teeth that were tiny, though beautiful.

"YES!" she said a little too loud, but he didn't seem to mind.

"Do you have a cell phone or something like that? You know, so that we can get together sometime?"

Tamara blushed a little and said, "No, not really. I'll find you. I'll always find you."

Cameron chuckled nervously and said, "I'll always find you, Mary Margret. When we found each other again, we can also go look for Emma and Henry."

"Yeah," she replied. "See you around, Cameron."

It was very obvious that she didn't understand the reference. Cameron left the pharmacy. He couldn't really remember how he got there in the first place, but he continued along the sidewalk for no more than a minute.

"Hey," Tamara shouted from the inside of the entrance. "I guess you don't know how to get back to that party, huh?"

"Not really."

As Tamara caught up with him, he filled her in on the details of where the party had been and what the house looked like.

Tamara sighed in frustration.

"Do you know where the party is, or are you just as lost as I am?" he asked, but saw that there was no amusement on her solemn face.

"What's wrong?"

Tamara sighed again and said, "Yeah, I know where that house is."

"You sound a little disappointed."

"Not really," she replied and went silent for a minute or two; she walked like a ghost beside him, all color from her face had disappeared.

"Hey, are you okay, Tamara?"

"I'm fine, Cameron. I know perfectly well where that house is, because I live there."

Cameron felt very dumbfounded. He frowned and put his hands in his jeans' pockets.

"Why is there a party at your home, but you aren't there?"

"Oh, my mom thought she would do me a favour and throw a party at our house for me. She wanted me to socialize more and make new friends. Maybe even screw a guy or something. She meant well, but I left the house even before the party started."

"But you were there earlier, weren't you? I mean, you thanked us for coming to the party over the intercom."

"Yeah, that was kind of a great trick. I bribed a girl from school to do it for me."

"Oh," Cameron replied disappointed. "I would have liked to meet you at the party, though. Why didn't you decide to stay?"

"I, uh, had other things to attend to."

"What did you do, if you don't mind me asking?"

"I run a soup kitchen every night of the week, especially on the weekends. I finished my volunteer work just down the street and was headed to the, uh, nowhere really. That's when we walked past each other and other events unfolded."

Immediately Cameron felt his heart thud louder in his ears. His palms were getting sticky with sweat. A line of sweat formed on his brow. He then understood that he felt an admiration for her which he had never felt for anyone before.

"Oh, I'm sorry," she said and frowned. "I tend to get really chatty when I get stressed out."

"Why are you stressed out?"

"I...I don't really know."

"Can I ask you a question though?"

She nodded her head and turned her face to look at Cameron as he spoke.

"Why did you feel the need to shoplift the other day?"

Tamara's cheeks burned with embarrassment. She looked down at her feet, not wanting Cameron to see the tears welling up in her eyes.

"I did it for excitement," she replied softly. "My mother is really rich. I can buy anything I want, but I just wanted to do it for the thrill of it. I don't expect you to understand, Cameron."

Cameron hugged her closer to him, slung his left arm over her shoulder and held her there for a moment, stopping on the sidewalk.

"You have nothing to be ashamed of," he replied. "I understand completely what the thought behind it was. You returned the goods anyway. No harm, no foul."

"This is as far as I go," she said and looked at Cameron's face. She noticed that his face was not full of judgement and resentment, but very well of happiness and excitement.

"Maybe we can go out sometime and do something fun, like *that*."

Cameron felt that he may have said and asked too many uncomfortable things. He sensed that there was a slight possibility that he was never going to see her again, not after embarrassing her like that. The things she had done up until that point were definitely red flags, but much like a bull in the ring, he was running right into it.

"Promise me that we'll see each other again," Cameron demanded.

"YES!"

"Okay then," Cameron said and let go of her. He studied her face for a second or two and noticed that she sucked back the tears that waited to spill.

"Are you sure you can't come with me?"

"Yeah, I'm sure. Goodbye then. See you soon."

"Yeah, can't wait."

With that Tamara left him to stand there all by his lonesome. He looked back at her one last time before advancing towards the big house.

"There you are, you big silly," Ira said as he walked through the parking area.

She was as drunk as a skunk and he was sure that she would wake up one morning pregnant. She was leaning against the side of her car.

"What took you so darned long?" Bruce demanded. "It feels like we've been waiting for hours for you to come."

"Are all of you super drunk?" Cameron asked sarcastically.

"Let me ask you this, Cam," Jaleel said. "Are we at a disco, moving around and swirling around the dance floor?"

"Not at all," Cameron replied.

"Well, then I guess I am super drunk."

The rest of the group burst into laughter. Cameron took a few steps backwards, looked down at his sneakers and almost ripped in half with laughter.

How was he going to drive them all home with a sprained wrist?

CHAPTER 6

There was a subtle knock on the door of the guestroom. Cameron looked away from his cell phone's screen and glanced in the direction of the door.

The door swung open, hitting against the side of the wall. "Hey," Ira said as she entered the room.

"Hey," Cameron said and smiled.

He was sitting on the bed, the purple duvet crumpled up at his sides.

"Want to sit down?" he asked her.

"Okay."

Ira made her way to the bed, half swaying; whether she was still drunk from the night's party, he could not tell.

"What can I do for you?"

"Oh," Ira said and seemed to be thinking pretty hard. Cameron was sure that steam would puff out of her perfectly rounded ears.

"I have no idea what I wanted to ask you."

Ira broke out in laughter for absolutely no reason at all. Cameron studied her for a moment, looking up and down at her. He was then certain that she was still as drunk as a skunk, maybe even a pirate.

"Oh, right," Ira exclaimed, pressing her head on his right shoulder. "Your mother wanted to see you in the living room."

Cameron sighed in disappointment, knowing exactly why his mother wanted to see him, so he started thinking of something to say.

When his mother finally spotted him, she patted on the open spot on the couch next to her. Cameron reluctantly sat down.

Once his mother finally spoke, Cameron's mouth hung open. "Did you have a great time at the party, Cam?"

It took him a couple of seconds to register before he answered her. "Yeah, it was great! I had the time of my life."

He knew his chances of getting away with the sarcasm were scarce, but he grinned, saying, "Thanks for making me go. I'm glad that I did."

Miss Williamson took his left hand in hers, studying it intently. Although it was still wrapped, she pictured how it would have looked.

"What happened to your wrist?"

"Oh, I, uh," Cameron babbled. "I sprained it when I fell down the stairs at the...*party*."

That seemed to be humorous for her, because she chuckled in a low tone. Her face was lit with amusement and happiness.

"Oh, did you meet any new people?"

"Yes!" Cameron said a little too loud.

His mother smiled in disbelief. "Wow, really? Tell me all about it."

"Her name is Amy. She's Ira's friend. We talked all night and had so much in common."

Cameron couldn't understand why he had lied to his mother. Something in the back of his mind told him to lie to her.

"Oh, that's so nice, Cam," she replied and put her hand on his left shoulder. "When will I meet her?"

"Oh, I don't know. She's really busy."

"That is great, Cam. I told you that you would make some friends if you went to the party."

"Would you mind if I went to sleep now, Mom?"

"Oh, be my guest."

Without any further ado, she kissed him on his left cheek. He left the living room, feeling disappointed in himself for lying to her once again. Lying was something he had become accustomed to, because she just didn't understand him. Sometimes he thought she didn't have any interest in understanding him.

Once he was inside the guest bedroom, he lied down on the bed. He picked up his cell phone and continued to play a piano tiles game until he was drained of all energy. He then went to sleep.

Cameron was back at the big house. He was talking to Amy, where they sat at the side of the pool; this time their feet dangled in the cold pool water.

"Yeah, uh," Cameron said and frowned as he looked at Amy. "I know it's not any of my business, but I am certain that you deserve someone that likes you for who you are."

"I know, but Jaleel...he's not like the other boys his age. I like him, maybe even love him in a way; why I do, I have absolutely no idea."

"Why don't you try talking to him? Just tell him that it's over and that you don't want to be his cover anymore."

It was at that exact moment that someone else was nearing them. This guy said, "Hey, Cameron! I was wondering where you went."

Startled, Cameron and Amy turned their heads to see Eric standing behind them. Eric had put on a red T-shirt and he had also changed into pink neon shorts.

"Talking about feelings," Amy said and smiled. "You should stay true to yours."

Cameron was bamboozled at what she said. "What...what do you mean?"

No answer came, because Amy had disappeared into the thin air.

"Hey," Eric said as he sat down beside Cameron; he also put his legs into the water, feeling gooseflesh creep up his arms.

"Hey, are you okay?" Eric asked.

Cameron snapped out of his daze. He looked at Eric's face, which was lit with a smile that could brighten any one's day.

"Yeah," Cameron replied. "I'm okay, thanks for asking." He couldn't help but smile too.

"Want to go for a swim?"

Cameron shook his head and said, "No...no thanks. I, uh, don't have swimming clothes on."

Without another word, Eric took of his T-shirt. Beneath his shirt, his torso was as smooth as his voice. His torso was also ripped. The brown tan on his skin was more than perfect.

Without further ado Eric made a double back flip into the pool. Water splashed into all directions; little waves of water splashed against the sides of the pool and wet Cameron's rolled-up jeans.

"Hey!" Cameron said aloud, but in a fun manner. That smile never left his face.

After a minute or two, Eric's head appeared at the surface. He swam closer to where Cameron was sitting.

Eric's short and dark hair stood up in spikes, looking almost like a porcupine.

"Do you know what a whale does in the ocean?"

Cameron nodded his head and said, "Don't you dare spray me with water!"

Eric sighed in frustration. "There's not much you don't know, is there? Well then."

Before Cameron could stop him, Eric pulled Cameron's legs towards him. Cameron pleaded as if though his life was about to end.

Before long Cameron fell into the pool. The water was chilly against his skin. Shivers shot down his spine.

Whilst he was still under water, he opened his eyes for a moment and saw Eric's face before him. Eric was grinning under water, which was odd. Little bubbles of air floated to the surface.

Cameron's eyes immediately shot open, staring at the white ceiling.

He rolled his head a little to the left to see what time it was. The clock on the bed stand read 06:57.

Cameron sighed and felt a wetness wash over his face as he rolled back to his original position. His pillow was soaked through with sweat; his dark brown hair was even darker and damp with sweat.

He tried so hard to remember what his dream had been, but as usual his dreams got lost once he opened his eyes.

Cameron decided to get out of bed. He made the bed until there were no creases or wrinkles on the purple duvet cover.

He walked past the other rooms that were upstairs. Ira was still snoring, sleeping off the previous night's party. His mother was also still sleeping like a little baby.

Cameron went down the stairs and was thankful that they didn't creak like the stairs at home. He was afraid of waking anyone, although he was certain that Ira wasn't going to wake up soon.

He found himself standing inside the kitchen. No more than five minutes later he went to the front door with a cup of coffee. With a cringing sound the front door opened.

It was a bright and fuzzy Sunday morning. The sky was clear of any clouds. The wind chimes that had been hung on the porch didn't make a single jingle or jangle.

Cameron sat down on the brown couch that was located to the left corner of the porch. He stared at the rest of his surroundings. He was about to take another sip of his hot coffee when he saw a familiar face running past the house.

When Amy spotted him, she waved her hand at him and sprinted towards him. He took two sips of coffee and put the cup down on the wooden floor.

"Hey, Cameron," she said, coming to a stop at the porch steps.

"Hey, Amy," he said and smiled at her.

"Can we talk?"

"Yes, we can."

Amy sat down on the porch steps, squinting as her buttocks made contact with the coldness.

Cameron noticed her discomfort and said, "There's a couch on the porch, if you would prefer to sit there."

"Oh, no thanks, I uh…"

Cameron sensed that her discomfort was in fact not where she sat, but very well what she bore in her heart.

"I want to apologize for the party. I had absolutely no right to try and kiss you. I guess I just had a lot to drink."

He hadn't thought that she would even remember that night. He was certain that she had forgotten everything that had happened.

"There's no need to apologize for that. I mean, you just had a lot to drink."

"No," Amy said softly. He could barely hear what she had said. "No, Cameron. I wasn't drunk. You are a great guy, I can tell. I guess I was just very lonely and I just wanted to feel close to someone."

"Like I said before, Amy, there's no need to apologize. I mean, I can definitely understand where you are coming from."

Amy didn't say a word. She just stared at her feet.

"Look, it's not really my business, so forgive me for the intrusion. Why don't you break things off with Jaleel? If he doesn't love you like a girlfriend, why bother?"

Amy shook her head and felt tears stinging her eyes. "No, I just can't do that. Like I told you before, I am his cover and he makes me popular."

Cameron nodded his head as if in understanding. He put his right hand on her left shoulder and squeezed a little.

"Things will get better for you, I just know it. You can never allow yourself to be suppressed by others' comments or peer pressure."

A tear rolled down her left cheek, cold against her brown skin. She wiped it away with the back of her left hand.

"I can't do it, Cameron. I'm not as strong-willed as you are. I care a lot about what others say."

"I know that it's hard sometimes to shut out others' words and comments, but you have to stay strong. I mean, soon you will leave and go to college or something and you'll leave Jaleel behind. It's just the way of life, Amy."

"I have to get going now," Amy said and wiped away more tears that rained down her face. "Just promise me something, Cameron."

Cameron studied her face intently and said, "Of course, Amy, what is it?"

"Promise me that you won't tell anyone about Jaleel and me."

"I promise not to tell anything if you promise to think about the things I just said."

A small tugged at her lips as she said, "I promise."

Without further ado she sprinted away from the porch. She had in fact felt much better after talking with Cameron. He just knew how to make her feel better.

Cameron watched her disappear around the corner of the road ahead. He sighed deeply and went back to his ever patient coffee, but made his way back to the couch.

He picked up the cup and took a sip. The coffee was cold by then, but he loved iced coffee. He sat down on the couch and drank the remaining coffee.

"Good morning, Sunshine," Cameron said as Ira made her way towards the couch. "Did you sleep well?"

Ira still had the previous night's outfit on. Her hair was an mess and looked like a minor explosion took place. Her face was pale in some places and in others her make-up faded and smudged, making her look like an train wreck.

"Yeah, whatever dude."

"Maybe you ought to get cleaned up."

Once she sat next to him on the couch, he almost gagged. The rancid smell of alcohol clung to her like a baby with a piece of candy.

Ira was bamboozled, because she studied herself and frowned. A shiny line of sweat dried on her forehead. She smelled her armpits, which was even weird for her.

"Yeah, I definitely need a shower," she said and when she stood up, she cried out in pain. "Damn, I hate the morning after. It feels like my head is going to explode."

Cameron, being a picture guy, imagined it actually happening. He couldn't help but laugh, clutching his stomach and almost doubling over.

"It's not funny, you asshole."

Ira left Cameron alone on the couch again. He studied the ever-green grass of the front lawn. They always say that the grass is always greener on the other side, which was true in this case. Ever since

he and his mother had come to visit Ira for summer break, his mother hadn't been the way she was at home.

Cameron let go of that thought and went back inside the house, stopping in the kitchen first to put away the cup and then headed to the guestroom.

He studied the clock again. This time it read 07:23. He sighed and went to the closet, searching for something to wear.

Once he opened the closet door, he was hit by a wave of sudden laughter that he couldn't explain. In the shoe rack next to his sneakers, was a dirty white sneaker.

He picked up the sneaker and held it for a moment or two. He suddenly had the craziest idea pulsing through his head: he was going to go down to the pharmacy in the hope of finding Tamara there.

He quickly threw on something he was fond of: blue jeans, a black T-shirt and black sneakers. He ran into the bathroom and brushed his teeth, combed his hair and made sure his outfit for the day was perfect.

As he made his way out of the room, he spotted his cell phone on the purple duvet cover. He quickly ran back and grabbed his cell phone.

Something inside him made him feel warm and fuzzy, a feeling he wasn't used to anymore. Had he ever felt it before?

There was some excitement and thrill in knowing (perhaps wishing) that he would see Tamara again.

He skipped along the stairs and once he reached the foot of the stairs, he was caught off guard.

"Where are you off to, Cam?" Miss Williamson asked from the living room, which was near the front door.

"Oh, I, uh, I'm going out with my friends."

He knew he was telling a little white lie, but he couldn't tell his mother the full truth, as she would ask too many questions, and grill him like a detective.

"Oh, well, enjoy it, Cam. Just be back by one o' clock."

"Of course I will, Mom."

Cameron sprinted over to his mother and kissed her on her rosy cheek. Just when he pulled back to leave, she pulled him closer to her.

He felt his heart jump a beat. She put her arms around him and hugged him fiercely.

"Just be careful, okay?"

"I'm always careful, Mom."

With that she let him go again. He turned around and walked towards the front door, but he stopped dead in his tracks.

He turned his head back to look at his mother. It was the oddest thing. Her face was lit with a smile that for once didn't look like it was plastered onto her.

She waved her left hand at him and said, "Go on now, Cam. Your friends are probably waiting for you and you don't want to be late now, do you?"

Without saying anything else, she left.

Cameron stood in front of the front door. He was feeling more bamboozled than he had ever felt in his entire life.

Perhaps she was just happy that he finally made some friends. Perhaps she actually drank a handful of happy chill pills. Who knew?

Cameron shook his head and left through the front door.

Once he was outside, he shook his head again in utter disbelief. He removed his cell phone from his pocket and looked at the screen. The digital clock read 07:47.

He pushed his cell phone back into his pocket and began walking down the sidewalk, whistling all the way, almost skipping along the sidewalk.

CHAPTER 7

No more than thirty minutes had passed when Cameron found himself standing in front of Kellerman's Pharmacy. How he got there, he had no clue.

He wasn't sure whether he would actually see her at her mother's store, but he hoped that he would.

In his right hand he held the white sneaker. He looked down at the sneaker in his hand and couldn't help but smile.

"Can I help you, weirdo, or are you just doing some window shopping?"

It was unmistakably a girl's voice. It sounded familiar as well.

Once he realized who the voice belonged to, his heart skipped a beat. He turned around and saw Tamara standing behind him.

It became obvious to Cameron that she was also very fond of jeans, because she wore torn jeans and a black T-shirt with red sneakers.

"Oh, I think that one belongs to me," she said and took the sneaker out of his hand.

She looked at his wrapped wrist and sighed. She smiled apologetically and said, "How is your wrist feeling today?"

"Fine, I guess I'll live."

"So, did you want assistance in the store?"

"No, I, uh," Cameron said. He hadn't the faintest idea of what he actually wanted to tell her when he saw her.

"What's the matter, cat got your tongue?"

"Not at all, I just...I..."

Tamara made her eyes big as if though she tried to compel words out of him. She snapped her fingers in front of his face.

"I just wanted to see you again."

"Oh, well, I hoped I would see you again today too."

"Yeah?"

"I wanted to thank you again for last night, you know, all that saving."

"I think you have thanked me enough for one night, Tamara."

"Well, there's kind of one more huge thank you coming your way. I hope you aren't busy with anything today, are you?"

"No, I haven't made any plans for today yet."

"Great," Tamara said and smiled at him. "We should get going then."

"Uh, where exactly are we going?"

"I can't tell you," she said and bit her lower lip. "Are you up for a journey or not?"

"I guess I am, but I would like it very much if you would just tell me where we were going."

"I can't tell you, Cameron, it's a surprise."

Cameron considered it for a moment or two. He didn't like not knowing where he was going at all. For all he knew she could be a psychopath or kidnapper or something. He considered the possible outcomes: kidnapped, death or serious injury could occur.

He decided that any form of excitement was worth having with her no matter the outcome.

Cameron nodded his head and said, "Yeah, why not? Let's go for it."

"Awesome," she replied and hooked her left arm around his right arm. "We are going to have so much fun today.'

Without any further ado she led him to a Jeep Jimny that was parked by the entrance of the pharmacy.

Once they reached the Jeep, she waved at it and said, "Baby, we are going for a ride."

"You call your Jeep 'Baby'?"

"Yeah, you got a problem with that?"

"No, not at all," Cameron said as he got into the Jeep. "I like it, because it reminds me of..."

"Dirty Dancing," Tamara finished for him.

Tamara looked at Cameron's face. She couldn't quiet read what he was thinking, so she frowned.

"You like Dirty Dancing?" Cameron asked.

"Yeah," she said and started the Jeep's ignition. "It is definitely one of my favourite movies of all time. It's just an *iconic* classic!."

Without any further ado she backed out of the parking space, constantly looking in the side mirrors.

"That's great!" he said and smiled. One could have sworn that he had just won a million bucks. "I mean, most of the people I know don't even know what Dirty Dancing is."

"You like it as well?"

Without hesitating one moment he said, "Yes! It is brilliant!"

Tamara widened her emerald green eyes and studied Cameron for a moment. She suddenly felt a new kind of admiration that she didn't feel the night before.

At last they were out of the parking lot and turned at an intersection. Tamara's hand reached for the radio and before she turned it on she said, "Do you mind if I put some music on?"

"Not at all," Cameron replied with barred teeth.

Even though she was an excellent driver without any flaws, he was petrified. The truth was that he could never stomach riding in a car, because he got car sick too quick.

"Hey, are you okay?"

"Yeah," he said and rested his head on the seat, closing his eyes. "I just get car sick real quick."

"Oh," she said and laughed a little.

"What's so funny?"

"Oh, I'm sorry. I didn't mean to be rude. It's just funny, because I downed two pills before getting into Baby."

"What *sort* of pills?"

"I get car sick too. Just open the glove compartment and take two of the pills. There's a bottle of water in there as well. The water is hot though, I'm sorry"

"Thanks," he said and opened the glove compartment. He rummaged through it and found a blue tube filled with pills. Without thinking about it, he took two blue pills and downed them with a lot of water. The rancid taste of medicine made his throat ache.

"Thanks," he said and suddenly realized that he had done something terrible: he just drank strange pills from a girl he had barely known.

"Are you okay? I mean, you are looking whiter than a ghost."

"Feeling much better..."

"Great! We are almost there."

Tamara turned on the radio. As the song started, Cameron couldn't help but smile.

"Now I, had...the time of my life, and I never felt this way before..."

She certainly was a fan of Dirty Dancing. Before long he felt much better and started to sing along; Tamara joined him.

No more than five minutes had passed when the Jeep stood still on a dirt road.

They were surrounded by the tallest trees Cameron had ever seen in his entire life. They were so high in the air that they blocked out most of the sun. The ground beneath their feet was a red colour and as they walked on it, it kept their foot prints in the moist ground.

"This place is extremely beautiful," he said in awe.

"You think this is beautiful?"

When Cameron nodded his head, she looked at him and said, "Oh, Cameron, you haven't seen anything yet. Come on, don't just stand there and look pretty all damn day now."

Cameron was too stupefied and amazed to realize that she was flirting with him. He looked up and tried spotting where the tree tops ended, but his efforts were unsuccessful.

Tamara realized that she wasn't going to be able to get him out of his daze, so she sprinted to him and hooked her left arm around his right arm.

"Come on, Cameron," she said and pulled his arm. "We can't stay here all day long."

"I'm sorry. It's just so beautiful here.'

She led him to the back of her Jeep and picked up the picnic basket. Cameron took the picnic basket from her and held it in his left hand.

"I'll lead the way to my favourite spot."

"Great," was all he could muster.

She plucked his arm and skipped into the woods. Cameron nearly tripped over huge rocks four times. He tried to study his surroundings, but he couldn't really make anything out, just images of evergreen trees flashed past him.

At some point the leaves of the trees got so close to Cameron's face that he had to duck down before getting hit in the face.

"Are we ever going to get there?"

Tamara giggled and said, "In a minute."

Tamara was right, because when the minute passed, they cleared the leaves. Cameron could stand up straight again.

He stopped dead in his tracks. The entire field was cleared of any trees. The sky above was as clear and without any clouds.

Once he spotted where Tamara was heading, he gasped in utter disbelief. A waterfall was situated ahead. Its crystal-clear water ran down a bed of rocks and formed a gigantic pool beneath the falling water. As the water rained down with force, it reflected tiny little diamonds which could be seen from where he was standing.

"Are you coming or not?" she shouted from far ahead. "It's your loss if you don't."

Cameron laughed with glee and ran after her. The picnic basket nearly fell out of his hand, but he clutched it harder and winced lightly as his left hand cramped.

His legs had never worked so hard before. With every step he took he squinted with terrible pain, but it was most definitely worth it.

As they neared the waterfall, the sound of water gushing against rocks sent shivers down Cameron's spine. He dropped the picnic basket carefully and studied Tamara's face.

"Surprise!" she cried out and threw her hands in the air. "I hope you like it."

"Are you kidding me?" he asked. "I love it!"

His mouth hung open in fascination and amazement. He studied her face again. He was certain that he could see excitement and a little bit of fear in her eyes.

"Come on," she said and waved at him. "Follow me."

He jogged behind her and suddenly forgot all about the pain in his legs and hand.

She ran up a little mountain and disappeared behind it. Cameron followed suite and almost fell backwards as he scurried to keep up with her.

"There you are," she said and pointed at something. She then walked closer to the edge of what seemed to be the origin of the waterfall.

He went over to her and gasped as he looked down at the waterfall. It was one of nature's wonders to him. The water rushed down in anger and made waves of foam atop the pool of water at the bottom.

"You said you wanted to do something fun and exciting," she said as she removed her T-shirt.

She threw her T-shirt on a gigantic rock that was next to her. She unbuttoned her jeans and removed them. She threw it on the rock as well.

Tamara was still wearing a black bathing suit. She smiled at him and said, "Well, this is exciting."

Without another word she ran towards the edge. Before Cameron could mutter a single word, she went over the top, yelling at the top of her lungs.

He could feel his heart skipping a couple of beats. Two seconds later he heard a splash. He ran to the edge and almost went over it. Staring at the spot where she had fallen into the water.

He was certain that she had knocked herself unconscious and was drowning. His heart thudded against his ribs.

Not a minute later her head popped out of the water. She wiped her hair out of her face and looked up to where Cameron was standing; he was as tiny as an ant to her.

"Are you coming down or what?" she cried out.

Cameron could barely hear her, because his heart was beating too loud. Soon he would have a heart attack (or so he thought).

He moved back from the edge and ran his hands through his dark brown hair.

"Shit!" he muttered to himself.

He studied the rock where her clothes had been thrown unto. He hadn't the faintest idea whether he should do it or not.

Before he could start thinking about all the terrible things that could happen as a result, he pulled off his T-shirt and threw it onto the rock. His jeans and sneakers were next to go. Luckily for him he had worn red boxers.

He stared at the edge where Tamara had taken a leap of faith. Before he could change his mind, he ran at full speed and jumped when he reached the edge.

He took a deep breath and never exhaled. The icy wind rushed against his body and made his hair flutter in the wind. Gooseflesh covered every inch of his body.

It felt as if time slowed down, like slow motion in a game. He was certain that his heart had stopped beating for the entire three seconds it lasted.

Once his body hit the water, the cold water was excruciatingly painful. His entire body was two metres down from the surface. Bubbles of air escaped his mouth and floated upwards.

About a minute had passed, when he needed to get to the surface for fresh oxygen. He swam upwards and when his head was out of the water, he breathed in air as if though he never had the pleasure of doing it.

"Hey, I was beginning to think that you wouldn't jump at all." Tamara said as she doggy-paddled closer to where he was.

Cameron wiped his hair out of his face. When he opened his eyes, he stared directly at Tamara's eyes.

"Yeah, well, I did it."

"Was that thrilling and exciting for you?"

"Well, it was most definitely thrilling..."

Tamara giggled in such a way that was almost deafening to the ear. Cameron chuckled and studied her face: there were no make-up smudges on her face. She hadn't worn any.

She smiled in such a way that reminded him of the Wicked Witch of the West. Before long she splashed water in all directions. Some of it hit his face.

He grunted and tried to get the water off his face, but he was unsuccessful. When the burning in his eyes stopped, he looked around and saw that Tamara had somehow vanished.

"Tamara!" he called out. He felt bile creeping up his throat. "Tamara! Are you okay?"

There came no answer, except for something that brushed past his left leg and pulled him.

"Tam..." was all he could get out before the water engulfed his mouth.

Once his head was above the surface again, he heard laughter that was similar to the Wicked Witch of the West.

"Oh, Cameron, I am so sorry. I just had to do it."

He studied her face for a moment, gnashing on his teeth, but once he saw her rounded and pale face, he just smiled at her.

"I will get you for that," he said and made a growl that sounded half like a bear and a zombie at the same time.

"Oh, you sound more like a zombie than anything else."

"Oh, it's not as if you can replicate the perfect growl."

"Well, talking about zombies. I am absolutely famished. I'm going to get something to eat. Are you coming?"

"Yeah, that sounds great."

The two of them splashed around the icy water and headed for the embankment.

Once they were out of the water, water ran down their bodies and leaked onto the green grass beneath their feet.

"I'll race you to the picnic basket," Tamara said and started running as fast as she could.

"Hey, that's unfair," Cameron said laughed. He ran after her and almost ripped in half with laughter when she tripped over her own feet.

She slammed down onto the ground, but she luckily didn't fall that hard. She merely brazed some of the skin off of her left knee.

Cameron stopped beside her when he reached her and said, "Are you okay?"

"Yeah, I guess I'll live," she replied and took the hand Cameron offered to her. He pulled her up and studied her face, which was lit with a wicked smile.

"Loser," was all she said before she pushed him as hard as she could.

Cameron fell onto his back. As she ran towards the picnic basket, he looked at her and guffawed. He had to admit it to himself: she had a dark sense for humour, much like him.

He picked himself up from the ground and ran after her, but she had already beaten him to it.

"I just had to do it, you know."

"Yeah, great move."

As she opened the lid of the wooden picnic basket, she said "I didn't really know what sort of food you eat, so..."

Tamara picked up a red and white chequered blanket, which she spread over the grass.

"Sit down," she said.

Cameron sat down across from her. He studied the plastic fast-food containers she packed out: one of them was filled with slices of pizza. Another had dumplings in. Another had salad in. Another had macaroni and cheese in.

"What would you like?"

"Macaroni and cheese sounds great."

She handed him the container and a pink spork.

"I'm going to have a couple of slices of pizza."

"We can share, if you want to."

"Great!"

She removed three slices of American pepperoni and eta and handed them to him. He scraped some of the macaroni and cheese into her container with the spork.

Cameron set down his container and said, "It's unbelievable how beautiful this place is."

"Yeah," she said and ate a slice of pizza. A piece of pepperoni fell on her lap, but she didn't notice.

"I love it here. I always come here for peace and quiet. You know, to get away from the loudness of the town."

"Yeah," Cameron said and nodded his head. "I can definitely see why you would come here."

He just studied her face as she took another bite of the pizza. He was certain that he could hear music somewhere, but that was just in his mind.

CHAPTER 8

"So, you mysterious creature," Tamara said (which was ironic). "Tell me about yourself."

Cameron sighed and said, "Well, my species is male. I'm seventeen years old. Some people say I'm rocket scientist smart, but that's an insult. I am not really a socialiser, much more of an introvert."

Tamara scoffed and frowned. "You know, that's not what I meant at all. I want to know your deepest and darkest secrets."

"Now why would I tell a stranger I met not too long ago my secrets?"

"Oh, I don't know, maybe because you...trust...me..."

Cameron hadn't the faintest idea of what to say next, so he only sat there and stared at Tamara, who was nibbling on a piece of chocolate.

"It's so beautiful and peaceful here," he heard himself saying. "I would have thought that it would be very crowded here, you know, like a regular party location."

"Yeah," Tamara said. By the way she said it and the way her face looked at the picnic blanket, Cameron could tell something was wrong.

"Are you okay?"

"Yeah," she said and looked at him. "Would you believe it if I told you that this place was in fact a regular party spot?"

Cameron nodded his head and said, "Yeah, I would. I mean, you have lived here for longer than I have been visiting, so yeah."

"About a year and a half ago the mayor's son drowned in that pool of water," she said and pointed her index finger to where they swam earlier.

"Oh, that's really sad. Did you know him?"

"Yeah, everyone knew him. I mean, he was the mayor's son. He was just so young when it happened. They found his body floating atop the water one day when they came to cool off."

"I'm really sorry," he said and frowned. He never really knew what to do in a situation like that, because he was not responsible for such things. He didn't have a reason to be sorry.

"Yeah, well. Ever since that this place has been abandoned. Nobody really comes here anymore."

The conversation went silent for a moment. It was not an awkward silence, but both of them knew that it was a silence of tribute.

Cameron ran his right hand over his left arm, feeling the scorching sun on his skin. He sighed and noticed that his arms were already sun burned to a rosy color.

"I really wish that you would have told me that we were going to be in direct sun," he said.

Tamara felt a surge of gratefulness that he had changed the subject so swiftly. It was as if his words were enough to make her forget about everything that was said before.

She got a hold of the picnic basket and removed a bottle of sun tan lotion. She grinned and said, "Here, I made provisions."

Cameron took the bottle from her, twisted the cap open and sprayed the lotion on his arms and over his face. He wiped the lotion until it was gone.

When he handed her the bottle, he noticed for the very first time that she had a perfectly good tan that made him feel jealous.

Tamara noticed that he was studying her body.

"Hey, my face is up here, you pervert," she said mockingly.

"Oh, no, I, uh," Cameron babbled and found that his tongue was tied in a series of knots. "I was, uh, just...admiring your perfectly tanned body, that's all."

"Oh, so you admit you were looking at my body?"

Cameron's mouth was open even though no words came out. Words formed on his lips, but no sound escaped them.

"Oh, lighten up, Cameron. I was just kidding around. I notice that you have a bit of a tomato burn going on yourself."

He sensed that she was just joking, so he said, "Yeah, sometimes I burn so badly that my skin shrivels up like burnt granadilla skin."

Somewhere near them a couple of bees zoomed past them. Tamara swatted at them and returned her gaze to Cameron.

Cameron returned her gaze and was almost hypnotized by the shade of green of her eyes. Tamara felt as if though she could get lost within his dark brown eyes. Brown eyes were certainly underrated and underappreciated.

Cameron's brown eyes glinted in the sun and looked like tiny pools of molten honey.

As the tension built between them, she moved closer and closer to where he was sitting. Cameron, not familiar with what was happening, just sat there like a statue.

Her face was so close to his that he could still smell a faint hint of macaroni and cheese. The corners of her lips moved upwards, uncovering one of the most beautiful smiles he had ever seen in his life.

In that moment both of them were breathing in ragged motions

Before long they stared deep into each other's eyes. Cameron felt anxious, but Tamara felt excited.

The faint hum of a bee zooming nearby entered Cameron's eardrum, but he paid no attention to it.

As Tamara leaned in to land the kiss on his faded-pink lips, Cameron's attention was lost to the beehive falling down from god knew where.

As the beehive fell on the grass, directly where they were sitting, it burst into shards. Swarms of bees protruded from within the leftover pieces of the hive. Their loud zooming noises were enough to send shivers down Cameron's spine.

Tamara cried out in pain when she felt two bees stung her. Her hand automatically went to the left side of her neck. She clutched the spot as if though she had to stop blood from flowing out, leaving her dried up like a prune.

Cameron yelled as he was stung by four bees at the same time, but different locations: one stung him in the neck, another stung him on his left arm, the other two stung him on his right cheek.

Everywhere they had stung him, little bumps formed and within them the stingers were still buried.

Cameron could feel his throat starting to close up. Breathing became a task of much difficulty.

"Tamara!" he cried out, feeling petrified for her safety. He couldn't see much, because his vision was slurring and the quantity of bees that were swarming past his head also made matters worse.

Cameron's hand closed around Tamara's hand. Their hands interlocked and five seconds later they were fleeing the picnic spot.

A couple of bees were very persistent and followed them as they barely escaped. Tamara swatted at them and managed to get the bees away from her.

"Cameron!" she cried out. "Are you okay?"

Cameron's vision was at that point where he could only see white, which then turned black with tiny stars twinkling.

"Allergic," was all he could get out from with his swollen throat before he fell on the grass beneath him. After that, everything was black...

"Cameron!" she cried out again and fell on her knees next to him.

She shook him a couple of times, sure that he would wake up, but that didn't happen.

Tamara's swollen and tear-streaked face made her look like she had taken a serious beating. Her hands trembled so badly that she could barely get a hold of his legs.

After struggling a moment or two, she finally got a hold of his legs. She dragged him along the way. He would surely have grass burns on his back and legs the next morning.

"Stay with me!' she cried out, but lost all faith. In that moment she was absolutely certain that she had lost him forever.

Tamara dropped his legs; they thumped down like dead meat.

Tears ached her eyes much more ferociously. She made an effort to wipe the tears away.

The truth was that Tamara really didn't possess the power to drag Cameron all the way back to the Jeep. She understood that it might all be over by then, so she couldn't do anything for him.

Tamara was so frustrated with herself for being useless to Cameron. The realization that Cameron could, *was*, dying in front of her brought up all sorts of nostalgic memories, but none of them were quiet as terrifying as the one before her.

"Hey," a man's voice said from behind Tamara.

The suddenness of another living presence made her heart skip as many as three beats.

"I need help!" she said and plucked at the man's brown shirt. "I need help! My friend, he's allergic to bees and he got stung multiple times. Please help him! Just do something!"

The man's eyes widened so much that Tamara was certain that they would pop out of his skull.

"Okay," he said in a tone that would be comforting in any normal situation. "We have to get him to a hospital as soon as we can, young lady, or else he'll go into shock and perhaps a coma."

The man didn't really do anything else that comforted her in any sense possible. He saw that he wasn't going to get any help from her, so he sat on his hinds next to Cameron.

It didn't take him more than two minutes to pick Cameron up. The truth was that even though Cameron didn't really work out, but being tall in stature made him heavy.

"Okay," the man said and looked into Tamara's eyes. "We have to go to my truck, because I parked it no more than five minutes from here. I know a short cut back to the hospital."

"Okay, please, let's just go. I can't let anything happen to him, please..."

Tamara was certain that she could see concern in his light blue eyes. "You have to remain calm and work with me or else he won't make it, do you hear me?"

Tamara nodded her head so many times that she was sure that she looked like a bobbling head. "Yes!"

"Alright then, let's go," the man said.

Without any further ado the man turned around with Cameron in his arms. He started walking away in a brisk pace; Tamara followed suit.

The man hadn't lied either, because they were standing beside his truck within five minutes.

Even though only five minutes had passed then it felt like hours to Tamara. She couldn't really see anything, because her vision was slurring.

Even though Cameron had been the one to faint first, Tamara would soon follow. So many bees had stung her, but she didn't even notice.

'Hey!" the man said and waited for Tamara to pull open the door of the back passenger's seat. "Open the door, would you?"

Tamara quickly pulled the door of the truck open. The man put Cameron's limp body onto the seat and said, "I think you ought to get into the back with him. You know, to make sure that he keeps breathing."

She nodded her head and quickly jumped into the right passenger's seat, nearly tripping on the bars that were mounted onto the side of the truck.

No more than a minute passed by when the ignition roared to life.

"Okay," the man said. He looked back at Tamara's tear streaked and swollen face. "Make sure he breathes, okay?"

Without saying another word the man started driving.

It was a very rocky and uneven road. Every so often Cameron nearly fell in between the gap from the front and back seats.

Tamara got a hold of him just in time when they went over a speed bump, which was a sign that they were already on a road.

She put her right hand's index finger below Cameron's nose and felt a tinkling sensation of low air being breathed out.

"He's still breathing," she said in utter amazement. She hadn't thought that he would still be breathing, but he had. It felt like a miracle.

Tamara put her head on his chest and whispered to him, "Hold on, Cam, you're going to be okay."

The faint hum of air escaping his nose sounded like the sharp sound of a train's wheels screeching to a hold.

Another five minutes passed. Tamara nearly fell asleep on Cameron's chest twice, but awoke both times when the man in front murmured something to himself.

"We're almost there," he said. "Is he still...breathing?"

Tamara heard the thudding sounds Cameron's heart made on the inside of his chest. Even though his heart raced a million miles an hour, he was still breathing.

"Yes," she replied and immediately sat up straight when she heard an ambulance's sirens blaring.

"We're here," he said to her.

The man didn't even bother to find a suitable parking; he parked right in front of the emergency unit entrance.

As the man got out of the driver's seat he yelled, "We need assistance right away! This boy was stung by bees multiple times! He's allergic from what I can tell."

By the time the man was at the passenger door, Tamara was out of the passenger seat. The man moved her out of the way and got a hold of Cameron again. He didn't even bother to close the door. He ran straight to a couple of doctors and said, "Please, help me!"

Not a second later a nurse came around the corner with a bed on wheels.

"Just put him on there, sir," one of the doctors said.

The man did as he was told and put Cameron onto the bed as carefully as he could have.

"There's no way that poor old boy is still alive," one of the nurses said to the other.

Without any further ado three doctors and the two nurses disappeared with Cameron through a set of white doors.

"I hope he's going to be okay," the man said to Tamara, but when he turned to face her, she was already sprawled out on the white tiles of the hospital.

"I need some help here," he said to the only doctor that was still standing by the entrance.

The doctor immediately rushed over to her and called for another nurse. A minute later another nurse came around the right corner with a wheel chair.

Once the nurse was close enough, the man picked Tamara up and put her onto the wheel chair as carefully as he could.

As the doctor and nurse pushed her away, the man stared at them. Once they disappeared through the same door, the man sat down on a black leather couch, which was located on the left side of the room.

One of the nurses protruded from the doors and skipped along the hospital floor as swiftly as an angel.

Once the nurse reached the man, she said, "Sir, we need to know exactly what happened to your kids. I also need you to come to the front desk with me to fill out some forms, if you don't mind."

The man scoffed in utter disbelief. Sure, his grey hair was kept short and his red and white chequered shirt was neatly tucked into his pair of blue jeans, but he sure didn't have any kids.

"I'm sorry, nurse," he said and spotted a name tag. "I'm sorry, Nurse Cornwell, but I didn't witness anything that happened to these poor kids. I was just a bystander."

The nurse looked utterly disappointed. She said, "Oh, I'm sorry to bother you sir. Thank you for being a good citizen. Are you sure there is nothing you can tell me that would help me?"

The man considered this for a moment and said, "I was down at the waterfall spot, you know, to cool down. That's when that young lady approached me and said that her friend was stung multiple times by bees and that he was allergic. I rushed him to the hospital as fast as I could."

"Thank you, Sir," she said and turned around to walk away, but turned back to him again. "Did she perhaps have a wallet or something with them so that we can try to contact the parents?"

The man couldn't help but smile. "No, Nurse Cornwell, I mean, they were both half naked."

"I understand," she replied and finally walked away. She disappeared through the white door again. Her shoes squeaked all the way.

I thought they closed that place down for good after that boy drowned there the man thought as he stood up from the couch. The leather made the same squeaky sounds the nurse's shoes had made.

The man spotted a vending machine and went to it. He studied the screen for a moment or two and decided that he wanted a Twix.

It was at that exact moment that the man's cell phone rang. He filched his cell phone from his pocket and said, "Hello, Darling."

The woman on the other end of the line seemed to be ballistic. The man could barely hear what she was saying.

"Calm down, Darling," he said to her.

The woman continued to babble, but immediately stopped when the man said, "I'm okay, Darling. Some teenagers were in desperate need of my help. Yes, Darling. No, I'm okay. Yes, I'm at the hospital right now. Alright, Darling. See you in a couple of minutes."

Without another word the man hung up the phone.

CHAPTER 9

The light inside the hospital room was so bright that one had to constantly shut your eyes. The walls of the room were painted a white colour. Even the curtains were white.

"Oh, my Baby," a woman said as she entered Tamara's room. "I am so glad to see that you are alright!"

The woman walked at brisk pace over to where Tamara was situated. She sat down on the end of the hospital bed.

"Hi, Mom, I'm okay," Tamara said and grunted as she did.

Her make-up had been dissolved, and smeared her tear stricken face. Her hair was an absolute mess; strands of hair stuck out of her bun.

Miss Kellerman took her daughter's hand into hers and said, "Baby, what happened to you? Your face, it's all messed up."

Tamara sighed and felt a sharp tinge of pain inside her throat. Her throat was as dry as a desert.

She spotted a jug of water and a glass, but when she reached to pour herself a glass, her mother did it for her. "I want you to tell me everything," Miss Kellerman said and frowned. She handed Tamara a glass of fairly hot water.

Tamara downed the glass of water as if though she was stranded in a desert for an entire month without water.

"My friend and I were at the spot by the waterfall. This beehive fell out of the sky from nowhere. We got stung multiple times, so we just ran...but..."

Tamara's mom frowned and nodded her head in understanding and said, "Oh, Hon, is there anything I can do for you?"

"What made matters worse, is the fact that my friend is allergic to bees..."

Before Miss Kellerman could say anything, a doctor and two nurses entered the room.

"Hello, Madame Mayor," the doctor said and smiled at her. "It is such an honor to meet you in person."

"Oh, please just call me Chloe. There's no need to speak so formally to me."

The way Tamara's mom was always able to speak to the community as if though they were equals was something Tamara admired about her.

"Can we speak privately, Chloe?" the doctor asked.

Before Chloe replied, she spotted the doctor's name tag. She smiled and said, "Doctor Cornwell, there's no need for privacy. My daughter can hear anything."

"It's about the health insurance coverage," Cornwell said shyly even though he knew he could speak freely.

"Oh my, is there a problem?"

Cornwell coughed to clear his throat of phlegm. He was very anxious to speak to the mayor. His hands were fiddling behind his back.

"You see," he said shakily. "There is no problem with your coverage, Miss Mayor, uh, Chloe, but it would seem that the boy's parents haven't been notified yet."

There was a moment's worth of silence between everyone in the hospital room. "It is because of that, that we have no choice but not to continue with the boy's treatment."

"Wait, what?" Tamara cried out. "You won't continue to treat him?"

"I'm sorry, Little Miss, but you wouldn't understand it even if I tried to explain it to you."

"Oh, I understand very well," Tamara said and flung her stiff legs out from beneath the blanket. "You want him to die just because you don't get your money, is that it?"

Cornwell's eyes bulged out of his skull. His body was trembling. His cheeks burned a bright red colour. A sweat line formed on his brow.

"We are a hospital, Little Miss, we don't do charity here," he said to her.

Without saying another word, he and one of the nurses left the room. The remaining nurse looked at the mayor and her daughter with apologetic eyes.

"Oh, I'm so sorry about Doctor Cornwell. He can be really unfair sometimes."

Tamara walked over to the nurse; her legs almost gave way twice.

When Tamara reached the nurse, she said, "Is he okay? The boy I came in with, is he okay?"

The nurse looked down at her white shoes for a minute before she looked at Tamara's petrified face.

"I'm not supposed to tell you anything yet, because it's against hospital policy to give out patient's information to non-relatives," the nurse said. "But because I like you, I'll tell you, but you have to promise to keep it our teeny tiny secret…"

Tamara nodded her head a number of times and said, "I *promise* I won't say anything."

"He's unconscious at this moment. The doctors were able to stabilize him. He's not completely breathing on his own yet. I have bad news though…"

Tamara felt tears forming in her emerald green eyes. Her eyes looked like a wet forest during raining season.

"If he doesn't continue to get treatment, he's not going to make it on his own," the nurse said and cleared her throat. "I suggest that you find his parents to clear up the health insurance stuff. I have to go make my rounds, but I'll be back later with an update."

Before Tamara or her mother could say anything to her, the nurse disappeared into the hallway.

Tamara looked at her mother's face. Tears rained down her red-spotted face. She understood very well what was going to happen to Cameron: he would die, and it would be all her fault.

"Baby, I have to ask you," Chloe said as she cupped her hands and took Tamara's face into them. "Do you know where we can find his parents?"

"No, I, uh, just met him a while ago. I don't know anything about his parents. He's going to die, and it will be my fault. I should have stayed away from that freaking waterfall. We already lost *someone* there, and now it's happening all over again."

Before Chloe could comfort her daughter, Tamara burst out in even more tears, followed by sobs. Tears and snot ran down her cheeks in rivers.

"Baby, I'm so sorry about everything. I'll be right back, okay?"

Tamara opened her mouth to protest, but before she could manage a single word, Chloe was already gone.

"Hello, Madame Mayor," the nurse said. "Can I help you with anything?"

Chloe smiled at the nurse that sat behind the nurses' station.

The nurse had also worn a white uniform, which was no surprise at all. Her black hair was made into a bun atop her round head. Her skin was fairly pale, but her blue eyes made her face pop with utter beauty.

"Yes, I would like to ask you a couple of questions, if you wouldn't mind."

The nurse smiled brightly and said, "Oh, Madame Mayor, that's what I am here for. What can I do for you?"

"My daughter, Tamara, came here with a friend earlier today. There's a problem, because his parents cannot be found in time to clear the health insurance issues. So, I would like to take care of everything."

"That can be arranged," the nurse said and rummaged through her desk drawer to find a pen and a form.

Once she found it, she handed it to Chloe with a smile. "You are a really good person, Madame Mayor."

"Thank you for the assistance," Chloe said and walked away with the form in her left hand and the black pen in her right hand.

"Where were you?" Tamara pleaded as Chloe walked back into the room.

"I just cleared something out with the nurse that's all. That friend of yours will be fine. They will continue his treatment."

"Oh, Mom, what did you do?"

It sounded more like she was disappointed than grateful. A frown appeared on her face, sweat decorating the creases.

"I just cleared out the situation, that's all."

"Thank you, Mom," she said and swallowed down her dry throat. "I will pay you back every cent; I promise."

Chloe sighed and said, "Oh, Baby, there's no need for that. I did it to make you feel better. How are you feeling?"

Tamara studied herself for a moment: several marks were on her arms, but they were only tiny red dots. Most of the spots on her face and neck had already cleared.

"It's like I'm going through puberty again, isn't it?" Tamara asked disappointedly. "I don't even wish to know how my face looks."

Chloe giggled in such high pitches that Tamara's eardrums nearly burst. "It's not that bad, Baby," Chloe replied. A smile formed on her lovely face. "Anyhow, I have some good news for you."

"What is it?"

"You made a friend, Baby. I want you to tell me all about him."

The room was filled with utter silence, except for the regular heart monitors and several other medical appliances that could beep.

The bed was in the middle of the room. Its sheet and pillows were white. The white curtains were wide open, and a ray of sunshine crept through the room and made its way to the bed.

Under the white duvet was Cameron's unconscious body. His mind was lost, perhaps in a dream...

"Rochelle," Mister Williamson said as he sat down on the bed next to his wife. "You are being very unfair to me."

Rochelle turned her head and faced her husband. Her face was lit with a scowl that made Jeff feel petrified.

"I will not have our children speak to us that way," she said and frowned. "God says that children should honour thy mother and father. I intend to keep it that way."

Jeff sighed deeply before he said, "I can't take this anymore. Ever since the...you found God in this unnatural way. Everything you say and do."

"Don't you dare condescend me. Everyone grieves in a different way. You didn't even grief, Jeff. You acted as if nothing happened."

Cameron was two years younger. He had been sitting on his bed, reading a paperback. His attention hadn't really been focused on the paperback, but very well his parents' fight.

Even though his door was closed, he could still hear them fighting, because they weren't really talking, they were raising their voices at each other with every sentence they said.

"It was hard for me too, you know that. You were never a church goer, but now you are a Jesus freak. He took our unborn child away, and you go on praising him."

"Don't you dare say stuff like that, Jeff. I found comfort in God, because my husband couldn't even do it. You couldn't even be there for me!"

"I can't take this craziness anymore, Rochelle. I want a divorce. I went to a lawyer's office on Friday and drew up the papers."

Jeff rose from the bed and went to the drawer at his side of the bed. He rummaged through it and found the papers tucked away neatly between socks and underwear.

He handed her the envelope. She sat with it in her hands, just staring at it.

"You would break your vow?" she asked him.

"What vow are you talking about?"

"The day we were married you took a vow: till death do us part. If you want a divorce, you are breaking this vow and God will punish you for it."

"Honey, death did do us part. That miscarriage was the death that did us apart. The day our unborn child died was also the day I lost the woman I had loved."

"I still love you, Jeff, but you are a sinner and God will punish you by sending you to the eternal fire pit."

"Stop it, just stop it! I don't want to hear any more of this bullshit. I'm leaving tonight. I'll find some place to stay. When I come back tomorrow, I want to see the signed papers. I also want the kids' stuff to be packed."

"Wait, what? Are you taking the kids away from me? You can't do that, Jeff! They are my kids as well!"

"I don't care what you want or think. I am done dealing with you. You are crazy, and the court will give me full custody of the kids when they see your record."

Without saying another word, he went to the closet and got himself a big suitcase.

He threw the suitcase onto the bed and plucked open his drawer. He didn't even fold his clothes as he tossed it into the suitcase and zipped it up once it was full.

"I'll get the rest of my stuff tomorrow. Oh, by the way, don't let me come here tomorrow and the kids aren't here."

"Oh, come on, Jeff. Let's just talk about this for a minute. Please don't do this to me, to us."

"I have talked to you enough. You don't ever listen to what I have to say. I am done! I just can't do this anymore."

"Please, I'm so sorry. Don't take the kids away from me, I beg you."

Jeff didn't say anything; he only nodded his head. He grabbed his suitcase and left the master bedroom.

Just when he walked down the stairs, Cat appeared at the foot of the stairs.

Her little face was pink. Her white nightgown made her look like a little princess. Her dark brown hair hung loosely on her shoulders.

"Where are you going, Daddy?"

"Oh, Cat, I just have to go away for a little while, but I'll be back tomorrow, I promise."

Cat's eyes turned into glass as she said, "Is this because of what I said at the table?"

Despite the situation that was going on, he smiled at her. "Of course it wasn't your fault. Mommy and I have decided to be apart for tonight."

"I will never say anything like that ever again, I promise."

"That's very good of you. Come give me a hug."

Cat ran to her father and hugged him fiercely. Tears ran down her pink cheeks and collected to form a drop below her chin.

"I have to get going now," he said as he let go of her, but she didn't do the same. "Oh, Cat, I really have to go now, but I promise to see you tomorrow."

At last, she let him go; her arms dropped to her sides. She stopped crying, which was a big relief.

"So, you're leaving then," Cameron said as he descended the stairs. "But you promised to see us tomorrow, right?"

"Of course I'll see you guys tomorrow. Come give your dad a hug, Big Man."

Cameron smiled and went to his father. He hugged him; his father patted him on the back as he said, "I'm sorry, I have to go. See you kids tomorrow."

Without any further ado, he left through the front door with his suitcase at his left side.

Cameron watched as his father got into his car and walked away. He went back to his room.

No more than five minutes later the ignition started. His father drove off.

Even though he knew it was against the law to text and drive, Jeff did so.

A moment later someone was calling him. He accepted the call and put the phone next to his left ear.

"Hey, I need a place to crash for tonight," he said to the person on the other end of the line. "Yeah, I finally had enough of it. Okay, are you sure? Great, thanks. See you in a bit."

Jeff hung up the phone and put it on his lap. Just as he reached to turn on the radio, someone broke the silence for him.

"Daddy!" Cat cried out.

She had been hiding in the gap between the seats. She popped up and sat on the seat.

"Cat!" Jeff cried out. He turned his focus from the road to look at her for a moment. "What are you doing here?" He looked back her, bewildered.

They were supposed to stop at an intersection, because the light turned a bright red color.

Jeff's attention hadn't been where it was supposed to, because when he looked back at the road, he noticed something that made his bladder loosen up.

A truck came searing down the road at fort speed, with its bright headlights on. The horns blared.

The very last thing Cat had said, was, "Daddy?"

The very last thing Jeff would see were the lights that came closer and closer until it was all over in a split second...

CHAPTER 10

Cameron's mind shut out of dreaming world. His eyes opened slowly, which felt like a mammoth task.

"Oh," Tamara said and squeezed Cameron's right hand. "You're awake."

"How are you feeling?"

"Like I've been stung multiple times by bees."

Tamara felt a smile form on her lips. Even though he could have died, Cameron didn't seem to be affected by it, because he smiled too.

"Cameron," she said. Her voice was so soft that it was almost suppressed by the wind that howled outside. "I'm so sorry about everything. I...I... didn't know..."

Cameron scoffed and said, "There's no need to apologize, Tamara. It was the most thrilling and fun day I've had in a very long time. Thank you."

Tamara's eyes filled with tears, but they were tears of joy and relief.

"Although, I think that's enough excitement and death-defying fun for a while."

She was unsure whether he was just kidding around, but when he chuckles a couple of times, her smile widened.

"I'm really glad you're okay."

"How are you feeling?" he asked as he sat up straight. Tamara saw his struggle and put a pillow behind his head.

"I'm okay *now*."

There was a moment's worth of silence between them, but it wasn't an awkward silence. Both of them took a moment to thank *whomever or whatever* for helping them escape what could have been a very tragic day.

"Cameron, I need to ask you a couple of questions, if you don't mind of course."

"Ask away."

"Nobody came to see you yet, or to find out what happened to you. Can I call anyone for you?"

Cameron realized that he had lost his cell phone somewhere along the way. It was hard to keep track of your property when hundreds of lethal bees were on your tail.

He sighed and said, "I ought to phone my mom, you know. I don't want her to be worried about me."

"Are you feeling okay to call her yourself, or should I call her for you?"

"I'll make the call, thanks."

Tamara filched the cell phone from her jeans' pocket. Cameron studied her as she did so: the last time he saw her, she had been wearing a bathing suit. Now she was wearing a clean pair of jeans and a white t-shirt.

"Here you go," she said as she handed him the cell phone. "I'll be back in a couple of minutes, okay?"

"Yeah, thanks."

Without any further ado she left the room. Cameron sat in the utter silence for a minute or two, just appreciating it.

He looked at the cell phone screen and sighed. He didn't really feel like making the call, but he knew it was the right thing to do.

He unlocked the cell phone and typed in his mother's number. He dialled and held the phone next to his left ear.

"Hello," a voice on the other end of the line said. It wasn't his mother's voice though. It sounded like Ira.

"Ira?"

"Yeah, it's me. What's going on?"

"Where's my mom?"

The only noise that could be heard was static. During this quiet period Cameron's body went cold. His heart throbbed so hard that he could feel it hammering against his ribs.

"Cameron, I'm sorry, but I have no idea. I was close by when I heard the phone ringing. The bed was unmade, and her purse was on the bed."

"Oh, I, uh...I kind of needed to talk to her, but I guess she's out. I don't want you to be alarmed or anything, but I'm in the hospital..."

Before he could manage another sentence, heck, even another syllable, Ira interrupted him.

"Oh my God, Cameron! Are you okay? What happened? Oh, I'm on my way."

"Calm down, Ira. It was just a little accident. Come to the hospital and I'll fill you in on everything. If you perhaps see my mom anywhere, tell her to come, okay?"

Ira seemed to consider this and said, "Yes, I'll see you in a couple of minutes. Bye."

She hung up on the other end. Cameron moved his hand away from his ear and studied it for a moment. On the home screen was a picture of Tamara and an older woman, presumably her mother.

Just as he put the cell phone down next him on the duvet, Tamara came into the room.

"Here you go," she said and held out a cup of hot coffee to him. Once she reached him, he took the cup and took a sip.

"And here you go," he said and handed her the cell phone. "Thanks for letting me use it."

"No problem," she replied and tucked the cell phone back into her pocket.

Cameron and Tamara just looked at each other. Their eyes met. He was sure that she was trying to hypnotize him with her glamorous eyes.

"Knock-knock," a voice said from within the doorway. "Can I come in?"

The woman had a slim design to her. Her blonde hair, visibly the same shade as Tamara's, was made into a bun atop her head. Her face was a rosy pink colour, which made her cheekbones pop with utter beauty.

"Of course you can come in, Mom," Tamara said and took another sip of her hot coffee.

"Hi," Chloe said as she reached the bed. She held out her hand to Cameron, but she withdrew it when she saw his right hand had clutched a coffee cup and his left was wrapped in gauge.

"Hi, you must be Tamara's mom?"

"That would be me," she said and grinned, revealing ever white teeth. "It's so nice to meet you. Not that I've heard anything of you before."

Tamara sensed that the silence that brooded between them would soon turn into an awkward one. She said, "Oh, mom, this is Cameron. We met like...a day ago."

"Oh my, that's such a beautiful name."

"Thank you, Miss."

"Oh, please call me Chloe. I don't like it when people say 'Miss Mayor' or 'Miss' or 'Madame'."

"Mom, can we please have some privacy?"

"Of course," Chloe said. She looked at them for a moment or two. "It was nice meeting you, Cameron. I'm glad to see that you're looking good."

Without any further ado she left the room. The two of them sat there in utter silence.

Cameron was the one to break the silence when he said, "Tamara, can I ask you a question? I mean, it's okay if you don't want to answer though."

She nodded her head and said, "Of course, Cameron. What is it?"

"You said that the mayor's son drowned in that pool beneath the waterfall..."

Tamara felt a sharp tinge of pain in her heart. For a moment she looked down at her chest, sure that blood was soaking her white t-shirt, but it was still dry.

"Yes," she said and looked down at the floor. "My little brother drowned there."

Cameron sensed that the conversation was going to turn into one that would end in tears and him having to comfort her.

Luckily for Cameron, he didn't have to do anything, because Ira ran into the room.

"Oh, here you are," Ira said as she sprinted towards the bed. "The nurse at the front desk didn't want to give me your room number, so I sneaked past her and looked through every room."

"Ira," Cameron said and frowned. "Just calm down, would you? I'm fine...How the hell did you get here so fast?"

Ira sighed and said, "Yeah, I came as soon as I could! I would have been here sooner had *someone* called..."

"Oh, Tamara, this is my cousin, Ira. Ira, meet Tamara."

The silence that brooded between them wasn't awkward, it felt feral. The two girls just looked at each other. Cameron was sure that both their heads would explode, because they glared that hard at each other.

"Yeah," Tamara said. "I know who this is. Excuse me."

Without saying another word Tamara left the room. The cup of coffee in her hand swayed a couple of times and spilled hot coffee onto her hand, but she didn't even notice.

"What the hell was that?" Cameron heard himself asking.

"Oh, just nothing," Ira said and sighed. "So, what happened?"

Cameron also sighed, but his was in frustration. "Don't try to change the subject, Ira! What the hell was *that* about?"

"I don't want to talk about this, Cameron."

"Just tell me what is going on."

"You're not my boss, Cameron. I don't have to tell you anything I don't want to. I said I don't want to talk about this, so just leave it, okay?"

After Ira spoke the room went silent for a minute or two. It was one of the most awkward silences both of them had ever experienced. Cameron was thinking of possible explanations to why Tamara left and why Ira didn't want to tell him what happened.

"Listen," he said and studied Ira's face. Her face was pale, and her eyes were red with tears. "I'm sorry that I tried to force you to tell me what happened. Can you forgive me? I mean, look where we are…"

A small smile formed on Ira's red lips. She sighed and said, "Of course I accept your apology."

"You really don't know where my mom is?"

"I'm so sorry, Cam, but I don't know."

Ira filched her cell phone from her pocket and unlocked it, using her password. She studied the screen for a minute and sighed in disappointment.

"She hasn't answered yet. She hasn't read the messages I sent her either."

Tamara fought hard to keep the tears back, but her efforts were unsuccessful. The moment she exited the hospital, cold tears spilt down her pale face.

Frustrated, she tried to wipe them off her face when she saw a familiar face approaching her.

"Are you okay?" the guy said, but she couldn't see who it was, because the tears made everything blurry.

Even though she had no idea who it was, she said, "Yeah, thanks."

"Are you sure?" the guy asked. "Maybe you should sit down for a minute or two."

Before Tamara could protest, the guy got a hold of her arm and led her to the nearest bench.

"Here," he said and sat on the iron bench.

Tamara sat down next to him. By then she had gotten a hold of herself. She looked up and studied the guy's face.

She smiled apologetically and said, "Oh, hi, Eric. For a moment there I didn't know who you were."

Eric nodded his head in understanding. He took her delicate hand in his and smiled at her.

"Are you sure you are okay? I mean, we can talk about it, if you want to..."

She shook her head three times. "No, I, uh, I'm okay, thanks for asking."

Even though Eric could sense that she clearly wasn't okay, her persistent tone of voice made him not interfere. She would talk to him when she was ready.

There was a moment of silence between them, but it was broken by Tamara's voice that seemed to have gone back to normal.

"How's your mom?"

Eric frowned and said, "She's fine, thanks for asking."

"How's your sister?"

"She's also fine, thanks."

Eric clearly didn't have the faintest idea why she was asking him all those questions, so he said, "Why do you ask?"

Tamara's mouth opened to speak, but the words didn't come out; her mouth just hung slightly open.

"I'm sorry if I'm being nosy, but what are you doing here if your family is fine?"

Eric bit his lower lip and smiled as if though he were embarrassed. He didn't have any control over his hands, because he fiddled with his fingers. His cheeks burned up a little.

When he spoke, his voice was a little shaky. "I, uh, I'm...I came here to check up on, uh, Cameron..."

Once he finished speaking, he cleared his throat and studied Tamara's face. She knew exactly what was going on, so she grinned so big that one could see the back of her mouth.

"Shut up, okay?" Eric said and looked away from her face for a minute or two.

"You like *him*, don't you?"

Tamara didn't say it in a mocking way. Her voice was serene, almost approvingly.

When Eric didn't speak for another two minutes, Tamara said, "It's nice of you to come and check up on him, Eric. He's perfectly fine..."

A smile appeared and just as quickly disappeared from his face. "Oh, uh, thanks. I guess I should get going now. It was nice talking to you, Tamara."

Eric rose from the bench and started walking towards the parking area of the hospital.

Tamara could see by the way his head was bobbing that he was probably cussing himself out.

"Eric!' she called out.

For a moment Eric stopped dead inside his tracks, but he probably thought that he was just imagining it. He continued to walk away.

"Eric!" she called out once more.

This time Eric stopped and turned his head to look at Tamara. He raised his eyebrows.

Once Tamara realized that she had Eric's undivided attention, she said, "I'm going back in to see him again. You are welcome to come with me, you know, say hi to him and see him for yourself."

Eric seemed to consider it for a moment or two whilst Tamara stood up from the bench. Her bum was as cold as ice.

Tamara made her way towards the entrance of the hospital but waited for Eric before entering.

"Are you coming, or what?"

"Uh, yeah," Eric said and jogged over to where Tamara was patiently waiting for him.

Together they walked into the hospital with mixed emotions. Tamara was concerned about her deepest and darkest secret with Ira. Eric was nervous, because he always got nervous in the presence of a gorgeous guy.

While walking along the long white hallways of the hospital, Tamara couldn't help but feel useless in multiple ways: she couldn't do anything to help Cameron and that she had had an encounter with her arch nemesis.

Walking beside her was Eric. He was also screaming at himself from the inside. He really didn't know why he had come in the first place.

"Excuse me, young lady," a nurse called out to Tamara.

Tamara tuned around to face the nurse. The nurse's black hair had been made into a bun atop her head. She tugged at her nurse's skirt to straighten it. She clearly took pride in her chosen profession, because she was standing as upright as a streetlamp.

"Oh my, is there something wrong with him?" Tamara called out nervously. Her breathing became ragged and not a split second later, sweat formed on her brow.

"Young lady, there is no need to conjure up any demons. Your friend is doing great. He just had his medicine a couple of minutes ago, so he is resting right now."

It was as if a big weight was lifted off Tamara's shoulders. She sighed and said, "Thank you, Nurse. Can I come back a bit later then?"

The nurse grinned, revealing perfectly white teeth. "Of course you can come back later. As a matter of fact: no matter what the patient's condition is, it is always positive to have support."

Tamara couldn't help but feel a great admiration towards the nurse. The nurse was pretty fantastic at her job, because she made her feel at ease, peace almost.

"Just remember," the nurse said and raised her eyebrows. "Please come back later during visiting hours..."

Without any further ado the nurse left the two of them alone. They looked at each other with eyes full of disappointment.

"Oh well," Tamara said. "I guess we'll just have to come back later then. He needs his rest."

Eric sighed in disappointment and said, "I won't be able to visit him tonight. I have to practice, and my parents and I have something on after practice."

"It's okay," she replied and put a hand on his broad shoulder. "I will tell him you stopped by."

Eric nodded and said, "Thanks, I really should get going now."

They looked at each other for another minute or two. Eric broke the gaze as he walked away from Tamara.

She stood there for five minutes, watching him disappear through the hallways of the hospital. She couldn't help but smile.

"Hey, Honey," Chloe said from behind her. "What are you doing standing here all by your lonesome?"

Tamara hadn't even noticed that she was the only one in the halls of that wing. In the distant hospital monitors and machines were steadily beeping.

"I, uh, I wanted to go see Cameron, but he's asleep at this moment. We have to go back during visiting hours tonight."

There was a tone of disappointment in her voice that made Chloe's heart ache. She wished she could wake Cameron up for her daughter's sake.

"Honey," Chloe said and put her right hand on Tamara's left shoulder. "Let's go home now. We can come back later..."

They walked through the long white halls of the hospital; neither of them said a word to one other. They continued to walk to the entrance of the hospital.

Tamara's sneakers stuck to the white hospital floor because of a piece of gum. Chloe's high heels made clicking sounds as she walked.

CHAPTER 11

Tamara spit the minty toothpaste into the sink and glanced up to check the time. The digital clock that hung on the bathroom's cream-colored wall read 06:23.

A little stream of toothpaste foam ran down the corner of her mouth. She used the back of her right hand to wipe it off.

That dreadful occasional meeting with the mirror came.

Her beautiful and glossy blonde hair was an absolute bird's nest. Her skin was shiny with the night's sweat. The emerald eyes darted back and forth in the mirror, studying the rest of her.

In that moment everything was silent: her breathing, the birds' songs outside and even the thoughts in her head.

She couldn't help but smile at the person in the mirror. She *loved* the reflection.

Tamara's smile of confidence made her facial features pop with utter beauty. Knowing that she was going to see Cameron soon, her eyes glinted with excitement.

Before long she pulled the sliding doors of the shower open. She removed her clothes and got into the shower; the glass sliding door made a squeaky sound as she closed them.

No more than ten minutes had passed when Tamara's tomato red arm peered through the steam covered shower door. She got a hold of her red towel and rolled it around her body.

Once she completely opened the sliding door, the entire bathroom was engulfed with the white mist; she could barely see in front of her.

Knowing that her mother would already be off to work, she went downstairs to fetch herself a cappuccino.

Her mom had a keen sense of style and decorating, but Tamara always wondered what on earth had possessed her mother to make the kitchen orange.

Something she always admired about her mother was the fact that she knew what her daughter needed in the morning after waking up: coffee. A cup of ready-made cappuccino was waiting for her in the microwave.

Coffee, as simple as it may sound, was something her body craved, a rather *compulsory* feeling, in the morning. She had a co-dependant relationship with coffee.

Tamara turned the microwave's knob and waited for the time on the rectangular display to tick down. The timer that ticked down always reminded her of a bomb. It was very immature of her, but she always opened the microwave door on the last second, believing that she had put an end to the reign of potential danger.

She took delight in the aroma of hot coffee. When she got a hold of the cup, she brought it up to her nose to engulf her airways.

"Nothing quite as good as that," she said.

As she took a sip of the sugarless cappuccino, she sighed with satisfaction. She took two more sips of the cappuccino before leaving the kitchen.

The digital clock in the living room read 06:59. It was almost time to indulge in another little treat...

Tamara put her cappuccino down on the glass table that was situated in the middle of the living room between the television and the couches.

She skipped to the window with a huge grin on her face; her perfect white teeth stuck out and shun like little diamonds in the sun.

Without being careful, she plucked the silver curtain open and waited for her piece of eye candy to arrive; one of the curtain hooks popped off and tumbled to the ground.

Not a minute later, her eye candy appeared. Her eyes darted to the right. She bit her lower lip and put her left index finger on her lip.

The guy was wearing black shorts with white sneakers. His bare legs contorted into various shapes as the muscles beneath them moved.

His short black hair was shiny with sweat. His face was flushed red and sweat trickled down his face in little streams.

His bare torso made her legs wobble like a plate of jelly. Tamara had to clutch her legs with both her hands to keep from toppling over.

That torso was apt to make any girl or guy's legs feel like jelly. What made matters even more erotic for her, was that perfect tan.

His pecs heaved up and down, and up and down. His abs were rock solid and didn't dare go flaccid. The sweat made each individual block look even more picturesque.

Just as quickly as he came, just as quickly he disappeared around the corner. Tamara sighed, disappointed.

Even though she knew he was gay, she still loved looking at Eric. He was total eye candy. She was sure that he would make her gain weight, because she loved that piece of candy.

Tamara sighed again and said, "Damn."

That one simple word could explain Eric thoroughly. He was in fact one of the best beefcakes in their whole darned town.

She stood there for another minute or two, just watching where Eric disappeared into. By the time she went back to her coffee, it was more like iced coffee, but she didn't mind at all.

As she entered the kitchen, she took the final sip of her coffee and put the mug into the dishwasher. A tiny cube of dishwashing soap was already propped into its place, so she turned the dishwasher on.

Unlike Cameron, she had no qualms choosing her outfit for the day. Even though she was different from all the other girls her age, there was one thing she had in common with them: clothes.

She found herself standing in her walk-in closet, staring at different blouses, even though she never wore them.

"Ah," she said with satisfaction. She grabbed the thing she loved wearing the most: jeans. The blue jeans went best with t-shirts, so she grabbed a blue one to go with it.

Although many girls her age would have a tremendous issue with shoes, she didn't. She grabbed the first pair of sneakers from the shoe rack and put them on; they were blue and matched the rest of her outfit.

As she looked at herself in the mirror to ensure her outfit was absolute perfection, her cell phone vibrated in her jeans' pocket.

She filched her cell phone from her right pocket and studied the screen. It was her mother. She swiped to accept and switched the phone to the other hand and held it against her left ear.

"Oh, hi, Hon," her mom said on the other end of the line.

"Hi, Mom, is everything okay?"

"Oh, I've never been better. I just called to tell you that I have to attend multiple meetings today, so I will probably be late tonight."

"That's okay, Mom. I understand."

"Get yourself some take out or something, but just be back at home before six, okay?"

"Okay, Mom. Can I get you anything?"

"No, thanks Hon. I will get myself something during the day. Enjoy your day."

"Thanks, Mom, I will."

"Oh, before I forget to tell you. The hospital called this morning..."

With that being said, Tamara couldn't help but feel anxious and nauseous at the same time. Did something happen to Cameron?

Her breathing became ragged. Chloe could hear it on the other end of the line.

"Sorry, Hon. There's no need to be anxious or anything. He made great progress. They are releasing him today."

Tamara immediately felt relieved and said, "Wow, you had me going there, Mom. Thanks."

"Have a great day!"

"You too, Mom."

Without another word, Chloe hung up the phone. Tamara stood there with the phone still held against her ear for two seconds.

That woman is going to give me a heart attack someday! she thought and sighed again.

It felt like a mammoth task for him to complete. Cameron tried opening his eye lids twice, but both times they fell shut again. It felt like weights kept pulling them down again.

Third time's the charm; this time his eyes stayed open. He was staring directly at the white ceiling.

It was at that exact moment that the nurse entered his room. She noticed that he was awake and said, "Good morning, young sir. How are you feeling today?"

The suddenness of someone else in his room startled him. With a shaky voice he said, "I'm feeling much better, thank you."

The nurse could hear the shakiness in his voice. She smiled apologetically as she stood by his bed.

"My apologies for startling you, sir."

"There's no need, Miss."

The nurse had three pills in her right hand. She handed them to Cameron; she poured him a glass of water as well.

Whilst he was drinking the pills, she went to the only window in the room and pulled open the white curtains.

Brighter than ever sunshine made its way through the room; Cameron had to squint.

"Well, I have some great news for you," the nurse said as she took the glass from him. "You are being released today."

"Great," he replied.

When he spoke the next sentence, it was much more serious, almost grave. "Have you heard anything from my mother yet?"

The nurse studied his face for a moment or two. Even though Cameron was looking great for someone that had been at the cusp of death, his face was still pale. Tiny red dots covered his face and arms.

She sighed and said, "Unfortunately not, young sir."

Without saying another word to Cameron, she left the room. He appreciated the silence, but in this case, it didn't help him with his anxiety.

Where the hell is she? He thought and sighed.

He sat up straight and propped one of the pillows behind his back to sit comfortably.

About five minutes had passed. The medicine made him feel very sleepy, so he closed his eyes and fell asleep.

"Cameron!" a voice said anxiously.

He immediately recognized that voice. It could belong to no other than his Ira. She shook him by the shoulders until he was awake.

"Oh, shit," she said. "I'm sorry. I thought you were like...uh...dead or something."

"No," he replied and laughed. "I was just resting."

"So, you are being released today."

"Yeah, I guess I am."

"I can't wait. You know, Amy can't stop talking about you, Cam. There's a party tonight, and well, she asked me to ask you if you wanted to go..."

Cameron laughed at that, not because it was funny or anything. Ira was very self-centred sometimes.

"No thanks, Ira. I think I should take it easy for a while."

Ira sighed disappointedly and made a baby face that Cameron could never seem to refuse. "Please, Cam, we really want you there..."

Cameron knew it was just a tactic to win him over, but he couldn't find it in his heart to refuse. It was one of the many reasons he thought he would be a bad parent someday.

"Okay, maybe I'll go..."

"It's not a definite yes yet, but at least it's a maybe," Ira said and grinned. "I guess I can work with that."

"But it's going to cost you."

Ira didn't even hesitate. She said, "Oh, yes, anything for you, my Lord."

Cameron chuckled and got a hold of her hand. "Can I ask you a favour?"

Ira nodded her head and squeezed his hand. "Of course, Cam. Anything for you..."

"I'm getting released today, as you very well know. I don't have any clothes here, you see. Can you go home and get me something to wear, please?"

Ira shook her head, making him feel a little angry. "I already packed a bag for you. It's in the car. I'll go get it for you."

"Thanks," he replied and smiled. Even though she could neglect important things sometimes, he admired the fact that she sometimes thought ahead.

Ira walked to the door, turned around and said, "I'm really glad that you are okay."

Without saying another word, she left the room. Cameron sat in utter silence once more.

The entrance of the hospital was ahead of her. She hoped to all the gods that it would be the last time she would have to visit Cameron in the hospital, forever.

Ira walked through the long white halls for what felt like hours, but it had only been five minutes. Once she passed the nurses' station, she took a left turn.

The fact was that even though they didn't see each other as often as they would like, they were very close. She couldn't bear the thought of ever losing him.

As she exited the hospital, a familiar face resurfaced. Ira's mouth hung open. Just when she thought that she would duck and hopefully not get spotted, but it was too late.

Tamara and Ira looked straight at each other. It was too late. If looks could kill, Ira wondered which one of them would have been dead first.

"Well, well," Tamara said and put her hands on her hips. "What the hell are you doing here?"

Ira sighed and felt her cheek blushing. "I'm visiting Cameron. What are you doing here?"

"I'm surprised that you even know him. You know, ever since you became one of the popular girls in school."

"He's my cousin. I don't understand how you know him. I mean, it's not like he's your type...is he?"

Ira was a good girl, but her mouth was the cause of her misery and trouble. She was never one to fumble her words.

"Just leave, why don't you?"

"I'm not going anywhere, Tamara."

"I'm done letting you trample all over me, Ira."

That seemed to be humorous because Ira nearly ripped in half with laughter. She had to clutch her stomach because it hurt pretty badly.

"Oh, what are you going to do? Talk me to death?"

"Just leave me alone! I'm warning you..."

"You hit like a girl, Tammy. Your threats are empty. You are *nothing*! You are *worthless*!"

Tamara laughed sarcastically and said, "You don't get it, do you Swallows?"

That seemed to bring the worst out of Ira. Her face was blood red. She was so furious that she actually balled her fists.

"Don't call me that!"

"I've had enough of your bullshit, Ira. We were once friends, more than friends..."

"SHUT UP!"

"I don't see why I should shut up, Ira. You are who you are. There's no need to deny it."

"I could say the same for you, Tamara. What do you want from Cameron?"

Tamara scoffed and said, "That's none of your business."

Ira looked down at her balled fists. She hadn't even realized that she had balled them in the first place.

"I think you should leave, Tamara."

Tamara scoffed again and said, "I don't listen to you. Now get out of my way."

Ira didn't do anything to stop Tamara from walking into the hospital.

Tamara walked past Ira, almost shouldering her. She muttered something to herself, but Ira couldn't hear what it was.

"What will your precious mom think about you when she finds out the truth about what happened at the waterfall spot that day?"

Tamara laughed hysterically. She laughed so hard that her stomach hurt.

"My mom already knows the truth, Ira. Your parents on the other hand, don't."

"YOU BITCH! Was that a threat?"

Tamara smiled in a way that made her look like a little princess. "What a stupid little girl you are, Ira. That wasn't a threat. I could never threaten you. This is a warning."

Tears formed in Ira's eyes. She sniffed and felt the first tear running down her cheek. "How did you get like *this?* The Tamara I knew wasn't like this..."

"*You* made me become this person, Ira!"

Ira shook her head multiple times and said, "The Tamara I knew..."

"The Tamara you knew is *dead!* You killed her! You left me alone! It's *all* because of you. I am so sick of your type, Ira. If you don't leave us alone, I will tell him everything."

Through tears and snot Ira said, "You wouldn't, Tammy."

"Try me," Tamara said. "And my name is Tamara, not Tammy."

Without saying another word, Tamara entered the hospital. Ira was still standing there, wiping away tears and snot from her face with her brown handkerchief.

CHAPTER 12

I ra stood there for a moment or two. Her brown handkerchief was wet with tears and snot. She carefully folded it once the tears quit leaking from her eyes.

She finally had herself under control, but she knew it was going to take more than that to mend her heart.

After the events that unfolded, she never realized that she had dropped the brown bag with Cameron's clothes.

Considering everything that had just happened, it was odd to see Ira grinning. Her teeth glinted like tiny diamonds in the morning sun.

Even though she knew in the back of her mind that Tamara was with Cameron in his room, she picked up the bag and sighed deeply before gaining the courage to continue making her way to the room.

It was a rare occurrence for her to feel self-conscious as she was one of the most popular girls in town. It was one thing to be popular and loved by all, but she was reduced to *fear* and *regret*.

"Hey, Cameron," Tamara said as she entered his room.

Cameron was not in bed anymore. He was staring out of the window; at what he was staring, Tamara couldn't say.

He turned around and studied her face. He noticed that all color had gone from her face. Her skin was as pale like a statue, almost ashy.

"What's wrong?" he asked her.

Tamara smiled nervously and said, "Nothing. I just want you out of this darned hospital, that's all."

She giggled nervously, but her efforts to seem normal were useless. Cameron could see that something was wrong, but he understood that she didn't want to talk about it at all.

"Yeah," he said and grinned, not revealing any teeth. "Do you know what the first thing is that I am going to do when I get back to my cousin's?"

"Nope."

"I am going to make me a mega-sized cup of Joe."

"Yeah, hospital coffee tastes like water, not coffee."

"Totally!"

There was a minute's worth of silence between them. Neither of them looked each other in the eyes.

"Listen," Tamara said at last.

Cameron looked directly into Tamara's eyes. He could *see* that she was hurting. Her emerald green eyes shone as tears formed in them.

"Look, there are no words to describe how sorry I am about what happened to you, so I am not even going to try. I hope you know that I..."

Before she could finish the sentence, the first tear spilt down her left cheek. Before long Cameron was standing in front of her. He wiped away the tear with his thumb.

Tamara was taken aback at how close he was standing to her. She could almost feel his lukewarm breath against her skin. In that moment her body temperature dropped below zero. Her breathing spiked. Her palms were sweaty. Her legs almost gave way.

Cameron took her delicate face into his hands as if though he was handling a priceless artefact.

As he got even closer to her face, she could smell a hint of medicine. She understood what was about to happen. It was something she was looking forward to ever since she had met him. Her loins ached for his touch, his closeness, the reassurance...

"There's no need to apologize, Tamara," he said.

Tamara was absolutely certain that he was going to land the kiss. He grinned and moved his face away from hers.

They stood and stared at each for another minute; Cameron still had her face in his cupped hands.

Suddenly Cameron dropped his hands and turned around. He walked to the window and stared out of it again.

Tamara's face contorted into a frown with lines creasing all over her face. She was certain that he would kiss her, but he didn't. Had she built it up in her head? Had she convinced herself that he was into her?

A feeling of discontent filled her heart. Her loins were on fire. Her entire body quivered like a wet Chihuahua would.

"Hey, Cam," a voice from within the doorway said.

Cameron turned around again and immediately his smile reappeared. He walked as swiftly as he could, because his entire body ached from being in bed for too long.

"Hey, Ira," he said as he took the bag she handed to him. "Thank you so much for this. I can't wait to get out of this darned hospital...I am going to go change."

Without saying another word, he left through the door on his left, which led to a bathroom. He closed the door behind him.

"Hey," Ira said.

"What do you want, Ira?"

"Look, I know I have been a real bitch to you in the past. If you be-friended Cameron just to get back at me, I urge you to stop. Cameron is a great guy..."

Before Ira could finish, Tamara said, "Yeah, you are right. Cameron is a great guy. He's not like the rest of them. I am not going to hurt him just to get back at you. The fact that you would even suggest something like that is, I don't know, absurd..."

"I don't get it...What *do* you want from him?"

Tamara scoffed and put her hands on her hips. "That has absolutely nothing to do with you. Just keep your fake nose out of my damn business."

Ira rolled her eyes and said, "Listen, Tamara, there's no need for us to fight like this. I mean, we both care about him. I think we owe it to him to not fight in front of him."

Tamara considered it for a moment. Even though she hadn't the faintest of love for Ira *anymore*, she had to admit that Ira made a valid point.

"Okay," Tamara said. She studied Ira's face with her emerald green eyes. Ira grinned at her; it was something Tamara hadn't seen in years.

"How about we call a truce?"

Tamara didn't answer but nodded her head in agreement.

The door inside the room swayed open and hit the wall by accident. Cameron poked his head out from the archway.

"That was a lot harder than I wanted it to be."

Tamara and Ira studied him; both of them had their hands on their hips. There was a moment's worth of silence between them.

"I want to get out of here," Cameron said. "I mean, I've been here for far too long."

"Cameron," Tamara said as she walked over to where he was leaning against the wall. "I guess Ira's going to take you home, so I will say goodbye, because I have somewhere I need to be."

"Uh, yeah," he said and grinned. "Thanks again for everything. I really appreciate it."

Tamara's arms closed around Cameron's body; she totally caught him off guard, because she could feel his tensed muscles. Reluctantly he put his arms around her.

"Don't mention it," she said as she let go of him. "Bye, Cameron."

"Bye, Tamara."

Tamara turned around and started walking out of the room; Cameron followed her with his eyes.

A sense of relief filled Ira's body, because she didn't know how much longer she would have the patience not to snap Tamara's neck.

Reluctantly Ira said, "I, uh, I'm having a party at my house later tonight. Promise me that I'll see you there, Tamara..."

Tamara stopped dead in her tracks and turned around. She studied Ira's face and waited for Ira to explode with laughter, but she didn't. Ira was being dead serious.

Tamara sighed and said, "Yeah, I promise. I guess I'll see you two tonight then."

"Yeah," Ira said, clearly fumbled as to why she had invited Tamara in the first place.

"Okay," Cameron said.

Without saying another word, Tamara left the room. Ira turned her head to look at Cameron.

"What the hell just happened?"

Ira looked confused. "What do you mean?" Her forehead was full of horizontal creases.

"I mean, what the hell just happened. The last time the two of you were in the same room, you two nearly gouged each other's eyes out."

Ira really didn't know what to say, so she said, "Are we going home or what?"

Cameron sensed that she didn't want to have a conversation about it, so he shook his head and walked over to where Ira was standing.

"Don't mind if I do," he said as he walked out of the room, but he realized that he didn't have the faintest idea where Ira parked the car, so he stopped. "Are you coming or what?"

"Yeah," Ira said as she snapped out of her memories. Some of those memories were the best days of her life, but others made her want to weep.

Even if he didn't live there, it was always good to be home. Home sweet Ira's home. The aroma of scented candles and Coco Chanel were scents he became all too fond of during summer vacation.

Cameron was sitting on the bed, reading a paperback, *as usual*. He was enjoying each and every moment of Stephen and Owen King's Sleeping Beauties.

The rays of sunshine that crept through the curtains were just enough to light up the room, which made it easier and more pleasurable to read.

There was a knock on the door, and when Cameron didn't answer it, the following knocks became louder and more impatient.

"Cameron!" Ira shouted.

Cameron sighed deeply and set his paperback down on the bed. "I'm on my way, Ira."

He opened the door for her and studied her face. Drops of sweat formed on her brow. Clearly, she had been a busy body getting her party on the go.

"What is it?" he asked irritably.

"Jeez," she said and grinned. "Someone poked the bear."

"Yeah, that bear's name is Ira."

"Sorry. What were you doing that is so darned important? Okay, don't even answer that, because it was only rhetorical."

"Oh my God," he said and held his left hand over his mouth as if astounded.

Ira's eyes widened. "What? What is it?"

"The great Ira knows a big word like 'rhetorical'."

Sometimes Cameron's sarcastic remarks made her want to scratch his face off, but she giggled in high pitches.

"You asshole," she said jokingly.

Cameron grinned in such a way that reminded Ira of the Grinch when he stole Christmas: so wicked and mischievous.

"I need your help..."

"With what?"

"I need you to help me set up the snacks and such for my party guests. I mean, it's not like you are going to, like, you know, engage in the party."

"Excuse me, Ira, who said that?"

"I did."

"I actually thought about engaging in this party, Ira. I really ought to get out more often. Anyway, I think it would be nice if I could see Amy again."

"Well, then you can still be in charge of the snacks. If you are going to party with us, you need to pull your weight."

Cameron couldn't help but grin, because he understood that no matter how hard he protested against it, she was right: he had to pull his weight.

"Okay then," he said and folded his arms. "What snacks would those be?"

"Oh," she replied in an energized manner. "Come with me."

She led him down the stairs and into the kitchen. All the lights were turned on inside the kitchen, which was a sight to see.

"Okay, so," she began. "The Vodka Jell-O moulds are inside the freezer. You have to take them out and get them out of the moulds. Secondly you need to get the rum-soaked cake out of the pans and cut them into little squares."

"Wow," he said. "That's what you call snacks?"

"Yeah, Cameron, those snacks are great. Then you have to take out the alcoholic lollipops. Oh yeah, and before I forget, you have to take out the rum and raisin ice cream without the raisin out of the freezer too."

Cameron sighed and said, "Oh my God, Ira. There really is something wrong with you."

"Shut up and listen Cameron. I need you to do all of this while I go get dressed. After I've dressed, we'll prepare the beverages."

"Okay, but I don't see the need to do that. Why don't we just serve everyone a bottle of rum and vodka each? Wouldn't that be much easier?"

"Cameron! We want people to have an enjoyable night, not one filled with vomiting, okay? Tonight's party is more low key."

"Okay," he said. Ira started walking out of the kitchen. "They will do that anyway."

"I heard that," she said from afar. He grinned and cussed at her Vulcan hearing ability.

Immediately he got to work.

Ira stood inside her walk-in closet. The smell of washing powder and softener agitated her nose, making her sneeze twice.

The moment of dread washed over her. She could never understand why finding an outfit was a problematical affair.

Her eyes glinted as they spotted a nice dress. "Yes!" she said and got a hold of it.

The dress was very short and barely covered her knobby knees. She couldn't help but smile, because the dress reminded her of when she was twelve.

Immediately she bellowed in disgust and threw the dress out of the closet. It was a marvellous dress to wear, *if you were a twelve-year-old girl.*

"Ugh," she cried out. "I am never going to find something to wear."

She looked at the silver watch that was on her left wrist. It read 6:38 pm. She was taken aback at the time. She didn't realize that the time flew by so rapidly.

"Shit," she muttered.

Cameron finished popping out the last of the Vodka Jell-O from the moulds. He put them on the platter and back into the fridge.

There was a soft, almost inaudible, knock on the front door. Cameron sighed and waited for Ira to get it, but when the visitor knocked again, he walked to the front door.

Once he stood in front of the front door, he opened it.

"Hey," he said.

"Hey, Cameron," Amy said. "Well, like, am I early or what?"

"Yeah, a little I guess."

Amy giggled nervously. Her hands were behind her back as if though she was a naughty child.

"You're welcome to come in, you know."

"Uh," she said as she snapped out of the daze she was in. "Yeah."

Amy walked into the house and ordered herself to stay cool in front of him.

"Where's Ira? I mean, this is her party."

Cameron grinned and said, "She's upstairs. I think she's having a wardrobe malfunction. She's been up there for quite a while."

She hated herself for what she was about to say. "Can you excuse me? I have to go help her. The guests are about to arrive, and she can't be late, you know. But I will be back in a while..."

Cameron frowned and said, "Yeah, go ahead."

Amy smiled nervously and walked up the stairs. She was mumbling something to herself, but he couldn't make out a word of it. He thought that it was strange, but he dismissed it.

There was another knock on the door, but this time it wasn't soft.

Cameron was still at the front door, so he opened it and stared at her. His mouth hung open in astonishment and his eyes nearly popped out of his skull.

It was the very first time that he saw Tamara in a dress. The dress itself was silver and cut off at the knees. It was so beautiful in its simplicity. She had a pair of silver high heels on that complimented the dress. Her blonde hair was loose and curled.

The lip gloss on her perfectly formed lips made Cameron's desire to kiss her burn bright. Her face popped with utter beauty, because she had applied a little bit of blush.

"Are you going to let me come in or should I just stand here in the cold all night?"

Cameron had to swallow a couple of times before he could speak again.

"I, uh," he said and shook his head. "Yeah, uh, come on in."

Tamara smiled anxiously as she walked into the house. Cameron closed the door a little too loud, making her tense up.

Cameron was also very anxious. He didn't know what to say. Hell, he would say anything to her, if he could. He was still too tongue tied to speak.

Suddenly two other voices grew thicker and louder. Ira and Amy descended the stairs. When they were at the foot of the stairs, they stopped.

Both of their jaws hung open. Their eyes bulged in their skulls. The way their faces looked, reminded Cameron of Jim Carey from The Mask.

In that moment Cameron was absolutely certain that that must have been how he looked as well. It made him smile.

"Wow!" Amy said astounded. Her right hand covered her open mouth. "You look amazing, Tamara."

Ira only stared at Tamara, who also looked at her with widened eyes. Ira stood as still and quiet as a statue. Her cheeks burned red. Her palms were sweaty.

A wave of nostalgia washed over Ira's body. It felt like a cold shockwave.

In the distance multiple cars could be heard. The faint hum of pop music also filled the street, so much for silence.

Multiple cars stopped in front of the house, and shortly after came multiple knocks on the front door.

The chatter of party goers grew louder and louder. More hands knocked impatiently on the front door.

Cameron looked at Ira and said, "Ira, are you going to get that or what?"

"Yeah," Ira said, but never took her eyes off Tamara.

CHAPTER 13

*T*wo years before...

The Jeep came to a gradual stop in front of Ira's house. Tamara switched off the ignition.

Tamara quickly looked at herself in the mirror to do her final check-ups. Puberty had its claws in Tamara, as her face was covered with acne spots.

"Ugh," she sighed and applied lip gloss.

A minute later she got out of the Jeep and started walking to the front door. She almost stepped on a poor lizard as she walked on the pathway.

Once she was in front of the front door, she knocked twice and waited patiently. She could hear Ira's voice through the door.

The front door opened. Ira stood in front of Tamara. She looked absolutely adorable.

Blush had been applied to her cheeks a little too thickly. Her hair was made neatly into a bun atop her head. The eye liner around her eyes made them pop with utter beauty.

"Are you ready to go?" Ira asked.

"Yeah, uh, I," Tamara said anxiously. "There's been a slight change of plans..."

Ira wanted to scream, because she needed *to get out of her house for fun; her parents' drove her insane.*

"My mom is basically forcing me to take my little brother with us today. She and my dad are going through stuff with the divorce attorney, and she doesn't want him to be there."

Ira nodded her head and said, "I understand, Tammy. I guess we'll make it work then."

Tamara's emerald green eyes glinted with exhilaration. Ira grinned and said, "Let's get out of here, shan't we?"

Ira walked out of her house and closed the front door. She walked at Tamara's left side. There was a moment's worth of silence between the two of them.

"Where is the little bugger?"

Tamara giggled and said, "He's in the Jeep. I am really sorry about this. I didn't want to ruin our special day."

"It's okay, Tammy. Don't sweat it too much."

Ira got into the passenger seat and Tamara the driver's seat. They shut the Jeep's doors at the exact same time.

Tamara looked into the mirror. Her little brother was asleep. She admired his ability to sleep all day, anywhere and everywhere.

"Shh," Tamara said softly.

Ira only grinned and nodded her head.

Not a minute later the Jeep's ignition started again. Before long they were off to the waterfall spot.

It took them about forty minutes to get there. The Jeep's ignition once again switched off.

The two of them looked at the scrawny boy on the back seat. He was snoring away like a tutu train.

Neither of them could find it in their hearts to wake him up, so they got out of the Jeep and closed the doors as softly as they could.

Tamara enclosed her right hand over Ira's left. Together they jogged into the wild bushes.

"Oops," Tamara said as she tripped over a piece of log wood. Gravity pulled her down as fast as it could.

Tamara couldn't help but laugh at herself. She laughed so hard that she had to clutch her stomach, because it hurt too much.

Ira giggled too. She held her hand out to Tamara. Tamara took her hand, but instead of using it to get herself up, she pulled Ira down.

Ira yelped and fell next to Tamara. Both of them burst out laughing again. They looked each other in the eyes. The silence that brooded between them wasn't awkward, but very well one of admiration.

"Aren't I just the luckiest girl in the world to have found you?" Ira said.

Tamara grinned and put her left hand on Ira's burning cheek. "I think I am the lucky one."

"Just shut up and kiss me," Ira ordered.

Tamara did as she was told and moved her face closer to Ira's. Their faces were so close that they could feel each other's ragged breaths against their skin.

Ira was the one that lurched forward and landed the kiss on Tamara's lips. Ira tasted the watermelon flavour of the lip-gloss; it was her favourite.

The one kiss turned into multiple. Soon desire turned into need; a desperate need to feel closer, to be one. Their breaths were short. They held each other's hands slightly sweaty hands.

Tamara's hair was covered in leaves and dirt, but she didn't seem to care the least. Ira was on top of Tamara. They kept going at it for seven minutes. Seven minutes in heaven.

"I think we ought to get going," Ira said through her teeth as they kissed.

"Oh, why," Tamara enquired. "Let's stay here and make out."

"We could," Ira said, but she stopped kissing.

Ira's mouth ached to kiss Tamara even more. Her loins were on fire. Both of their breaths were still ragged, but Tamara also stopped kissing.

Tamara made her best baby face and in a baby voice, she said, "Do we have to go?"

"Yeah," Ira said disappointedly. "We have to get going if we're going to get to the theatre."

"Fine."

Ira got off of Tamara and stood up. She held her hand out to Tamara. This time Tamara took it and hoisted herself up.

"You have some dirt on you," Ira said and started swatting at Tamara's butt and legs.

"Thanks," Tamara said and grinned. "You don't have any dirt on you."

Ira's left hand closed around Tamara's right hand. They walked back the way they came. In no more than three minutes the Jeep became more visible.

Once they were at the Jeep, they got in and slammed the doors. It completely went by them that Danny might still be sleeping.

"Hey, Buddy," Tamara said as she started the ignition. "You have to get up. We'll be at the theatre in no time."

Danny didn't answer.

Tamara looked into the mirror. Her entire body went cold.

Danny was no longer sleeping. He wasn't even in the back anymore.

"Where the hell is he?" Tamara cried out.

Ira turned her head to look at the back seat. Danny was really not there anymore. Her eyes widened and almost popped out of her skull. A sense of dread filled her.

"I don't know," Ira said and immediately got out of the Jeep. "Danny! Danny! Where the hell are you, Danny?"

Tamara also jumped out of the Jeep and started running into the wild bushes, calling out to Danny.

Never in her entire life had Tamara felt so nauseous before. Her stomach made all sorts of knots and turns. A sour taste filled her mouth.

Where could he be? Was he going to be alright?

"Danny!" Ira called out again. Neither of them realized that they had split up. "Danny!"

Tamara was also calling out to Danny. Somehow the blush she had applied to her face was gone, because the colour had been drained from her cheeks.

Her body was stone cold and shivered uncontrollably. She ran so much that she could no longer feel her legs or her feet. Her hands were weak and scraped raw from removing bushes out of her face.

"DANNY! DANNY! WHERE ARE YOU? CAN YOU HEAR ME, DANNY? DANNY!"

She cried out so loud that the metallic after taste of blood was in the back of her throat. It wasn't a taste she was very fond of, but she continued bellowing until she could barely muster a word.

Before long she felt a little lightheaded. Her vision slurred before her eyes; if it were the tears, or her light headedness, she wasn't sure.

It became all the more difficult for her to see out in front of her. Another minute passed. Her eyes closed completely. Gravity pulled her down once more...

When Tamara opened her eyes for the first time in ten hours, she was in her bed.

The black duvet cover was pulled over her cold body. It was an absolute mess.

"You're up," Chloe said softly. "How are you feeling?"

Tamara didn't even answer her mother. She burst out in tears. Tears and snot ran down her pale face in streams. She tried talking, but her sobs muffled out her words.

"Just calm down, Hon," Chloe said and put her right hand on Tamara's shoulder. "Everything is going to be...okay."

"Mom," she said. "I'm so sorry. I know we were supposed to watch him, but he was asleep. We left him alone for only ten minutes tops."

"Hon, I need to tell you something..."

"Did they find Danny?"

"Yes, Hon, they found him."

"Is he okay?"

When Chloe didn't answer, Tamara could feel the vomit creeping up her throat. It became all the more difficult for her to breathe.

"Is he okay?"

Chloe shook her head. The first tear rolled down her left cheek. Her nose became runny.

"They found him in the pool by the waterfall spot. He, uh, drowned."

There was no time for Tamara to say anything, because she was already out of bed and running for the bathroom.

Once she was inside the bathroom, she locked it and threw up multiple times. She could barely see anything, because tears blurred her vision. It came to a point that she was still vomiting, but nothing but air came out.

There was a sudden and soft knock on the door.

"Hon, open the door. I need to talk to you."

Tamara really didn't feel like talking at all, because she opened the cabinet door and removed a razor blade from it.

She held the razor blade in between her middle and index finger, pressed against her left palm.

She wanted to end it all, because she was the reason that it ended for Danny. How could she possibly have known that that would happen?

"Hon," Chloe said anxiously. "Open this door. Don't do anything stupid. I know how you must feel. Let's just talk about this."

"There is nothing to talk about, Mom."

*She started pressing the blade into her palm, but she didn't-*couldn't-*bring herself to make the cut.*

"Open the door, Hon. Let's talk. I know how you feel..."

"You can't possibly know how I feel. I hate *myself! I wish I could just* die *and get it over with."*

"Hon, don't do that. Just listen to me, okay?"

"I can't do this," Tamara said and pressed the razor blade against her left palm again; once again she couldn't build up enough courage to do it.

"Did you know that you had another brother?"

Tamara immediately dropped the razor blade and said, "Mom, what are you talking about?"

"I never told you, because I was so mortified. You had an older brother. He was four."

"Are you lying to me?"

"No, Hon," Chloe said and slid down the bathroom door until she sat down on the floor with her back still against the door.

"He wanted to play outside, but I was too busy with work and every-thing. He, uh, went out by himself. Some drunk asshole ran him over..."

"Oh my God, Mom, just stop. I can't do this right now."

"Hon, what I'm trying to say is that we all make big mistakes, but it's how we pick ourselves up after it that counts. We pick up the broken pieces and try to mold them together as much as possible."

"Mom, I'm so sorry," Tamara said and unlocked the bathroom door. She opened the door and looked at her mother.

Chloe was still just sitting there. Tears and snot also ran down her face. She looked absolutely defeated.

Tamara sat down next to her and said, "Mom, I really am sorry. I don't know why we didn't just watch him like we were supposed to."

"It's going to take some time for me to forgive you, Tamara. Why weren't you watching him?"

"I don't want to talk about it, Mom. Please don't make me."

"Danny is dead. I think you owe it to me. You owe it to him, okay?"

Tamara sobbed and wiped away the hair that hung in her face. Her eyes were bloodshot as if though she were in an epic fight.

"Ira and I were going to the theatre to see a movie. The movie didn't start until much later, so we decided to stop at the waterfall spot for a picnic, but we didn't go that far in."

Chloe studied Tamara's tear-streaked face and said, "What do you mean by that?"

"Danny was asleep, so we didn't go far away. We were about five minutes away from the Jeep."

Chloe frowned, because she struggled to put two and two together. "What were you two doing out there?"

Tamara sobbed even more than before. "Mom, I have to tell you something."

Reluctantly Chloe said, "Okay."

"I understand if you'll hate me and not love me anymore..."

"Tamara Kellerman! Don't even say those things. You are my daughter, and I will always love you, no matter what."

"Ira and I were there together, as a couple. I love her, Mom. She loves me too."

There was an awkward silence between the two of them. Neither one knew what to say to the other.

"I guess that means that you are a, uh, lesbian then."

"I don't know who or what I am anymore, Mom. I wish I could turn back time and just come home from primary school and eat a grilled cheese sandwich and worry only about what toy I want."

"Hon, growing up can be pretty exhausting. You're changing in all these tiny ways. You're starting to learn who you are and what your place in this world is."

"I don't know what I want yet, or who I want. I hate the fact that I don't know who I am anymore. I hate the fact that I am rediscovering who I am. Mom, I can't do this..."

Chloe wrapped her arms around Tamara's trembling body. She hugged her daughter fiercely.

"Tamara," Chloe said. "Look at me."

Tamara looked at her mother with weary eyes. A tear rolled down her right cheek and collected with the rest of them below her chin.

"I love you more than anything else in this world, Tamara. You should always remember that. I will be at your side for as long as I live. I accept you for who you are."

"Really?"

"Yes, I promise, Hon. We'll get through this together."

"We will?"

"I want you to know that it wasn't your fault. It could have happened to anyone. I want you to make me a promise..."

"Anything."

"I want you to promise me that you will not beat yourself up over this, okay?"

Silence brooded between them again, but this time it wasn't an awkward silence. It was a silence of acceptance.

Before long Tamara fell asleep with her head on her mother's lap. Chloe grinned and slowly caressed Tamara's hair.

Dear Lord, *she thought as she looked up at the roof. She was absolutely certain that* someone *was looking down on her.* Please help me and my daughter. I will do anything in return. I need your strength in order to help her.

Chloe looked at her sleeping beauty. Somehow, she knew that they were both going to be fine.

She continued to caress Tamara's hair for ten more minutes. At last, she put her arms under Tamara's body and stood up.

The bones in her back and arms and legs crackled. Luckily for her Tamara wasn't a heavy load to carry, not physically anyway.

She carried Tamara to the master bedroom and put her down on the bed as softly as she could so that she didn't wake Tamara. She turned off the lamp that stood on the little night table.

Before long she lied down next to Tamara on the bed. She was on her back with her arms folded on her stomach, staring at the ceiling.

She understood very well that hard times were ahead for her and Tamara. Danny's funeral. It would take up a lot of her time and exhaust her, because she didn't want anything less than perfection for her little prince.

Chloe didn't think that she would be able to ever forgive Tamara for what happened, but as she looked at Tamara's still trembling body, she understood that she had already forgiven her.

Being a mother was never going to be easy. No one ever said it would be, but oh my. No one ever said that it would that darned difficult.

In that moment she realized that although she had just lost her son, that she still had her daughter. If she didn't get Tamara back on track as fast as she did, she might have lost her too.

Chloe put her hand on Tamara's trembling body, but that didn't help at all. She rolled onto her side and moved closer to Tamara. She put her arms around her and squeezed Tamara's body.

They were in the spooning position. They were so close to each together that Chloe could hear Tamara's ragged breathing. A tiny whistling sound escaped Tamara's nose.

In that moment she felt gratitude to the higher being. She understood very well that everything was about to change: she would have to be more supportive towards Tamara. She would have to turn a new page with her life. She would have to become a new person for her daughter.

She realized that she had to become a better person and that she would start as soon as possible.

One of her greatest achievements in life was her kids. She brought them into this life, and she would guide them as much as she could.

When Tamara's nose whistled again, Chloe put her head on Tamara's back. In that moment she knew that everything was going to be fine.

CHAPTER 14

Ira reluctantly opened the front door. She was absolutely thwarted, because she was no longer interested in her own party.

"Hey, Ira," a guy said as he and his friend entered the house with a keg.

Many others entered the house as well. Many of them greeted Ira and Amy, but Ira was disinterested in anything going on; it was as though someone had turned the lights down in her mind.

The party had officially started. As the music grew louder, Cameron started walking up the stairs. His delicate eardrums could no longer bare the thunderous music.

As he went into the guestroom, someone came in after him. Cameron fell down onto the bed; the springs inside the mattress croaked.

"Hey, Cameron," the voice said.

Cameron's heart skipped a beat. In that moment his entire body went cold.

He sat up straight and looked at Amy. "Jeez, Amy. You almost gave me a darned heart attack!"

Amy grinned shyly and said, "Oh, I, uh, I'm sorry, Cameron. I really didn't mean to."

Cameron nodded his head and ran his right hand through his brown hair and said, "Is something wrong?"

Amy shook her head. "No, nothing's wrong, Cameron. Would you mind if I sat down?"

Cameron frowned; his forehead wrinkled. Amy pointed to the bed with his index finger.

"You want to sit on the bed?"

"Uh, yeah."

"Okay."

Amy sat down next to Cameron. The moonlight that came through the window made her face pop with utter beauty.

She must have dyed her hair to a chocolate brown colour; her hair hung loose around her shoulders. The tone of her brown skin was complimented by it.

"So, I want to talk to you about something."

Reluctantly he said, "Okay."

"The talk you and I had the other night inspired me to talk to Jaleel. I just couldn't go on with it."

Cameron grinned. "That's great, Amy. Good for you."

"I left him, Cameron, because you were right. I deserve somebody that I love."

"I'm really glad for you, Amy. You are a very striking girl. Any guy would be lucky to have you."

Amy looked down at her hands and anxiously said, "Really?"

"Yes."

"Do you mean it?"

"Of course I do, Amy."

Amy looked up and studied Cameron's face. The last time she looked so intently at him, she was drunk as a skunk. This time she studied him thoroughly.

For the first time since meeting him, she realized that Cameron was eye-catching. His brown eyes, brown hair and perfectly formed lips made her want to kiss him more than ever.

There was something about the way he smiled. That smile could brighten anyone's day.

His neatly kept hair was cut short. She could never understand why guys would let their hair grow out long. She wanted to grab a hold of his hair and pull him closer to her.

"Are you okay?" he asked, because she went completely silent on him.

She hadn't even realized that she had grown silent. She smiled sheepishly and said, "I have never been better, Cameron."

"Okay, I'm glad."

"Cameron."

"Yes?"

In a way they could sense what was coming. Amy braced herself for the worst-case scenario, but Cameron braced himself to disappoint her.

"Do you find me attractive?"

"Amy," Cameron said anxiously. "You are a very attractive girl."

"Do you want to be *with* me?"

"Amy, don't..."

"It's a simple yes or no question, Cameron."

Cameron grew silent for a moment. He didn't really want to break Amy's heart, but he didn't have a choice.

"Cameron..."

Cameron tried to form the words, but he couldn't. Once he finally formed the words on his lips, they simply didn't come out.

He cleared his throat and said, "Like I said, Amy: you are a very attractive girl, but I don't see us together, I'm sorry..."

Amy could feel the tears pooling inside her eyes. She did her best to conceal them, but her efforts were useless. A tear rolled down her left cheek and then one on the other.

She spoke softly. "Is it..." She was cut off immediately by him.

"I really like you a lot, Amy, but just as a friend."

"I'm sorry, Cameron, I don't know what I was thinking. You are a great guy, but you're obviously not interested in me. I get that."

Cameron tried to find the right thing to say, but he couldn't think of anything.

"My heart belongs to another."

Amy didn't look astounded at all. It was as if though she could sense who it was. She sighed and said, "I know."

"Why did you ask then?"

Amy grew silent again. The tears that formed in her eyes evaporated. She actually smiled again.

"It's like I said, Cameron. You are a great guy. You can't blame a girl for trying."

Cameron moved closer to Amy and put his arms around her. He wasn't sure if it was the right thing to do, as he didn't want to send her mixed signals, but he did it anyway.

Amy put her arms around him too and hugged him fiercely. They sat like that for two whole minutes.

"I guess we ought to get back to the party."

Cameron didn't know what to say. He sure as hell was going to need earplugs or something if he went down there again.

Reluctantly he said, "Yeah, I guess so. Why don't you go down? I'll be there in a minute."

"What are you going to do?"

Cameron chuckled as he said, "I'm going to need earplugs if I were to go down there again."

Amy giggled and said, "Yeah, okay. I'll see you down there."

Without saying another word, Amy left the room. Cameron could hear the faint clicking sounds of her high heels on the wooden stairs.

He rummaged through the desk drawer that was situated next to the bed until he found a pair of earplugs. God only knew what they were doing there. He smiled victoriously and plunged them into his ears.

The party downstairs was raving. Everyone was having an exceptional time, but others couldn't quite enjoy themselves.

Ira sat inside the kitchen on the marble counter opposite the zinc. She clutched a plate in her left hand. With her right hand she forced alcoholic treats into her mouth.

Cameron came into the kitchen to fetch himself a bottle of cold water. Luckily for him no one really talked to him, so he didn't have the need to take out his earplugs.

Once Ira saw him coming in, she tried to hide her face behind her Jell-O smudged hands.

"I saw you," he said and walked over to where she was sitting. "You were too late."

"Damn it," she cried out. "I wish this darned party would just end already."

Cameron barely heard what she said. For a moment his body went cold, because he was absolutely certain that he had suddenly became deaf.

Once he realized that it was the earplugs, he removed them and studied her.

She was clearly stuffing herself with treats because she was feeling blue. She wasn't just feeling blue, but her tongue was lightly stained too.

"Okay," he said and sat down next to her on the marble counter. "What is it? Tell me."

"No!" she protested.

Cameron used his stern voice with her. "Tell me."

"Jeez, Cam. There's no need to yell at me."

That made him smile, because he didn't nearly yell at her. He understood that it was something else working in on her, making her feel that way.

"Have you like, uh, ever did something that you totally regretted?"

Cameron could think of numerous things. Attending this party was one of the most recent regrets.

He nodded his head and said, "Yeah, of course I have, Ira. No one's perfect."

Ira scoffed and said, "Oh, Cam, not you. You're absolutely perfect. I wish I was more like you."

The smile that was on his face, disappeared. The conversation was about to get more grave.

Cameron shook his head three times. "Ira, I'm nowhere near perfect. Why don't you try to explain to me what's wrong?"

"I did something a while back. I have regretted it every moment of my life. I wish I could turn back time and undo it, but I can't."

"I know what you mean."

"Cameron?"

"Yes."

"Can I ask you something?"

He immediately felt a little uneasy, because recently every time someone asked him that, they wanted to know if he was into them. *Hopefully it would be a completely different thing with his cousin.*

Ira closed her eyes. Cameron was absolutely certain that she had fallen asleep.

"Am I a good person?"

Cameron was flabbergasted. He looked at her face. She had cried before, he could tell, because her eye liner had dissolved and ran down her face.

"Yes."

Ira opened her eyes. She looked Cameron in the eyes and said, "Really?"

Cameron couldn't help but smile, because he always loved the way her eyes resembled those of a puppy's when she was feeling down.

"Yes."

"Promise me."

"I promise Ira. Who was the one that was constantly at my side when I was in the hospital? I mean, that's just something that happened recently."

Ira didn't realize that it was actually a rhetorical question. "I was."

Cameron grinned. "Who was the one that picked up a dog with a broken leg once and didn't let go of it until her mother paid the Vet's bills to have it in good health?"

Ira giggled softly. "That was also me."

"You see," he said and put his left hand on her shoulder. "You are a good person, Ira. One of the best I've ever had the pleasure of knowing."

"Really?"

"Yes."

Ira went silent again. She rested her head on Cameron's shoulder. She held his left hand in her right one.

Out of the blue Ira said, "Do you think she'll ever forgive me?"

Cameron frowned. Neither Tamara nor Ira told him what happened between the two of them, but his intuition told him that it hadn't been pretty at all.

"I don't know, Ira," he said and waited for a reply, but none came.

Ira had fallen asleep on his shoulder. He smiled again as he thought of the major hangover she would have in the morning.

Her nose whistled and low snores escaped her. Even though he didn't really like interaction with others, he had to admit that it was pretty adorable that she had fallen asleep on his shoulder.

No more than five minutes had passed. Cameron got a hold of Ira's legs and put his arm under them. He put his right arm around her back.

It was exceptionally difficult for him to hoist himself off of the marble counter, but he did it.

He walked with her in his arms like a character from a wedding day movie.

There was something humorous about the way her head bobbed and weaved. Cameron couldn't help but smile, because she was out stone cold. Nothing could wake her.

Another thing he didn't think of was the stairs. He didn't have much upper body strength, but somehow, he managed to get her up to her room.

He found himself standing in front of her bedroom door. He sighed deeply because there was only one way he was going to open that door: he would have to put her down and open it.

What made matters even worse was the fact that he was certain that he wouldn't be able to pick her up again.

Just when he had lost all faith, a familiar voice spoke to him.

"Do you need some help?"

Cameron couldn't make out who it was, but he was all too obliged. He couldn't turn his head to look either, because he would have dropped her.

Cameron sighed and said, "Yeah, please. Just open this darned door for me."

"Certainly," he said.

He came over and opened the door for Cameron. Cameron could smell his scent. It was a smell he would not soon forget. Somehow it smelled like lavender, but somewhere hidden within it was a masculine smell. He couldn't quite explain it.

Cameron walked into the room at snail's pace. Once he was in front of Ira's bed, he put her down as cautiously as he could.

He hadn't been inside Ira's room in years. He looked around the room and couldn't help but admire her taste.

The walls were painted a black colour. Her duvet cover was covered in patterns of red and black, which was eccentric.

Absolutely no moonlight came in through the closed curtains. Cameron remembered that Ira could never sleep if any sort of light disturbed her.

"Wow," he said to himself.

"Hey, by the way," the other guy said.

Cameron was startled, because in his daze he had totally forgotten that someone else was present.

In the dark he couldn't make out a face, but he said, "Hey. Let's get out of here."

Once he was outside in the hallway, he could finally see who it was. His eyes widened, because it was totally unpredicted.

Eric was standing opposite Cameron. His short black hair was neatly combed. He wore a pair of black skinny jeans. His perfectly cut abs stuck out even though he wore a red T-shirt.

"Hey," Cameron said again.

Eric grinned and said, "Aw, you're such a good cousin."

Cameron closed the door and said, "Come on, you would have done the same thing."

Eric chuckled anxiously. "No, I wouldn't have. I would have left her where she was sleeping."

"If you say so."

Eric was still grinning. He looked down at his red sneakers. Clearly, he showed signs of being shy, which Cameron thought were endearing.

"So, uh, is there somewhere private we can go to?"

Cameron didn't have the faintest idea what to say. His head bellowed to him to say no, but his heart roared for him to say yes.

"Yeah," Cameron said at last. "We can go to my room."

Cameron led the way to his room. Once both of them were inside, he closed the door.

Eric sat down on the end of the bed. Cameron reluctantly sat down on the opposite end.

"I, uh, got you this," Eric said as he revealed a teeny box with a red bow on it.

Eric held the box out to Cameron. Cameron was too far away, so he moved closer to Eric.

That darned scent could seduce him.

"Eric," Cameron said. "What..."

"Just open it."

Even though he didn't like it when his own mother barked out orders at him, he found it irresistible when Eric did it.

He took the teeny box and studied it for a moment. It was one of the tiniest boxes he had ever seen in his entire life.

"Eric, I," he said.

"Just open it."

Cameron's heart skipped a beat when Eric said that.

Cameron removed the red bow and opened the box. His mouth hung open at what he saw.

Inside the box was a little chipped teacup necklace-which resembled Rumpelstiltskin and Belle's love from his favourite television show, Once Upon a Time.

A gasp escaped Cameron's mouth. His hand automatically went to cover his mouth.

"Do you like it?"

"'Do you like it?' Are you kidding me, Eric? I freaking love it! I, uh, what..."

Eric grinned shyly and said, "I found your Facebook profile and I saw that you love that series. I got you this gift."

"I don't understand..."

"Happy-birthday, Cameron. I hope you enjoyed your day. I saw that it's your birthday today."

Cameron's eyes filled up with tears for many different reasons: no one knew it was his birthday; even Ira forgot. The more serious reason was that he hadn't celebrated his birthday for the past two years.

"Eric, I, uh, don't know what to say. I don't think you know how much I appreciate this."

Eric grinned. He was absolutely relieved to hear that, because he felt insecure. He didn't have the faintest idea whether Cameron would find it bizarre that he went onto his Facebook profile, or whether he would think it was a romantic gesture.

Cameron couldn't take his eyes off of the chipped teacup necklace. It was one of the most paramount things anyone has ever given to him.

The teacup itself was made out of steel and was about the size of his thumb. The chain it was on was made out of silver.

It was so picturesque in its simplicity, which Cameron found striking.

Cameron was lost in the fantasy world that was Once Upon a Time. By just looking at the chipped teacup he could see the entire series of it unfold before his glassy eyes.

He took the necklace out of the teeny box and held it in his right hand.

Cameron looked at Eric with huge puppy eyes. Eric was certain that he could see the excitement inside Cameron's eyes.

"Would you care to put it on for me?"

Without hesitation, Eric moved even closer to Cameron. Cameron turned around so that his back faced Eric.

Cameron was sure about a lot of things in his life, but he didn't have the faintest idea whether only girls were allowed to ask their boyfriends to put on their necklace. Was it a taboo question to ask?

What Cameron found even more perplexing, was the fact that Eric barely knew him. What did *this* make the two of them?

That was a question that both of them had on their minds, however a sense of relief washed over Eric, as he was relieved that Cameron didn't have an adverse reaction to the situation.

Eric moved his face closer to Cameron's neck. As he breathed, Cameron's heart hammered against his ribs. He could feel Eric's lukewarm breaths against his neck, which sent his arms into a state of absolute gooseflesh.

When Eric's hands moved over Cameron's head, a wave of cold air washed over his fuming body.

It became all the more difficult for Cameron to breathe.

As the chipped teacup fell gently against his chest, he realized that the teacup wasn't the only thing he was falling for...

CHAPTER 15

Three years before on Cameron's birthday

"*Happy birthday, my boy,*" *Jeff said.*

Cameron looked up at his father. He grinned. His eyes glinted with excitement.

Jeff grinned too. "I got you a little something."

Jeff held out a huge square box to his son. Cameron took the box and put it down on the dining room table.

"*Can I open it?*"

"*No, Cam, you are not allowed to open it. You may only look at it for an hour. Only then you can open it.*"

Cameron grinned in a wicked way. He knew his father was only goofing around, so he picked up the present again.

He studied the shape. His heart was almost broken, because he didn't want to ruin the beautiful glossy red wrapping paper.

He ripped it open and gasped in utter disbelief. It was an X-Box One, which was something he had wanted for quite a while.

"*Aw, this is the best thing you've ever given me, Dad. Thank you so much.*"

Cameron jumped up from the seat and gave his father a hug. He kissed his father on the forehead and went back to his assigned seat.

"Oh, my goodness, Jeff," his mother said with disgust. "Why did you get him that awful piece of technology? Do you realize that the Lord doesn't approve of that?"

Jeff sighed and said, "Jesus, woman. It's just a gaming box. It's not evil or anything."

Cameron's mother put her hand on her hips. "You will not take the Lord's name in vain. You bow your head and pray for forgiveness; you too, Cameron."

"Cameron, would you excuse us for a while?"

Cameron nodded his head and left the dining room. So much for a great birthday...

He went into the living room, but he could hear both of his parent's voices clearly.

"I will not have my son play with that rubbish; do you hear me? You ought to throw that out immediately!"

"I will do no such thing."

"You have to in order for the Lord to forgive you, Jeff!"

"I will do no such thing, okay? Let's just enjoy our dinner and celebrate our son's birthday, okay?"

She only looked at Jeff. If looks could kill, Jeff would have been dead. Surely her Lord wouldn't have liked that...

She picked up the X-Box and threw it into the trash. "Dinner is ready, guys!"

Cameron was utterly perplexed. He didn't really understand why his mother had to be like that. The most miniscule thing would have spiral and lash out.

He sat down on his assigned seat and looked at his father. His father mouthed something to him that looked like 'I'm sorry'. Cameron shook his head in approval.

No more than two minutes had passed. Cat slid into her chair. "Sorry, I is late. I was at a party."

Her mother walked over to her and stood next to her. "You have to say, 'I am' not 'I is', okay?"

She looked at Jeff and shook her head. "What are they teaching the kids at that school?"

Jeff shrugged his shoulders, because he knew that was the right thing, the only thing, to do.

In no more than five minutes another fight broke out, and in no more than an hour Jeff packed his suitcase and kissed the kids goodbye.

After Jeff left through the front door, Cameron and Cat went to their rooms. Neither one of them had something to say to their mom.

Cameron was asleep; his mind deeply shut into the dreaming world.

In his dream his mom didn't have the faintest issue with him having an X-Box One. In fact, she was playing Grand Theft Auto V with him, shooting people in the head and running them over.

It was one of those dreams that you just didn't want to end, but if there's one thing Cameron learned, is that all good things come to an end.

His eyes shot open when he heard his mother screaming at the top of her lungs.

"CAT! CAT! WHERE ARE YOU? CAT! CAT!"

Immediately he jumped out of bed. He didn't even bother to put on his slippers.

He ran out of his room and met his mom in the middle of the hallway between his room, Cat's room and the master bedroom.

"What is it, Mom?" he asked, but she didn't answer. "Mom?"

His mom's face was paler than a piece of white paper. Her hands were trembling. Her eyes twitched and looked like glass.

She stumbled to talk. "Your...uh...Cat...she's gone."

He could only make out several of the words she said.

He ran into Cat's room and looked everywhere for her; under her pink bed, in the closet, behind the drawers, but he didn't find her either.

He searched the entire house for Cat, but he couldn't find her Time continued to move along and was not waiting for anyone. Cat had been missing for more than 2 hours.

He could hear his mother screaming at the top of her lungs. She would surely not be able to speak in the morning.

That's when the call came. The telephone inside the kitchen rang and rang and rang, but neither of them picked it up.

Who could be calling them at that hour?

Cameron's mom finally went into the kitchen. She plucked the phone of its stand and held it closer to her left ear.

It was at that exact moment that their lives would forever be changed.

She sobbed and let the phone drop to the floor; it shattered into shards of plastic and wires. Before long she fell on the floor.

Cameron went closer to his mom, to comfort her, but she didn't want him to.

"GO AWAY, YOU BUGGER! IT WAS YOUR FAULT! YOU'RE THE REASON THEY'RE BOTH DEAD!"

Cameron could feel his eyes fill with tears. If it wasn't bad enough to not know what was going on, it sure as hell was no picnic to hear that it was his fault.

"Mom, what are you talking about?" he asked dryly.

His cheeks were red and hot. Tears started spilling down his cheeks and formed a big drop underneath his chin.

"Mom," he said softly.

"JUST GO AWAY, YOU RUNT!"

"Mom, stop saying those mean things..."

"YOUR FATHER LEFT BECAUSE OF YOU! HE'S HATED YOU FOR QUITE A WHILE! IT'S ALL BECAUSE OF YOU! I WILL NEVER FORGIVE YOU!"

Cameron sobbed uncontrollably. He tried to wipe away the tears and snot on his face, but he didn't succeed.

Instead of trying to comfort his mother, he left her alone on the kitchen floor. He ran up the stairs and almost tripped over his feet twice, because he couldn't see. His vision was blurred with tears; his eyes stung.

Once he was inside his room, he locked the door. He walked over to where his bed was situated and fell down onto it.

Even though he was awake in his bed for two hours, he eventually fell asleep.

Miss Williamson came into the room and put the spare key on the night table next to the bed. She sat down on the bed and looked at Cameron.

He was still asleep like a little baby. He rolled himself into the fetes position; it made him look vulnerable.

Miss Williamson ran her right hand through Cameron's hair. She caressed the top of his head until his eyes shot open.

"Hey there, little guy," she said softly, almost inaudible.

Cameron's eyes were bloodshot. He really wasn't the Snow White type. He frowned, because he absolutely hated it when she called him 'little guy'. He's fifteen for goodness sake.

"Mom?"

"Yes, Hon, it's me. I need to talk to you about something."

Cameron's eyes were finally fully open. He stared at his mom in utter disbelief.

Her hair was made into a neat little bun atop her head. Her dress and shoes were covered in their usual flower patterns. She was herself again. Prim and proper.

"Your father and sister," she began, but had to stop to gain control of her emotions. "They were in an accident. I'm so sorry, Hon."

There was something off about her. Cameron couldn't completely understand it. The previous night she hated him and now she talked to him as if though he's a baby.

"Mom, are you feeling okay?"

Miss Williamson frowned and said, "I know they may no longer be here with me, but my Lord always has a plan."

Even though he knew that that was the way she had coped with it, he couldn't help but be furious at her. Even through everything she still stayed her Lord's little Sheppard.

"Everything is going to be okay, Cam."

She lied down next to him and put her arms around him.

Two years ago, on Cameron's birthday

Cameron's eyes opened slowly. He stared at the ceiling of his room. A deep sigh escaped him. He pulled the duvet cover back over his head.

He tried to go back to sleep, but he couldn't. Snow White's deadly apple *came to mind.*

Just when he finally fell asleep, he got woken up by his ringing cell phone.

He sighed and tried to get a hold of the darned phone, but the more he tried to get it, the more it moved.

He was forced to get out of bed in order to get to the cell phone. He threw the duvet cover off of his body. The coldness of the room against his scorching skin sent his arms into a state of gooseflesh.

At last, he got a hold of the cell phone. He held it up to his face and looked intently at the screen. It was his grandmother.

He thumbed accept and held the phone to his left ear.

"Hello, Cameron," his granny said.

"Hey, Gran."

"Why is your mother not answering her cell phone?"

Cameron was flabbergasted, because he expected his granny to sing him a happy-birthday song, but she didn't. She didn't even say happy birthday.

"I, uh, don't know. I'll go tell her to answer her cell phone, Gran."

He walked like a zombie out of his room. He just couldn't function in the morning before having his first cup of coffee.

As he walked into his mother's room, she was no longer in bed. The bed hadn't been made yet; the brown duvet was shrivelled into an absolute mess.

Cameron walked down the stairs while constantly rubbing his eyes. He almost tripped over his feet twice.

"Mom!" he called out, but there was no answer. "Mom, where are you?"

He walked through the entire house but couldn't find any trace of her. He went into the garage and noticed that her car wasn't in the garage anymore.

He held the phone against his left ear again and said, "I can't find her. I think she might be out to the grocery store or something."

His granny said something to herself, but he couldn't hear what it was.

"Gran, what's going on?"

She cleared her throat and said, "Don't you worry about a thing, Cam. She just parked in my driveway. Cameron..."

"Yes, Gran."

"Just be safe at home, okay?"

"Yes, Gran."

"Goodbye, Hon."

Cameron couldn't even say goodbye, because she hung up the phone. It was out of the ordinary for his granny to be like that on the cell phone. It was even more peculiar that his mother would just leave like that.

He walked to the kitchen to make himself a cup of Joe, which he surely needed.

Cameron was sitting in the living room, watching television when his cell phone rang again.

He picked up his cell phone and held it in front of his face. It was his granny, again...

He accepted the call and held the phone against his ear.

"Hello, Cam. I am on my way over."

Before he had time to ask why, she said, "Your mother was just admitted to the hospital. I'm coming to get you to go see her."

"What?" Was that really all he could muster?

"I will explain it later. Just be ready when I get there. I'm around the corner."

This time it was Cameron who hung up first.

Luckily, he had already gotten ready for the day. All he had to do was slip on his shoes.

He grabbed his shoes and hastily tried putting them on, but the shoe he had in his hand did not fit his foot. He sighed when he realized that he tried to put the wrong shoe onto the wrong foot.

As he pulled on the last shoe, his granny pulled into the driveway. He grabbed his cell phone and ran out the front door.

As he reached his granny's car, he plucked the door open, got in and slammed the door shut.

At first his granny didn't say a word. She just drove and continued to drive until Cameron broke the ice.

"What's wrong with my mom?"

His granny swallowed and said, "I think she just, uh, this day is very traumatic for her, Cam. When she knocked on my door, I could sense that something was wrong."

Cameron nodded his head and said, "What happened?"

"She was a total mess. She cried and didn't stop crying. Then she was on the floor, having a seizure."

"Is she going to be okay?"

"The doctors stabilized her for the time being, Cam. But you will have to be her moral support. It's up to you to help her."

"What do you mean help her?"

His granny went silent again. Cameron didn't have the faintest idea whether that was a good thing or a bad thing.

"I think your mother is in denial, the first stage of grieving."

"Cam," she said and looked to her right for a second before looking back to the road ahead. "I simply don't have the words..."

Cameron couldn't help but feel furious again. The last time he tried to help her, to comfort her, she blamed it all on him.

"I can't help her, Gran. She has to help herself."

His granny went silent again. She understood very well that Cameron was different from other people. But couldn't he do at least this one thing to help his mother?

"You will help her, Cameron Williamson! Do you hear me loud and clear?"

When Cameron didn't answer her, she repeated herself in that stern voice of hers.

"You are the only one that can help her out of the situation, Cam. You have to stay strong for the both of you. It's been hard on her."

Yeah, *he thought.* Like it hasn't been hard on me losing the only parent that loved and accepted me for who I am.

Cameron looked out of the passenger window. Tears stung his eyes, but he didn't want his granny to see him like that.

After a while his granny said, "I know it's been hard on you too, Cameron. You're just a lot stronger than she is, that's all."

When Cameron didn't answer, she sighed. "I know everything's going to turn out like it's supposed to."

"How can you say that?" he said, but he never looked at his granny.

"I can say that, Cam, because she has you.*"*

In that one sentence were all the words he dreaded to hear. His detestation for his mother only grew bigger. Loathing her became more of a passion.

His granny parked her car and said, "Come on, Cam. We have to go."

They finally arrived at the hospital. His granny got out of the car and slammed the door shut.

Cameron tried his best to fight away the tears that longed to roll down his cheeks again. He closed his eyes for a minute and opened them again.

Get yourself together, *he forced himself.*

He got out of his granny's car and slammed the door shut. He walked over to where she was standing. They walked side by side into the hospital.

Cameron had an intense dislike of hospitals. He understood that there was a certain aspect to one's life cycle: being born, growing old, getting a serious illness that would chip away at your health in an agonising way, and then finally, death.

There was one thing that he was very fond of, and that was that strange chemical smell of a hospital.

The lady at the nurse's station was delighted to help them.

"Hi, how are you? Is there anything I can assist you with today?"

Cameron wanted to stop, but his granny just continued to walk along the long white halls. He shrugged apologetically and followed his granny.

In no more than five minutes they were standing in the entry way of his mother's room.

Miss Williamson was on the hospital bed, unconscious. The heart monitor continuously beeped.

His granny went inside the room and sat down on one of the chairs next to the bed.

When Cameron didn't immediately go in, she called out to him. "Come on in, Cam."

"Yeah," he said and spotted a chemical hand wash dispenser that he cherished.

He went to the dispenser and waved his left hand underneath it. The dispenser dispensed a liquid onto his hand. He rubbed his hands together. All he could smell was the beautiful aroma of sanitized hands.

Reluctantly he went into the room. Even though he loathed his mother, it was heart breaking to see his mother like that.

Her face was pale. Blue veins were visible on her cheeks. Every part of her body was limp in that unconscious state.

The heart monitor continued to beep steadily.

He stood next to his granny and intently looked at his mother.

No one said that it was going to be easy. No one said that he was going to have to give up his birthday every year. There was no way that he would ever be able to have a decent or normal birthday again.

The wicked part of Cameron wished that she could feel every little bit of pain. But the humanitarian part of him wished that he could pilfer the pain from within her body.

As he moved closer to her, her hand reached out to him. He took her icy hand within his and felt a light squeeze as she said, "Cam?"

"Mom." he said. Any negative thoughts he had about her up until that moment dissolved. A wave of shame washed over him too.

Chapter 16

Automatically Cameron's left hand shot up to his chest. He could feel the cold steel against his scorching hands.

When he turned his body back to face Eric, tears stung his eyes terribly. He was moments away from bawling like a little baby.

"What's wrong, Cameron?"

Cameron shook his head as if though he wasn't going to say anything, but then he said, "Oh, Eric. This is the nicest thing anyone has ever done for me. I really don't know what to say..."

Eric grinned and brought his face closer to Cameron's. "Then don't say anything..."

He said it as softly and as mysterious as he could. In that moment Cameron's heart skipped a beat, more than one beat. It was as if though everything around them disappeared, white noise surrounded them.

Eric moved closer to Cameron until his nose brushed Cameron's. Cameron could feel Eric's lukewarm breath against his lips.

Eric put his left hand on Cameron's right cheek. Cameron turned his head down in that direction. When he looked up, he was entranced in a sea of Eric's blue eyes.

Eric made his move. He felt his lips against Cameron's supple lips...

Cameron didn't know what to do at all. He sat as still as a statue. The color from his face had been drained out. He didn't dare move nor speak.

Eric realized that he was the only one doing the actual kissing, so he immediately stopped. He thought that the feeling might not be mutual.

He moved his head back and looked as if he might die from humiliation. His eyes nearly bulged out of his head. A sense of dread and regret washed over him. Had he read the signs incorrectly?

"Oh, Cameron, I'm so sorry. I...I misread the situation completely."

Eric's face burned red, he fumbled nervously with his fingers. He couldn't dare look Cameron in the eyes. His anxiety took over, as Cameron remained quiet for what felt like an eternity. He said, "Really, Cameron. I am so sorry. I have to go."

Just as Eric stood up from the bed to leave, and probably to never come back again, Cameron looked at him.

"Just shut up and kiss me," Cameron demanded. It was sudden. It was shocking. There was a strange hint of dominance in his voice, which was something he didn't often hear himself do.

Eric looked at Cameron and said, "What?"

Cameron rolled his eyes and got up from the bed. This time around he wasn't going to hesitate, so he walked over to where Eric was standing.

Once he stood still in front of Eric, he said, "I said shut up and kiss me, Eric."

Without saying another word, Cameron cupped Eric's face into his hands and pulled him closer.

Eric cupped Cameron's face in his hands and pushed Cameron backwards. Cameron fell onto the bed with his back; Eric fell on top of him. Neither of them seemed to feel anything but the desire to feel closer to each other.

Their lips made contact. It was a sensation Cameron had never felt before.

Their breathing became ragged and the more they kissed, the less they started to breathe. Desire, passion, lust, senses that were unusual to Cameron, overwhelmed him. It was as if though his senses were no longer his own.

It was the first kiss Cameron had ever had in his life. He wasn't sure what to do when he felt Eric's tongue slip into his mouth.

An anxious little breath escaped Cameron, but he handled the situation pretty well. He pushed Eric off of him with ferocity and got on top of him.

This time Cameron made his first move and kissed Eric on the lips, slipping tongue.

They were no longer breathing. Those breaths had become something far greater. It was a growing need to become one. It was almost as if the two of them were becoming one organism.

Neither of them had their hands on each other's faces anymore. Cameron grabbed Eric's left hand in his and squeezed it. Eric didn't seem to mind that at all; if anything, it seemed as if though he yearned for it.

Cameron's right hand went up Eric's T-shirt. He traced the lines of Eric's hard abs. To Eric it felt almost like a tickle, but it was ticklish in an erotic way, because a gasp of satisfaction escaped his mouth.

Cameron's left hand left Eric's. His hands were on Eric's T-shirt, he pulled it upwards. Eric threw his arms into the air.

Cameron pulled off Eric's T-shirt and threw it onto the floor. This time a gasp of fulfilment escaped Cameron's mouth.

Even though Cameron never was a guy that liked a lot of guys that had muscles, there was absolutely no way that he could deny that it was more alluring on Eric.

It was the way Eric's torso was covered in rock hard abs that stuck out like little pale bricks.

Cameron used his index finger to trace each line of the flawless abs. Eric's breathing became all the more jagged as Cameron did so.

Cameron chuckled nervously and moved his hand all over Eric's godlike torso. He could feel Eric's rapid heart drumming on the inside of his ribs, much like his own.

Eric's hands slipped up Cameron's back. Gently, he pulled Cameron's T-shirt over his head; in such a swift way that Cameron barely knew it happened. He threw it somewhere into the room.

He looked at Cameron's scrawny body, free of any bulging muscles, but he liked Cameron that way. It was something entirely different than what he was used to.

Cameron's body wasn't resting on his, so he put his hands around Cameron's back and pulled him closer to him.

Cameron's stomach brushed against Eric's; the abs were like little massaging stones, which made Cameron shudder with pleasure. Another gasp of satisfaction escaped him.

Eric's left hand moved all the way down to Cameron's lower back, sliding down Cameron's jeans.

Cameron gasped anxiously. Immediately Eric's hand went back up to Cameron's lower back.

"I'm sorry," Eric whispered, barely audible.

"No," Cameron said. "It's okay."

"Are you sure?"

"Yes." They made direct eye contact.

Eric's left hand moved down Cameron's back again and down into Cameron's jeans. Even though Cameron had feared that one day the time would come for *such* things to happen, it didn't frighten him. Not with Eric anyway.

Eric was so gentle, hand resting on Cameron's butt cheek without trying to grope any further. Cameron's underwear prevented Eric from touching his bare butt cheek, but Eric didn't seem to mind.

He squeezed his hand a little. His eyes filled with tears of joy. Cameron's cheek felt like a stress ball, and with every squeeze, satisfaction filled each of their bodies.

He squeezed again and felt a tinge of pleasure as Cameron's mouth moved down his chin and into his neck.

Cameron started kissing the nape of Eric's neck. His right hand gripped Eric's short black hair. He got a handful of that silky hair and pulled it.

It was something that he had wanted to do ever since he saw Eric for the first time. That short black hair was apt to make any man or woman's knees wobble.

"Cameron?"

"Yes?"

"Are you still feeling okay about this?"

Cameron sighed in disappointment and studied Eric's face. Eric's face was red, and concern occupied his blue eyes.

"Let me give you something to occupy that mouth of yours..." Cameron said.

He moved his head closer to Eric's again and kissed him. Cameron didn't have the faintest idea how to describe the taste of Eric's lips, but he sure was digging it.

Eric pushed Cameron off of him this time. It happened so suddenly that Cameron gasped.

Eric got on top of him and started kissing the nape of Cameron's neck.

It felt to Cameron as if he became an uncultivated animal, and he wasn't sure whether he liked it.

"Eric?"

Eric moved his head down the nape of Cameron's neck and started kissing his chest. He didn't seem to hear anything, because much like Cameron, that uncultivated animal escaped its cage.

"Eric?"

Even though he didn't really want to use his mouth for anything more than kissing, he said, "Yes?"

Eric's scorching breath against Cameron's stomach sent Cameron's arms into a state of gooseflesh.

"Would you hate me if I wanted to stop?"

Cameron felt unsure whether Eric would be able to control himself, considering the fact that he himself could barely instil self-control.

Eric immediately stopped what he was doing and crawled his way back up to study Cameron's face.

In that moment Cameron's entire body yearned for Eric's touch, but he didn't want to go *further* than what they were doing.

"Cameron, are you okay? What is it?"

Cameron looked into Eric's deep blue eyes. A breath of dissatisfaction escaped his mouth. Whilst looking into those picture-perfect eyes, his chest heaved up and down.

"Are you okay, Cameron?"

For a moment Cameron didn't know what to say. He couldn't mutter a single word let along a complete sentence.

Even though he knew the dangers of unprotected sex, especially gay sex, he couldn't deny the fact that he absolutely *wanted* his first time to be with Eric. He had no prior knowledge on how things would go, or what would be expected of him. It was all new to him, and that frightened him.

"Be gentle," Cameron whispered. His need for Eric, to feel him, to *have* him was much stronger than the fear of the unknown.

Eric's deep blue eyes nearly popped out of his skull. He frowned, which made him look even more charming.

"Cameron?"

"Yes?"

"Are you sure?"

"Yes." There was no hesitation in his mind.

It was like something right out of a movie. In a way it sounded cheesy, but Cameron didn't think it was cheesy at all. He thought Eric was being considerate and adorable.

Eric's head moved down Cameron's chest. He kissed Cameron's chest lightly and made his way down to the front of Cameron's jeans.

Cameron studied Eric whilst he moved all the way down. He was sure that he would have a heart-attack soon. He could feel his heart throbbing inside his throat. It was a feeling he hadn't ever felt before, but it was a feeling that he took pleasure in.

Eric's hands moved along Cameron's legs until they reached the jeans' button. Eric looked up with eyes that pleaded consent.

It was as if Cameron understood what it had meant. He nodded his head more than was needed.

Eric unhooked the button but immediately stopped when Cameron gasped.

"Don't stop," Cameron ordered.

Eric unzipped the fly and folded it open as if though he was unfolding a napkin from a fine-dining restaurant.

He started tugging the jeans off all the way to Cameron's feet. They chuckled nervously. Eric grinned when he saw Cameron's underwear. It was a plain Calvin Klein black brief, but to Eric it seemed exquisite; he was never keen on anything too over the top.

Eric stood up from the bed to pull his own jeans off, but Cameron protested against it. It was hard to explain, but Cameron felt the need to do it himself.

Cameron sat up straight on the end of the bed. He looked directly at Eric's hard abs, which forced a groan out of him. He kissed Eric's chest, with Eric putting his left hand on Cameron's head, lightly playing with his hair.

He hooked his hands into the pockets of Eric's jeans and pulled him closer to him until Eric was standing an inch away from him.

Eric ran his right hand through Cameron's hair again.

Cameron unhooked the button and zipped open the fly. He didn't struggle as much as Eric had to pull of his jeans. In no more than ten seconds, Eric's jeans were off and tossed into the abyss of the room.

Cameron couldn't help it but to sit back and admire Eric.

Eric's short black hair looked glossy with sweat. His perfectly tanned face was grinning, revealing perfect teeth. His torso was a little paler than his face, but his abs stuck out in perfect symmetry. The bulge of his jock strap pricked Cameron's interest, because it was kind of like opening a present on Christmas. Those darned legs were apt to drive anyone crazy.

"Cameron?"

Cameron looked up to Eric and grinned. Seeing Eric looking so picturesque made his desire for Eric to make love to him burn bright.

Cameron could feel his affection and lust for Eric more clearly, because his crotch throbbed.

Eric pushed Cameron backwards and got on top of him. They were on top of each other and could *feel* each other as they brushed their bodies together.

In that moment they became one...

About forty minutes had passed.

Cameron and Eric were spooning; Cameron was the little spoon, held by *his* muscular spoon. Neither of them said anything for five minutes.

"Cameron?"

"Yes?"

Eric's arms loosened up. Cameron turned his body to look at Eric.

"How are you feeling?"

Like I made love for forty minutes to the best-looking guy ever he thought.

Cameron grinned and said, "I don't know what I am supposed to say, Eric."

Both of them chuckled. Eric's right hand brushed Cameron's left cheek.

Even though Cameron was usually pretty pale, he didn't seem to be pale at all. Color had flushed his face and made him look terrific. It was amazing what a little bit of color could do to your appearance.

Cameron looked at the chipped teacup necklace that was still on his neck. Neither of them really noticed that it was there the whole time whilst they were making love.

"Cameron?" Eric said.

"Yes?"

"What's your deal?"

"What do you mean?"

"I mean, tell me more about yourself that I couldn't see on your Facebook profile."

Cameron couldn't help but grin apprehensively. He was still dumbfounded that Eric had even gone through the trouble to find him online.

"Like what?"

Eric grinned and said, "Let's start with the basics..."

"Okay."

"Favorite color?"

"Red, yeah, definitely red."

"Mine too!"

"Seriously?"

"Yeah. Your crush?"

"Oh," Cameron said as if though he was shocked. "There's this really cute guy."

"Yeah? I'm listening..."

Cameron chuckled and said, "He's got short black hair. Ugh, that perfect tan of his is exceptional. But do you know what?"

"What?"

"He's built like a Greek god. His body is so muscular and makes my legs wobble."

"Oh?"

"Yeah, he goes by a very sexy name too..."

"What is it?"

"ERIC!"

Both of them almost ripped in half with laughter.

Neither of them spoke after that, but they looked deep into each other's eyes. It wasn't necessary for either of them to speak, because they admired each other physically and mentally. Their body language did the talking on their behalf.

Cameron lightly played with Eric's hair, which he took great pleasure in.

The silence was broken by Eric. "I really like you a lot, Cameron."

Cameron rolled his eyes because he didn't really have the faintest idea why Eric, a muscular athlete, would be interested in him, a scrawny Mr. Smarty Pants.

"Why?"

The question came to Eric as a sudden shock. He frowned, which wasn't as cute as it was much earlier that night.

"What do you mean?"

"Why do you like me?"

"Why would you ask something like that?"

"I mean, you are this popular and gorgeous guy. Why would you be interested in me?"

"Oh," Eric said and cupped Cameron's face in his warm hands. "I like you because you are different than the rest of the guys."

Cameron grinned shyly and said, "Thanks."

Eric didn't answer. He moved his face closer to Cameron's and landed a kiss on his cheek.

"You just can't get enough, can you, Eric?"

Both of them chuckled. Cameron didn't know where this new-found confidence came from at all, but he did know one thing: he loved the way Eric made him feel when they were together. Perhaps he even loved Eric, a feeling that he's never been interested in before.

"Maybe," Eric said and grinned. He kissed Cameron again before putting his head on the pillow.

They went back into that silenced period in which they only looked at each other. Cameron realized that he could never grow tired of looking at Eric, because he was the finest guy he had ever seen.

Cameron put his arms around Eric and pulled him closer. Eric kissed him on the forehead and closed his eyes.

Cameron lied awake for the next hour thinking about everything that had happened. He always thought that his first time would be with someone he knew for five years. Someone he had known from the inside out.

Other things also ran through his mind. He couldn't answer most of them, but one pressing matter didn't dare go away: what exactly were they? *What* exactly was he? *Who* was he?

They had only met two or three days ago, where Eric flirted with him. They haven't even gone on a first date yet. Heck, he didn't even know what Eric's last name is; where he lived; what he liked to eat; what his ambitions were.

Cameron sighed, because another pressing matter came into his mind: what would his mother think of it?

In the first sense, his mother wouldn't be satisfied with him for losing his virginity whilst he wasn't married.

But Cameron knew what the real problem was...

What would his mother think of him for having sex with a guy?

He was certain that she would disown him for being different than what the default was. She, a 'Jesus Freak', would pluck out her Bible and pray for his soul.

It was in that moment that Cameron realized that perhaps he had made a mistake. He shouldn't have slept with Eric...

There was just one problem. Cameron didn't regret doing what he did. He loved every moment of it. Perhaps it was because it was rebellious or perhaps just sexual pleasure.

Screw whatever she thinks he thought. *This is my life, and I can fall in love with whoever the heck I want to, and if she has a problem with that, she can build a bridge and get over it!*

In no more than five minutes Cameron fell asleep in the company of Eric.

CHAPTER 17

Eric's eyes shot open. He rubbed his eyes with his free hand and looked at Cameron, who was still sleeping like a baby.

His other hand was caught between the mattress and Cameron's back. He carefully tugged his hand out. He shook it a couple of times, because it was asleep; pins and needles pricked his hand.

"Hey," Eric whispered as Cameron's eyes opened at snail's pace.

Even though he tried hard to keep his eyes open, they fell shut again.

Eric moved unhurriedly past Cameron's body to get out of bed. When he finally succeeded, he stood up from the bed.

Both of his feet were also pricked by pins and needles. He wobbled a couple of times, almost falling back onto the bed.

As he walked to recover his jeans from the corner of the room, every bone in his body crackled.

Once he picked up the jeans, he pulled them on. He searched the room to find his socks, which he found on the nightstand. They were neatly folded into one little ball, which made Eric smile. He knew that Cameron was a perfectionist.

On the other end of the nightstand was the chipped teacup necklace. It gleamed as a ray of sunshine, which came in through the window, shun on it and made it look like a golden teacup instead.

He found his T-shirt and pulled it on. It didn't smell very good, almost rancid. His face contorted in disgust.

"Where are you sneaking of to?" Cameron asked.

Eric's heart almost went still for a moment. He thought that Cameron went back to sleep, but he was wide awake.

"Can I take a shower?"

Cameron's eyes opened once more. If Eric didn't know any better, he would've thought that Cameron was a demon of some sort. His eyes were bloodshot, but what made it even more sinister was Cam's gaze; it seemed that he didn't have to blink at all.

"Yes."

"Are you sure?"

"Yes."

"Are you okay?"

"Yes."

"Are you sure? I mean, you don't look so good..."

"What's with the third degree?"

In that moment Eric caught on. He understood that Cameron wasn't a morning person at all. He couldn't help but grin.

"Okay, I'm going to take that shower now."

"Whatever."

Eric grinned all the way out of the room. He made a left turn and then another one.

He walked into the bathroom and closed the door.

He was amazed by the design of the bathroom. The walls were painted an orange colour. The tiles beneath him were also orange, only a lighter shade. It was strange to see paintings on the walls, but they made the walls pop with utter beauty.

The tub was in the left corner of the bathroom and the shower on the right corner.

He walked over to the shower and opened the pristine sliding door. He never liked it when he got into the shower and opened the hot water tap and cold water rained down on him, so he opened the tap and waited for the water to get hot; something he and Cameron had in common.

He took off his jeans and underwear and put it on the laundry basket next to shower. He got in and closed the sliding door.

Cameron's eyes finally stayed open. He got out of bed and walked to the walk-in closet to get dressed.

He didn't like the way he smelled at all. He hated the smell of sweat on himself. It was at that moment when he thought of something absolutely crazy.

He started walking out of his room and made a left turn and then another left turn.

He found himself standing in front of the bathroom door. He was sure about most of the things in his life, but not this.

He opened the bathroom door and went inside. When he was inside, he closed the door as softly as he could.

Cameron couldn't help but grin, because Eric was singing 'Look What You Made Me Do' in the shower.

He walked closer and closer to the shower. Once he stood still in front of the shower sliding door, he could barely see through it, because it was covered in steam.

His heart throbbed inside his throat. His palms were sweaty. A thin line of sweat formed on his brow. Perhaps his heart was not the only thing throbbing.

Cameron's hand clasped around the shower sliding door handle. It was then or never. He pulled it open...

Eric's body turned around immediately. His hands were on his head, scrubbing his hair.

"Cameron?"

"Care if I joined you?"

Eric grinned and said, "Not at all. The more, the merrier."

Cameron got into the shower and closed the sliding door. Luck was on their side, as there was plenty of room in the shower.

"Here," Eric said.

He handed Cameron a bar of soap and said, "Wash my back, would you?"

Cameron took the bar of green soap and started rolling it around in his hands to get foam. Once he got a large amount of foam, he rubbed it on Eric's back and started moving all the way up and down in even strokes.

Eric turned around and faced Cameron. "Thanks."

"Yeah, no problem," Cameron replied. He foamed up his hands and started rubbing Eric's shoulders. His hands moved all the way down to Eric's abs.

"I guess I'll have to wash each individual block," Cameron said.

Eric grinned and said, "Yeah, I guess so."

The bathroom door opened and hit the wall.

"Hey, Cam," Ira said as she came in. "Don't worry, I'm not peeking or anything. I just came in to get the laundry."

"Ira?"

"Yes, Cam."

"Get the hell out of here!"

"Jeez, Cam," Ira said as she walked closer to shower to get the laundry basket. "One could swear that you are in there with someone..."

Even though it was only a joke, Cameron said, "Get out, Ira!"

Ira chuckled and picked up the laundry basket. She noticed that there was a pair of jeans and a black jockstrap on the top.

"What the hell?" she whispered to herself.

She looked up from the laundry basket and looked at the shower. Even though it was covered in steam on the inside, she could see two shadows.

"Holy shit, Cam! Is there someone in there with you?"

Cameron sighed deeply and said, "Get out, Ira!"

"Oh my God, I'm so sorry whoever's in there with my cousin."

Ira cackled like the wicked witch of the west. She said, "Who is in there with you, Cam?"

"Ira!"

"It's me, Eric."

Ira's mouth nearly hung on the floor. A thin stream of spit actually started running down the corner of her mouth.

"Oh, I'm sorry, guys. I'll get out of here."

"Just go!"

"Enjoy yourselves."

"Ira!"

"I'm going, I'm going. Jeez!"

Ira still cackled as she closed the door. One could hear her even when she walked down the stairs.

Cameron looked at Eric apologetically and said, "Eric, I'm so sorry about that. She's so nosy..."

Eric grinned and said, "It's okay."

Eric took Cameron's face in his hands and kissed him on the lips.

"I'm sorry," Cameron said and chuckled. "It's too weird to do this now."

Both of them chuckled, tears spurting out of their eyes.

Eric turned off the taps and opened the sliding door. Steam puffed out of the shower like mist on a cold morning.

"Uh, Cameron," Eric said.

Cameron turned around and looked at Eric. Eric was completely dry, but he was also buck-naked.

"Yeah?"

"She took my clothes..."

"Oh, I see," Cameron said. "I think you don't need clothes."

Eric grinned anxiously and said, "I need to get to practice..."

Cameron frowned. He looked fumbled. "Practice? What could you possibly be practicing for in summer break?"

"My football scholarship. I have to train in order to..."

"Yeah, yeah, I get it, Eric. You can borrow something of mine for the time being."

"Thanks."

Cameron folded the towel around his waist and started walking out of the bathroom.

"Cameron!"

Cameron turned around and looked intently at Eric. "What?"

"Can I at least get a towel to put around me?"

Cameron grinned and said, "No..."

Eric's mouth hung open. "Cameron," he said in a playful way. "Please?"

This time it was Cameron who cackled like the wicked witch of the west. He looked at Eric, from head to toe. Why would anyone with a great package like that ever want to cover it up?

"Top drawer," Cameron said and pointed at the wooden cabinet next to the tub.

"Thanks."

Eric went over to the cabinet and got himself a red towel.

Cameron looked at Eric's butt, which made all of him yearn to hold it between his hands again.

Cameron looked around inside the walk-in closet and found a pair of black jeans that was a few sizes too big for him to wear.

"Here you go," he said and handed it to Eric.

"Thanks, but I, uh," Eric said.

"Yes, the oppressing matter of underwear."

Cameron looked everywhere to find an unused pair of underwear. He found a jockstrap, which he had never used before (he wasn't a sporty person at all) and handed it to him.

"Thanks," Eric said. "Why don't you wear it?"

"I don't really do a lot of physical sports, so I don't need it."

Eric sighed in disappointment and said, "Well, if you would wear it, it would definitely make your butt sexier..."

"There's nothing wrong with my butt..."

"I didn't say that at all, Cam. I'm just saying that it would highlight your butt more..."

Eric moved closer to him, pulled him in and landed a kiss. He squeezed Cameron's butt cheek through the towel.

Things were so different for Cameron when he was around Eric. He had been at ease, the voices in his mind were quiet, satisfied even. He had gained more confidence and felt secure with Eric.

"Oops," Cameron said as he pulled Eric's towel. The towel fell to the floor around Eric's bare feet. "I think you dropped your towel."

They walked down the stairs together, side by side, holding hands. It was such a pure and intimate act, surely one of the most underrated.

"Hey, guys," Ira said as they entered the kitchen. "Did you *sleep* well last night?"

"Ira!"

Ira grinned and said, "You know what, Cameron, I am getting pretty tired of you saying my name like that."

Cameron walked over to the marble counter and turned on the kettle.

"You never answered my question."

"I guess I can ask the same of you, Ira. Did you sleep well? You know, considering the amount of alcohol you ate and drank, I'm surprised you're even awake yet."

"Cameron!"

Cameron frowned. Ira said, "Yeah, you don't like it when I do it to you, do you Cam? Uh, who made sure everything didn't burn down here last night?"

Cameron and Eric shook their heads in unison. "I don't know," Cameron said.

"Cameron," Eric said. "I really have to get going now. I'll call you later."

"Yeah, I'd like that."

Eric kissed Cameron on the lips and walked out of the kitchen. A minute later the front door opened and closed.

"So?"

"So what?"

"How was it?"

"How was what?"

Ira sighed deeply and said, "Oh, come on, Cam. You and I both know something happened between the two of you last night."

Cameron chuckled. "That has got nothing to do with you, Ira. You're so darned nosy..."

"Oh, come on, Cam. Your love life is much more exciting than mine. I mean, mine is basically dead."

"You have your own boyfriend, go do stuff with him..."

"No, nope, I don't. We broke up a couple of days ago."

"Ira, I'm...I'm so sorry to hear that."

"No, don't be sorry. He was a total asshole."

"Oh."

"So, how was Eric?"

"I am seriously not discussing this with you."

"I'm your cousin, Cam. We are like...best friends. Just tell me already, okay?"

"I am not discussing my sex life with you, Ira, forget it."

"Oh my God, Cameron," Ira said and put her hand in front of her mouth. "You just said it."

"Said what?"

"That you have a sex life. Did you guys really...you know, have sex?"

"IRA!"

"Cameron, you dirty little one. Just tell me one thing, okay?"

"What is it?"

"He's like a, what can I say, he's like a sports car. But like, does he ride like a sports car?"

Cameron frowned. He didn't have the faintest idea what Ira meant. "What?"

"Well, he's got the perfect body, but did he have enough horsepower to satisfy your need for speed?"

"IRA! I am seriously not even going to answer that."

"Whatever, then I guess I will be left to make my own assumptions..."

Cameron was about to tell Ira exactly what she wanted to hear when the doorbell was rung.

"I'll get it," Cameron said. He walked out of the kitchen and to the front door. He didn't even bother to look who it was before he opened the door.

"Hey, Cameron," Tamara said.

"Hey, Tamara," Cameron said and grinned. "What's up?"

Tamara was wearing her usual clothes: blue jeans with a blue T-shirt and matching blue sneakers. Her golden blonde hair was made into a bun atop her head.

"Can we talk privately?"

"Yes," Cameron said sharply, but he didn't mean to say it like that. "Would you like to come in?"

"No," Tamara said. "I thought we might go for a walk and a coffee, if you wanted to."

"Uh, yeah, sounds great. Just give me a sec."

Tamara's face looked a little bit paler than her normal tone. Something was definitely up.

"Hey, Ira! I'm going out for a while. I'll be back later. Bye!"

Cameron came out of the front door and closed it behind him. "Are you ready to go?"

"Yeah, I am."

"Great."

They walked on the sidewalk, side by side.

"What happened to you last night, Cameron?"

"What do you mean?"

"You just disappeared..."

"Oh, I, uh, I'm sorry. I had to put Ira to bed. She had a little too much to drink. I'm sorry that I left you down there alone."

There was a moment's worth of silence between them, but it was broken by Tamara. "Did Eric find you up there?"

Just by hearing Eric's name a shudder shot through Cameron's entire body. Every part of him once again ached for Eric's touch.

"He came to the party last night. He was looking for you. He said that it was something very important."

"Oh, yeah, he found me. Thanks."

It was at that exact moment that they found themselves standing in front of the Coffee Co. (one of the best coffee houses in town).

"After you," Cameron said and pointed towards the door.

Tamara walked into the coffee shop; Cameron followed suit.

Once they entered the coffee house both of them indulged in the rich aroma of various coffees. It was one of the few aromas that made Cameron want to fall victim to its submission, except for Eric's faint sweet and sweaty smell, of course.

"Welcome," the woman in the Coffee Co. apron said. "A table for two?"

"Uh, yes, please."

"Right away, young sir."

She took them to the back of the shop where there was a table empty in the right corner beside a window.

They sat down on either ends and opened their menus. Tamara seemed to be scanning the menu, but she already knew what she wanted to order.

"One jumbo size iced coffee with cream, please," Tamara said.

"Okay," the waiter said. "What would it be for you, young sir?"

"The very same, thanks."

"Coming right up."

The waiter disappeared from the table.

There was another moment of silence between the two of them. Cameron felt that he might explode ff neither of them talked.

"It was you, wasn't it?"

Tamara frowned. She looked fumbled. "What?"

Cameron couldn't help but grin, because he knew it was true. In a way he could feel it. "You made sure everyone got home safe last night. You made sure that everything went smoothly, didn't you?"

"Yeah, I did. How did you know?"

"Oh, I just knew."

"So, did you and Eric have a good time?"

There it was again. Cameron was astounded once again. It felt to him as if though he had a sticker stuck on his forehead which read, 'Oh, My name is Cameron and I slept with Eric! Have a nice day!'.

"I, uh," Cameron said, but was interrupted.

"It wasn't that hard to figure out, Cameron. He went upstairs to look for you, whom he obviously found. It was very suspicious that neither of you came down..."

Cameron nodded his head. He understood very well that there was absolutely no way that he could deny it. Even if he could deny it to everyone that asked him, he knew that he couldn't deny it to himself: he was falling for Eric pretty big time. He also didn't feel the need to deny it.

Automatically his hand went to his chest. He pressed his hand against the chipped teacup and couldn't help but grin.

"Yeah," he said. "I really like him a lot. We talked a lot last night."

"Oh," she said. "If you don't mind me asking, Cameron, but are you, you know, gay?"

"I don't know *what* I am yet, Tamara." Cameron was silent for a moment before he looked at her intently. "I am just...*me.*"

"Oh."

"It's okay if you don't want to be friends with me anymore, Tamara, I completely understand that."

Tamara looked astounded. She frowned and felt her eyes filling with tears, but she tried her best to conceal them. How could he think something like that of her?

She took Cameron's hands in hers and held them as tightly as she could. She grinned.

"I will always stay at your side, Cameron."

"You promise?"

"Yes, I do."

"You promise that you will stay at my side?"

"When I make a promise, I intend to keep that promise. It might not happen right away, but it will be kept. That I promise you..."

CHAPTER 18

*T*wo years before.

It had been two days after Danny's heart wrenching passing. Tamara and Chloe sat in the Jeep, waiting to go into the church.

Even though she would never admit it, Chloe was frazzled. She didn't have the faintest idea who would actually show up for Danny's funeral.

It was a gloomy morning. The weather mirrored the tone of the day: a day of loss and melancholy.

"Do you think she will come, Mom?" Tamara asked.

Chloe threw the stub of the cigarette out of the driver's window. She looked at her daughter and frowned. "I guess we'll have to wait and see."

Tamara nodded her head and said, "We should probably go inside..."

Chloe sighed. She was in no mood to go into the church. It was easier said than done. If she had gone into the church, it would mean that everything up until then hadn't been a dream, and that Danny was waiting for her at home. Going into the church would destroy this illusion.

Tamara opened the passenger door and got out of the Jeep. She slammed the door shut and studied her mom's face.

Even though Chloe had been wearing blush she still looked paler than a statue.

Chloe reluctantly opened the driver's door and got out. Her legs were almost freezing in the chilly weather. How she had wished that she had worn something a little more suited for this weather.

"Mom?"

Chloe looked at Tamara. "Yes?"

Tamara walked over to where her mother was standing on the sidewalk. She held her hand out to her mom. Chloe took her daughter's hand and squeezed it.

"Thank you," Chloe whispered into Tamara's ear as they walked side by side.

Just as they approached the church door, it flew open. The reverend stood in front of them. He was wearing his usual white robe and had a Bible in his hand.

"Welcome, Mayor Kellerman."

Tamara wanted the punch the reverend's stupid face, because he was grinning. Out of all the days that he could have grinned, why would he choose that *particular day to do it?*

"Call me Chloe, please."

"Come on in, Miss Chloe."

As they walked into the church Chloe squeezed Tamara's hand even more than before.

Tamara closed her eyes. She feared that she would burst out crying inside the church. It was, after all, partly her fault for being there in the first place.

Behind them other people arrived. All of them wore black.

The reverend walked up to the front podium and talked into the microphone. "If everyone would be seated, we can commence this ceremony."

Everyone immediately sat down and stopped conversing. Tamara and Chloe sat in the first row, which was unnerving.

As the reverend commenced his ceremony, Tamara was thinking about a lot of other things that shouldn't have been on her mind.

The most oppressing thought that came to mind was the fact that Ira didn't even have the decency to attend Danny's funeral.

Four days later.

It was one of the longest school days that Tamara had ever experienced in her entire life.

She was standing at her locker, packing away her books at the end of the day, when a familiar face surfaced.

"Hey, Tamara," the boy said. "I, uh, heard about what happened the other day. I am so sorry for your loss."

Tamara shut her locker door harder than she had intended to do. She looked up to Eric. "Thanks."

"How are you feeling?"

Tamara sighed. It was the darned question that she dreaded. She bit the inside of her mouth and immediately tasted the metallic taste of blood.

"I'm fine, thanks for asking. It's been hard for my mother and I, but we are coping with it."

Eric put his hands into his jeans' pockets and leaned against locker number fifty.

"I am here for you, Tamara. If you want to hang out or just, you know, talk about stuff..."

Tamara would have gouged Eric's eyes out if she didn't already know that Eric was being sincere. Ever since her brother's death many boys were 'concerned' about her, but they only wanted to get into her pants. It was different with Eric, because he was gay.

"No thanks, I'm fine. Eric, I, uh, really appreciate you coming over here to talk."

Eric shook his head and said, "Yeah, no problem."

Tamara clutched her Science textbook to her chest. She could still taste blood in her mouth.

She frowned. "I really have to get going, Eric. I guess I'll see you around."

Eric looked fumbled. He frowned, which just made him look more adorable. "You mean I won't see you tonight?"

"Why? What do you mean?"

"Tonight is Ira's birthday party, don't you remember?"

Tamara shrugged, because she had totally forgotten about Ira's party. Ever since she didn't show up at the funeral, she hadn't talked to Ira.

"No!"

"Tamara, what's going on?"

It was at that exact moment that Ira stood still in front of them.

"Hey, guys, what's up?"

Eric scooted over so that Ira could put books into her locker, which was situated next to Tamara's.

When Tamara looked away and didn't answer, Eric put his arms around Tamara. "Go easy on her, okay?" He hugged her fiercely and let go of her. He disappeared into the hallway.

"What's up with you?" Ira asked. "You haven't spoken to me in days..."

The rage that fuelled Tamara's trembling body would soon explode, and Ira's death would be the outcome of it; luckily it didn't resort to that at all.

"Seriously?" Tamara heard herself asking. It was as if though it wasn't she who was speaking at all, but very well a girl with fire in her belly.

Ira looked gobsmacked. "What?"

"You are a real piece of work, you know."

"Hey, whoa, Tamara. What's your problem?"

"You're my problem!"

Ira didn't have time to finish packing her locker, because Tamara shoved her fists into the door. The locker slammed shut, almost catching Ira's arms in it.

"What the hell?"

"You are a real bitch, you know. You didn't even have the decency to come to Danny's funeral!"

Tamara didn't even realize that she was shouting. Other teens in the hallways stopped dead in their tracks, looking at the two of them. Things had escalated quickly.

"Tamara, let's go somewhere private and talk about this like rational beings," Ira whispered.

Tamara drove her fists into Ira's locker's door again. The steel caved in, leaving tiny cuts across Tamara's knuckles.

"I thought you cared about me, Ira. I thought you really cared enough to come to Danny's funeral, considering that you were a part of his death!"

"Tamara!"

Ira glanced anxiously around the hallways and noticed that they were being watched, like a mouse being watched by a hawk.

She put her right hand over Tamara's mouth. Tamara continued to shout into the palm of Ira's hand.

Tamara's right hand shot up and got a hold of Ira's palm. She twisted Ira's palm until Ira finally let go.

"I thought you loved me," Tamara said. "Obviously I was wrong."

"Tamara, don't..."

"We're done, Ira. I never want to see you again. I never want to talk to you again. If you come my way, I will kill you!"

"Don't say such things, Tamara. Don't say something that you're going to regret..."

It was at that moment that the principal came around the corner of the hallway, carrying a notebook.

"Miss Kellerman," he called out to her. "I want to see you in my office immediately."

Tamara shoved Ira against the lockers as hard as she could. Ira cried out in pain, because one of the handles caved into her back.

"Miss Kellerman, get to my office now!"

Tamara continued to walk the opposite way. She wasn't interested in anything anyone had to say to her.

"Tamara Kellerman!"

Tamara laughed senselessly and said, "Go screw yourself!"

Some of the teens in the hallway almost ripped in half with laughter, but when the principal shot them a look, they quieted down.

In that moment Tamara knew that everything was going to be different. She would become a different person all together...

Cameron felt his eyes filling with tears that waited to be spilled, but he controlled himself pretty well.

He cleared his throat and said, "I don't know what to say, Tamara. I really appreciate you standing by my side..."

Before Tamara could say anything else, the waiter appeared with their Iced Coffees.

She put their glasses onto the table as carefully as she could to not spill anything.

"These are on the house," she said as she put two chocolate sundaes on the table.

"Oh," Cameron said as he looked at the waiter. "That is very generous of you, thank you very much."

The waiter grinned and left them alone.

When Cameron looked down at his coffee, he was no longer interested in the coffee.

Tamara grinned and said, "Are you going to eat that sundae, or what?" She pointed to the sundae with her spoon.

It was so amazing to see her smile again. He was absolutely certain that things would soon be awkward between the two of them, but none of that happened, which he was very grateful for.

"Uh, are you kidding me?" Cameron said and picked up his spoon. "Of course I will eat this totally free sundae!"

Tamara took a heaped spoon of chocolate ice-cream and chocolate sauce and propped it into her mouth.

"Wow," she said through eating. "That is pretty darned good."

"Tamara?"

Tamara frowned, because she sensed that things would turn grave again. She swallowed the melted ice-cream and looked intently at Cameron.

"I just have to ask," he said as he brought the spoon closer to his mouth. A drop of melted ice-cream dripped from the bottom of the spoon.

"Yes?"

"Does this sundae contain nuts?"

Tamara was a little dumbstruck, because she didn't expect that at all. She grinned and said, "Oh, I don't know. I think so...Why?"

"I am allergic to nuts, so I just want to avoid another hospital close call situation."

Just as he was about to put the spoon into his mouth, Tamara slapped the spoon out of his hand.

The spoon clattered on the table, smudging the table with chocolate ice-cream and sauce.

He studied her face. She was grinning, which turned into giggles.

She shrugged her shoulders and said, "Rather safe than sorry."

Both of them burst out laughing, which seemed to attract the attention of some of the other customers. They only looked for a minute or two before going back to their conversations.

"So?" Tamara said.

"What?"

"You never did say what happened last night between you and Eric."

Cameron rolled his eyes and said, "Nothing happened last night, okay? Let's just leave it at that."

Tamara pursed his lips and made kissing sounds. Cameron burst out laughing. His pale skin became a red colour.

"Oh," she said. "You see, you're turning into a tomato. So, something did happen?"

Before Cameron could say something, his cell phone started vibrating. A second after that Demi Lovato started singing about how there's nothing wrong with being confident.

He looked at Tamara apologetically and filched his cell phone from his pocket. He held it up in front of him.

He frowned, because the impossible just became possible.

He thumbed accept and held the phone against his left ear.

"Eric? How the hell did this happen?"

Eric burst out laughing on the other end. He knew that Cameron would be amazed by what he had done.

"It wasn't very hard to figure out that your password is Rumpelstiltskin, so I unlocked your phone and put my number on your contacts' list."

Cameron was astounded. He didn't know whether he should be upset or amazed by it. Eric could have just tried to be adorable, or he could be a creepy weird stalker for all he knew.

"Cameron, are you still there?"

Cameron nodded his head, because he was still too astounded to actually form any words.

"Cameron?"

"Uh, yeah, I'm still here."

"Anyway, I just wanted to say that last night was...was really great. I was just, uh, wondering if you'd like to, uh, go out tonight..."

It was as if whatever was keeping him from having a conversation with his 'boyfriend', let go its grip on his vocal cords.

"Yeah, that would be great."

"Uh, like a date? I mean, our first official date?"

"Yes, that sounds great!"

"Great, I'll pick you up at Ira's at eight, if you are down with it..."

"Yeah, eight is great!"

"I guess I'll see you tonight then..."

"Yes!"

"Cameron, do me a favour would you?"

Even though he had been burned before by that question, he didn't even hesitate. "Yes."

Eric seemed to gather himself at the other end of the line. He cleared his throat and said, "Wear a jockstrap tonight."

Cameron chuckled and said, "I guess you'll have to wait and see, won't you?"

Cameron hung up the phone. He wasn't sure whether Eric would take it the wrong way, but he thought that it would keep things a little mysterious. But how mysterious could it actually be, considering what had happened the night before?

"So, let me take a wild guess at who that was," Tamara said. "Was it...Eric?"

"No," Cameron said, but he nodded his head.

Tamara broke out in laughter. She laughed so hard that everyone in the room looked at her. She sounded so masculine when she laughed, which Cameron thought was adorable.

Cameron grinned and took a sip of his Iced Coffee. Tamara ate another spoonful of ice-cream and sauce.

"Cameron Williamson!" someone shouted from within the entrance of the coffee shop.

Of course it was too good to be true...

Miss Williamson was standing in front of their table. Her hands were on her hips. Her face was red with anger. Her eyes nearly bulged out of her skull.

"WHERE HAVE YOU BEEN?"

"Mom," Cameron said. He was more astounded to see her than he was actually terrified of her bawling.

"I come back here to find out that you were in the darned hospital for days! I demand you to tell me what happened! You are such an irresponsible child, Cameron, you have always been!"

"Mom, just stop it, okay? I could ask the same of you. Where the hell have you been? I was worried sick about you."

Miss Williamson laughed manically. "It doesn't look like you were worried at all. I mean, you are sitting in a coffee shop, sipping iced coffee like some spoiled little brat!"

"Mom, would you just chill out?"

Miss Williamson's hands flew up in the air. "Don't you dare speak to me like that, Cameron! Get in the car this instant!"

Just as her hand slid to the left, she knocked over Tamara's iced coffee. The glass fell on its side, spilling all the content onto Tamara's lap.

Cameron looked at Tamara. "I am so sorry, Tamara. I don't know what's gotten into her."

"GET IN THE CAR!" she bawled.

Cameron barely got up from the red leather seat. His mom grabbed his arm and plucked him to her side; surely his arm would be bruised in the morning.

"Mom," he said. He didn't have time to finish before his mother slapped him with her flat hand.

Cameron looked astounded. His mother had never slapped him before. His hand went to his burning face; whether it was to feel his face or to stop her from hitting him again, no one knew.

"Hey, Miss," the waiter said. "You aren't allowed to do that anymore. It's against the law, you know..."

Cameron's mom swung around as swiftly as she could. She faced the waiter and said, "You better keep your nose out of my darned business, or else I will break it!"

Somewhere in the Coffee Co. someone shouted for someone to call the police. Many of the people plucked out their cell phones and took a video of this charade.

"Mom! Just stop, okay? What the hell is wrong with you?"

His mother didn't answer. She grabbed the collar of Cameron's shirt and plucked him to her side. She continued to do this until they were outside in the parking lot.

His mother pointed to the car and said, "Get in!"

Cameron shook his head. "I'm not getting into the car with you, not when you are like this."

"I don't give a shit, you little brat!"

It wasn't the first time he heard his mother say anything like that. The last time he saw her anywhere near as crazy as that, was when his father and sister had passed years prior.

"Mom, you have to calm down...I am here."

"I will not calm down anytime soon, Cameron! Just get into the car."

Cameron noticed that some of the shop's customers were standing outside, still making videos and taking pictures.

"I am not getting into the car with you..."

Miss Williamson bit down on her teeth. Cameron was sure that her teeth would shatter like cobble stone being hit by a hammer.

"I...SAID...GET...IN...THE...CAR!"

Cameron felt as the first tears rolled down his cheeks. They weren't tears of sadness, but very well rage.

"And I said that I am not getting into that car with you!"

Miss Williamson ran down on Cameron in her state of rage. The audience was sure that she would strangle the life out of him.

Just as she reached Cameron, a cop from behind her said, "Step away from the boy, Madam."

She turned her head to look at him and snorted. She turned her head back to face Cameron.

She continued to try to get a hold of Cameron's throat, but she didn't succeed.

She fell to the ground.

There was something satisfying in the way she rattled like a fish out of the water.

Cameron looked at the cop and nodded his head to show his appreciation.

She continued to rattle as the stun gun continued to shoot out its electric rays.

CHAPTER 19

Cameron sat beside his mother's bed.

It seemed to him that the hospital would soon have an entire room ready for the Williamsons. The hospital had become their second home.

The heart monitor that was attached to his mother continued to beep rhythmically.

"Mister Williamson, I presume," the doctor said as he entered the room.

Miss Williamson was still sleeping like a little baby. Apparently, her heart was too weak for the stun gun which caused her to have a seizure afterwards.

"No, I'm her son."

The doctor seemed to find it very humorous, because he laughed. He tried his best to conceal his laughter but failed epically.

Cameron frowned. "What's so funny, Doc?"

"Oh, I, uh," he said. "I'm sorry, that was very unprofessional of me. I thought you looked a little too young to be *Mister Williamson*. Please forgive me. As a doctor you don't get to laugh often."

Cameron grinned, but he didn't think that it was humorous at all. His mother almost attacked him to do god knows what to him, and here a doctor is laughing about it.

"Is she going to be okay?" Cameron whispered.

The doctor was taken aback by that. He frowned. A frown didn't look quite as good on him as it did Eric.

"Yes, for now she's stable. I need to ask you something, young sir."

"Okay..."

The doctor removed his pen from his jacket's pocket and clicked it. He then brought his clipboard closer to him.

"I need you to tell me exactly what happened."

Cameron cleared his throat, and when he spoke, he whispered, "I was in the hospital the other day, but I couldn't make contact with her."

"Why's that?"

The doctor seemed to be writing it down. It became clear to Cameron that the man before him wasn't a doctor, but very well a psychologist.

"She just disappeared a few days ago."

"Do you know why or where she went?"

Cameron sighed deeply. He fiddled with his fingers. "I don't know for sure, but I can guess."

"And what would that be, young sir?"

"This week marks the anniversary of my father and sister's death."

The psychologist continued to scribble notes onto the paper without even having to look down to do so; he kept eye contact with Cameron the entire time.

"Oh, I see." He continued to scribble.

Cameron felt very uncomfortable to make direct eye contact with the psychologist, so he bowed his head and looked at his fingers.

"Every year around this time she gets...a little crazy, but this year she went way too far. I am no psychologist, but I think she's still in denial..."

"How is that?"

"It's like, she, uh, she never talks about him or my sister anymore. But when she does, she speaks as if they were still alive, but just not there."

"Do you ever feel like...like she's blaming you for what happened to them?"

Cameron snorted and said, "Yeah, all the time. The night she found out about the accident, she said that it was my fault..."

He continued to make notes.

"Do you sometimes blame yourself for what happened?"

Cameron frowned. "No, I wasn't responsible for the accident, so I don't blame myself. I blame her..."

He pointed to where his mother was peacefully sleeping on the bed. The psychologist followed Cameron's finger and returned his gaze to Cameron.

"Do you hate her?"

"Sometimes I do, but...sometimes I don't. I just want her to get better, that's all."

The psychologist nodded his head and said, "Thank you, young sir. I have to get to my office now, but I will see you soon."

Without saying another word, he left.

Cameron looked at his mother and almost died of a heart-attack. Her eyes were open.

"Cameron?"

He walked over to her and studied her face. Purple veins bulged beneath her chin. Her eyes were red and her skin paler than ever before.

"What...what happened? What am I doing in a hospital?"

In a way Cameron was glad that she couldn't remember what she had done. He knew that she would never forgive herself for it.

"You had a seizure, Mom."

"What?"

"I have to ask you something, Mom."

She nodded her head and took his hand in hers. The coldness of her hand against his scorching hand made him shudder a little.

"What happened to dad and Cat?"

She frowned. She didn't seem to understand the question at all. "What do you mean?"

"What happened to them, Mom?"

"Your father left us and took Cat with him. He remarried and has another life. Why do you ask?"

"Why do you think that?"

"Because that's what happened, Cam."

"Mom," Cameron said softly. "You know they died in a car accident years ago, don't you?"

His mother looked astounded. She squeezed his hand and said, "I know it's been hard, Cam, seeing your father with another family, but that doesn't mean that he's dead..."

A cold tear ran down his left cheek. "Mom, they are dead. He didn't move in with another family. They died..."

She shook her head and frowned. "That...that can't be, Cam..."

"Where were you the past few days?"

She seemed to think long and hard about it. After two minutes of silence, she said, "I visited your father and sister."

"What?" More tears spilled down his cheeks.

"Oh my God," she said. The missing pieces in her mind started falling back into place. "I visited their graves. They really are dead, aren't they?"

Cameron nodded his head and watched his mother cry. She pulled him closer and when he was close enough, he lied down next to her.

Ten minutes passed. Neither of them said anything. She put her arms around him and said, "I *need* help, Cam."

"I know."

Cameron couldn't help but smile, because he finally made good on his promise. His granny made him promise her that he would be there for his mom and after years of trying, he could finally get through to her.

"Thank you, Cameron," she said and kissed his forehead.

"For what?"

"Thank you for being there for me all this time. I'm sorry that I took you for granted. I am so sorry..."

She began crying. Tears and snot ran down her face. Cameron couldn't help but cry himself, because she finally realized that she had a problem.

"Sorry?"

"I'm sorry for everything I did, Cameron. I'm sorry for never being there for you. I'm sorry for being mean to you all these years."

"Mom, just stop, okay? It's in the past..."

"I'm sorry for hating you when I should have instead hated myself all these years. It was because of me that they weren't home."

"Mom, don't blame it on yourself, it's in the past now. What you have to focus on is to get better, okay?"

She continued to sob. Cameron caressed her hair, but that didn't seem to calm her down at all.

"I'm sorry for being a shitty mother."

"You're not a shitty mother, Mom. You are a great mom, but you just went through a rough patch, that's all."

"Promise me?"

"I promise, Mom."

"Oh, Cameron!"

She continued to sob. Her tears and snot soaked Cameron's t-shirt. Her head rested on his shoulder.

In that moment he let go of all the anger he had had towards her. He knew that everything was going to be fine.

They dosed off in each other's arms.

Cameron woke up because his jeans vibrated. At first he didn't know what was happening, but when he finally realized what it was, he grinned.

He filched his cell phone from his jeans' pocket and looked intently at the screen. His eyes widened and nearly popped out of his skull.

He got out of bed as quickly as he could; luckily his mother had let go of him when they had fallen asleep together. It was such an odd thing that one would sleep so well after crying; it was inexplicable.

He jogged out into the hallway and immediately thumbed accept.

"Hello, Miss Jeanine," he said. His heart hammered against his ribs.

He realized that his entire life depended on this very phone call. Everything that would happen to him in the future depended on this phone call.

He cleared his throat and ran his left hand through his hair.

"Good afternoon, Cameron. I apologize sincerely for calling you at this hour, but you said that you wanted to know as soon as I got an answer. It usually isn't customary for us to make personalized calls..."

Cameron had to clear his throat again. "There is absolutely no need to apologize, Miss Jeanine."

"Cameron, are you ready for it?"

Immediately Cameron thought of one of his favourite songs by one of his favourite artists: 'Ready for It?' by Taylor Swift. He grinned and said, "Yes, Miss Jeanine, I have been waiting for quite a while."

Miss Jeanine giggled on the other end of the line. "I will put you out of your misery then, Cameron."

Cameron braced himself for the worst scenario. It could either be a yes or a no, and if it's a no, he was absolutely certain that he would be able to get into another...

Miss Jeanine got silent on the other end of the line. She was building the suspense.

"Miss Jeanine, are you still there?"

Another moment went by. Cameron didn't know whether it was good for his health, but at least he was inside a hospital if he needed medical attention.

"Congratulations, Cameron Williamson. You have officially been accepted to Harvard."

Cameron shouted in delight, but he didn't mean to. He grinned brighter than he had ever done before.

"Is it official?"

Miss Jeanine laughed on the other end. She thought that Cameron could be such a pessimist sometimes when he wanted to be one.

"Yes, Cameron. It's official. You are going to Harvard on full scholarship. Congratulations."

"Oh, Miss Jeanine, thank you very much for everything. I really appreciate it much more than you can ever know."

"It has been a pleasure to work with you, Cameron. You are very welcome."

Cameron was ecstatic, because his dream of studying to become a Neurosurgeon was already one step closer.

"Cameron," she said. "Just remember one thing, okay?"

"And that would be?"

"We all have something that starts a fire within our souls. All you have to do is find the thing that ignites the spark."

"That is so inspirational. Thank you very much, Miss Jeanine."

"It's been a pleasure, Cameron Williamson. I will not keep you up any longer. I am sure that you have to go update your Facebook or Instagram profile to 'ACCEPTED TO HARVARD'."

"Goodbye, Miss Jeanine."

"Goodbye, Cameron."

Cameron hung up the phone and continued to stare at the screen. It was mindboggling. He pinched himself twice to ensure that he wasn't dreaming.

"Are you okay?" a nurse asked.

Cameron didn't even notice that someone was standing next to him. He looked at her apologetically.

"I am fine, thank you."

He continued to grin, revealing his teeth.

The nurse looked at him and said, "You sure look jovial. Do you mind me asking why?"

Cameron tucked his cell phone into his right pocket and looked intently at the nurse. She must have been around twenty-four, perhaps a little older. Her blonde hair was made into a bun atop her head.

"I, uh, don't mind at all," he said. "I just got the phone call that I've been accepted to go to Harvard next year."

The nurse looked astounded. She covered her mouth with her right hand.

"Wow," she said. "That is some great news, huh. Well, congratulations on your achievement."

"I wouldn't call it an achievement, but thank you anyway."

The nurse sighed deeply and said, "Why wouldn't it be an achievement?"

Cameron nodded his head. He didn't really know who this nurse was. He hadn't ever met her, and if all things went well for him, he would never have to see her again. What he didn't know, was that it was a sign of his self-confidence growing.

"I, uh, have rounds to do," she said and grinned. "Congratulations again on your *achievement*. Perhaps soon we'll meet again. Bye..."

"It was nice talking to you. Bye."

The nurse continued along the long white hallways of the hospital. Her shoes clicked all the way.

If there was one thing that Cameron admired about hospitals, it was the silence. He knew that it was more of a morbid silence, but he didn't mind that at all.

He stood outside his mother's room for another hour, just indulging in the silence and the smell of chemicals.

His cell phone vibrated once. He filched his cell phone from his pocket and looked at the screen.

His battery was on fifteen percent, which triggered a warning that he had to charge it soon.

He looked at the time. It was 20:06 pm. It felt to him as if though he had forgotten something, but he dismissed it just as quickly as it came.

He put his cell phone back into his pocket and went back into the room.

Miss Williamson was still sleeping like a baby. The doctors didn't have the need to sedate her at all.

He sat on the chair that was situated next to the bed. He got his cell phone out and unlocked it. He didn't really know what he was going to do, but in no time, he found it.

The Fruit Ninja app opened, but there was no sound, because he had turned it off. He continued to play Fruit Ninja for forty minutes until his phone died.

"Ugh," he said to himself.

It was at that exact moment that he realized that he had forgotten about something very important.

"Shit!" he said and picked up his phone. He tried to unlock it, but then remembered that it shut off.

He frantically ran out of the room and made a right turn. He didn't quite know what he was going to do or where he was going, but still he continued to jog.

As he jogged past the nurse's station one of them said in a calm voice, "Sir, running is not permitted in this hospital. Please walk, and be careful as the floors may be wet and slippery."

Cameron didn't hear a word she said. His heart hammered against his ribs and after jogging three more minutes his heart was inside his throat. Perhaps he had a thing or two to learn from Eric's rigorous fitness routine.

He had to stop to take a break or else he would faint and most likely crack open his skull.

"Whoa there, Cowboy," a voice said from behind him.

Cameron turned around and looked at the nurse he spoke to earlier. She grinned and put her left hand on his shoulder.

"Are you okay?"

Cameron's chest heaved up and down. "Yeah," was all he could manage under his jagged breathes.

"Are you sure?"

"Yeah."

"Why are you running inside a hospital?"

"I just, uh, remembered...something very, uh, important, that's all..."

"Wow, it must be pretty important if you'd risk cracking your skull on these pristine floors."

"Yeah."

"Well, at least the wound wouldn't get infected..."

She giggled in high pitched sounds that were unnerving to the ear.

At last Cameron caught his breath again. "I just remembered that I had a date tonight."

"Oh my gosh," she said disappointedly. "You are going to break her heart."

"*His* heart," Cameron said. "I think it's too late already. He was supposed to pick me up at eight. Do you know what time it is?"

The nurse looked at her watch and said, "Yeah, it's nine o' clock."

"Shit!"

Cameron looked at the nurse and grinned shyly. "I am so sorry, that was bad language to use. It's just..."

"Oh, don't worry about that at all. 'Shit' is a pretty common word amongst us nurses. 'Oh, shit, I have to go clean that', 'Oh, shit, his artery exploded all over my uniform'."

Cameron understood that she was only trying to lighten the mood. He chuckled and said, "I guess I'll have to reschedule, won't I? He'll understand the situation, won't he?"

The nurse studied Cameron's face. She could see that sparkle of love inside his eyes. His eyes glinted with it like tiny little diamonds.

She grinned and said, "Well, if he doesn't, he's definitely a fool."

They were standing by the entrance of the hospital. Outside it looked very gloomy. The clouds intertwined with one another, creating dark purple waves. Even though the entrance sliding door was closed, they could still hear the blustering wind; every now and then plastic bags swirled past.

"Hey," the nurse said. "Do you want to go get a cup coffee?"

"Yeah," he said and grinned. "Are nurses even allowed to drink coffee?"

It looked as if though he might have actually hurt her feelings by what he said.

"Of course we are allowed to drink coffee, silly. What do you think fuels our bodies?"

Both of them broke out in laughter, but Cameron's laughter wasn't sincere.

She hooked her left arm into his right arm and guided him to the cafeteria that was situated on the bottom floor.

Cameron was annoyed with himself. He looked forward to going on his very first date. He cussed himself out several times inside his head.

How the heck could I have been so darned stupid to forget about our date? He thought to himself. *I can sometimes be such an amnesiac!*

The nurse somehow sensed it, because she said, "It'll be okay, you know. I'm sure he'll understand the situation when you explain it to him."

Yeah, he thought. *That's if he ever speaks to me again.*

Cameron sighed and frowned.

Eric would understand, wouldn't he? Surely, he would understand the situation Cameron was in, wouldn't he?

CHAPTER 20

C ameron's eyes slowly opened as he heard several voices inside the room. It felt like a heavy burden to open them, because it felt as if though he hadn't even slept yet.

"Hey," Miss Williamson said. "You're up."

He looked at the two doctors and nurse that were inside the room.

He didn't even hear a word the doctor was saying, because his eyes immediately shut again. He tried his best to open them and succeeded.

As he rubbed his eyes he said, "What's going on, Mom?"

His mother looked at him and said, "I'm getting released today, Hon. Isn't that just great?"

It sounded as if though she was being very sarcastic, but she had in fact not meant it like that at all.

Cameron got up from the chair because he understood very well that if he continued to sit in the chair, that he would surely fall asleep again.

He looked at his mother and saw that she was already dressed, which he appreciated a whole lot more than she could understand. He just wanted to get out of there to go talk to Eric.

In that moment he was reminded of his so called 'transgression'. He sighed deeply and grinned even though he had to force it.

"I'm glad," he said and took his mother's hand in his. "Let's go."

He didn't even realize it, but he tugged her hand. She studied him and said, "Whoa, there Cowboy. Why are you in such a hurry?"

Cameron's eyes moved around and looked at the entire room, but not once into his mother's eyes.

"I, uh, just want to go, you know. I think I've had enough hospital visits this week to last me a lifetime."

She only grinned and put her arms around him. She squeezed as hard as she could and said, "Oh, Cameron, I'm so sorry for not being at your side like I should have been. I really..."

He looked her in the eyes. "Mom," he said softly. "I understand what happened, okay? There is no need to constantly apologize to me, okay? What matters now is that you get better and go through with the recommended treatment."

"Okay," she said and went silent. After two minutes of hugging she said, "Who is it?"

Cameron frowned. He didn't have the faintest idea what she had meant with those words. "What do you mean, Mom?"

Miss Williamson chortled and said, "Oh, Hon, I can see that sparkle in your eyes."

"What sparkle?"

When his mom spoke, she spoke in a mocking and enthusiastic way. "The sparkle of love!"

The room got quiet. For a moment his mother only looked at him. She grinned victoriously.

"Well," she said. "Let's get out of here."

It felt as if though he was safe with her, considering recent events. It was a feeling that he hadn't been used to in a long time. It felt more than a weight being lifted off his shoulders. Could things possibly go back to the way it used to?

He didn't really know how to break the romantic news to her at all...

"Let's go home. Then you can tell me all about *her*..."

Cameron appreciated the fact that he didn't have to say goodbye to anyone at the hospital. He was never one for goodbyes, because he was simply not good at them.

His mother had arranged for Ira to pick them up. Even though her healing journey had yet to commence, Miss Williamson was acting much more like herself.

Ira was waiting patiently by her car, leaning against the side.

"It's about time, Cam," Ira said as they approached her. "Did you remember to book your next visit? Have they named a wing after you yet?"

Cameron grinned and shot her the finger.

"Hey, Auntie," Ira said to Miss Williamson. "I'm glad to see that you are well."

The three of them got into the car. Ira got into the driver's seat. Miss Williamson sat in the passenger seat and Cameron in back.

Cameron wasn't very fond of the smell inside the car. It smelled like someone had thrown up in there. The faint smell of Vodka hung around the air too.

"So, Cam," Ira said in her mocking, yet adorable, voice. "Eric was at the house last night..."

Cameron's eyes nearly bulged out of his skull. He glared into the mirror and shook his head a couple of times. The way he was glaring at her in the mirror, she was sure that there would be a hole in her head.

In a way she understood exactly what he was ordering her to do, so she shut her trap. She looked into the mirror with eyes that said she's sorry.

"So, who's Eric?" Miss Williamson asked.

Cameron didn't really want to tell her yet. He was terrified to tell her about Eric. He didn't know whether she would accept him. He had just gotten his mother back. He was petrified that any new information would make her spiral into old habits again.

"Oh," Ira said. "He's a close friend, that's all."

"That's nice."

"Yeah," Ira said. "He is, isn't he, Cam?"

Sometimes Cameron swore that he would strangle the life out Ira. She really needed to learn when to keep her darned mouth shut.

Cameron cleared his throat. He knew very well that he was going to have to tell her sooner or the later. *Later*, he guessed would be best.

Ira parked the car in the driveway.

Home at last all of them were thinking at the same time. They got out and walked into the house.

It took Cameron four hours to build up enough courage to speak to his mother.

When he entered the living room she was sitting on the couch, enjoying a cup of tea and some biscuits.

He sat down next to her in a slow and soft manner, almost as if though she was made out of fragile glass that could tip over and shatter at any moment.

Cameron started tearing the skin off of his left thumb with his index finger. It was one of his anxiety tell-tales.

"Mom," he said softly, almost inaudible. "There's something I need to tell you."

She studied his face. She could see the anxiety in his eyes. His face was as pale as a statue's, maybe even paler. He didn't even look her directly in the eye.

Miss Williamson could sense something was wrong with Cameron. She understood very well that this was going to be an awkward conversation, so she put her teacup on the coffee table.

"What is it, Cameron?"

Cameron cleared his throat and swallowed, but there was absolutely nothing to lubricate his throat.

"You were right, Mom. There is someone special in my life."

His mother's right hand covered her mouth as she said, "Oh, I'm so glad that you finally met a girl that you like."

Cameron shook his head. "Uh, yeah, Mom; that's the thing..." He had to clear his throat again before speaking. It became all the more difficult for his mouth to form the words. His palms were sweaty; a thin stream of blood ran down his thumb from picking at the skin.

"What is it, Cam?"

"I met *him* a while ago."

His mother nodded her head as if though she understood exactly what was going on. She sensed that the longer she kept quiet, the more awkward it would be.

"I see."

"Mom, are you okay?"

"Do you like him?"

"Yes."

"Do you *love* him?"

Cameron didn't even hesitate. "Yes."

It was the first time that Cameron openly admitted that he had feelings for Eric. Was it too soon? Love came burning bright, and it hit him in the face so quickly that he didn't even see it coming.

"I see."

Cameron studied his mother's face. It didn't look like she was astounded as much as he thought she might be.

"Mom?"

"I am very glad to you met someone, Cam. When can I meet him?"

"You want to meet him?"

"Of course I do, Cam," she said and grinned. "I want to meet the guy that stole my boy's heart."

"And you're okay with it?"

"Oh, Hon..."

"I mean, isn't it like against everything you believe in?"

The moment the words left his lips he wished to God that he didn't say them, but it was too little too late. His mother was silent. Had he triggered her again?

Finally, she said, "God created Adam and Eve, not Adam and Steve."

Cameron's eyes filled with tears; they stung his eyes terribly. He rubbed his eyes. In that moment he knew that everything was about to change again, and he wasn't sure whether he would be able to adapt this time.

"But."

A silver lining, perhaps?

"God gave *you* to *me*, Cameron. You are my son, and I will always love you, no matter what, okay?"

"Okay."

"Mom?"

"Yes?"

"There's more I need to tell you..."

"I'm listening."

"I think I'm gay, I am not even sure yet. I am still figuring things out."

"I know."

Those two words were enough to send his arms into a state of gooseflesh, which he didn't like this time at all.

"What do you mean, Mom?"

His mother grinned, revealing teeth. It was the first time in a very long time that he saw her smiling, but he didn't mind at all. It made her look youthful.

"Do you remember when your father had *the talk* with you when you were going to high school?"

Cameron frowned and said, "Yes, I do."

"That was the day you asked your father what it meant if you liked boys just as much as girls. He told you everything he could."

"How do you know this, Mom?"

His mother grinned, which turned into high pitched chuckles. "You made your father promise not to tell me, but he told me that same day."

"What?"

"Yeah, he made me promise not to tell you that he told me."

Cameron had mixed feelings. He didn't know whether to be furious at his father for telling on him, or whether he should be thankful that he had told her.

"I promised him that I wouldn't say anything. I was planning on talking to you about it, but a while later I had the miscarriage, and everything changed."

There was a minute's worth of awkward silence between them, but it was broken by Miss Williamson.

"I love you, Cameron Williamson. Always remember that, okay?"

"Okay, Mom, I love you too."

"So," she said. "When can I meet him, Eric I mean?"

"How did you know his name?"

"I'm old, Cam, not stupid."

"I, uh, don't know, Mom. I need to sort something out with him first."

Miss Williamson put her arms around him and hugged him fiercely. He put his head on her chest and nearly wept.

All those years he was petrified to tell her about his sexuality, but she had known all along. Heck, he didn't even know his own sexuality, and he was figuring it out as he went along, it was all a new experience to him, and it scared the shit of him.

"Mom?"

"Yes?"

"I missed you."

"I missed you too, Cam."

Both of them were only seconds away from weeping, but luckily Ira came to a rescue.

"Hey, Cam," she said as she entered the living room. "I am going to go watch some football practice. Do you want to come with me?"

Cameron shook his head. "No thanks, Ira. You know I'm not really into sports, so..."

"Yeah, I know, Cam, but maybe you can tag along and resolve your eight o' clock problem..."

Cameron's eyes widened. He was so caught up in the moment, *this perfect* moment that he had forgotten all about his problem.

"Yeah," he said and got up from the couch. "I think I'll join you, Ira."

"Great. Get your ass in gear then, okay?"

Cameron looked at his mother and kissed her on the cheek. "I'll see you later, Mom."

Ira and Cameron left through the front door.

The air outside was chillier than it had been when they arrived home. The sun was hidden behind light purple clouds.

Ira got into the driver's seat and Cameron into the passenger seat.

"So," Ira said as she started the ignition. "What's up with you and Eric?"

Cameron cleared his throat. "I don't know what's up with us, Ira, especially not after last night, okay?"

"Okay."

In no more than thirty seconds they were on their merry way to wherever the heck Ira was taking them.

Just before Ira turned the ignition off, the radio played 'Girlfriend by Avril Lavigne', which was very ironic.

"What are you looking at, Cam?"

Cameron didn't even realize that he was staring at Ira with a grin on his face.

He thought he understood why she loved that song so much. Maybe that song referred to that *special someone* that was on Ira's heart.

"Uh, nothing," he said at last.

"Whatever you say, Cam."

They got out of the car and slammed the doors shut. Cameron's heart skipped a beat when Ira's car alarm beeped.

It was humorous in a way, because the tiniest of things made him jump. It was probably the most anxious he had ever felt in his life before. His heart was throbbing in his throat.

"Just follow me," she said and hooked her arm into Cameron's; his hands were inside his jeans' pockets, which made it much easier for Ira's arms to hook into his.

"Have you thought of what you're going to say to him?"

It was one of those questions that usually popped up in exams that you didn't know the answer to, so he guessed that he was going to have to wing it. There truly was no handbook to guide love, but he wished that there was, since he would be able to ace it.

"Yeah," he said even though he knew he was lying through his teeth.

As they walked through the quiet hallways of the school, Cameron's mid raced a hundred miles per hour.

They made so many turns through the hallway that Cameron felt sick to his stomach, but he knew that that wasn't the real reason for it.

If there was one thing that was true, it was that he would surely not be able to get out of this school without Ira by his side.

Five minutes later they were walking on shocking green grass, which at first was displeasing to the eyes; the combination of freshly cut grass and breezy air would flare up anyone's allergies.

They were on the field where about eight guys were practicing football. Four of them were shirtless, which made the scene even more picturesque.

Cameron spotted Eric amongst the four topless guys. He also didn't wear a shirt.

He waved at Eric four times which didn't seem to capture Eric's attention at all. Eric just stared at him as if though he was translucent.

If it weren't for his one team nudging him and pointing to Cameron, Eric wouldn't even have gone over to where Cameron was standing.

Eric started sprinting over to Cameron. It looked like something out of a very steamy movie. Muscle heaved up and down.

Two minutes later Eric was standing in front of Cameron, looking sweaty.

Eric's short black hair was wet with sweat, which made his black hair shine with utter beauty.

Sweat dripped from his chin and covered his entire torso.

When Eric raised his arms to run his hand through his hair, a tiny bush of black armpit hair could be seen, which made Cameron breathe a little faster.

"Eric," he said wryly.

"Cameron," Eric said. "What are you doing here?"

Cameron and Eric both frowned. Eric put his hands on his hips, which he seemed to think made him look fierce, but to Cameron he only looked superb.

Finally, Eric spoke again. "What are you doing here?"

"What do you mean, Eric? I came here to see you."

Eric chuckled. "You came here to see me, is that right?"

"Yes, I did, Eric."

"Where the hell were you last night? I mean, I said I'll pick you up at eight. I was there last night. I waited for an hour, Cameron, but you weren't there."

"Eric," Cameron said and walked closer to Eric until they faced each other. "I'm so sorry about last night, really. Just give me a chance to explain, would you?"

"No," Eric said. "I want you to answer me something, Cameron. I mean, after last night I think you owe it to me."

Cameron nodded his head. "What is it, Eric?"

"The other night when we slept together and talked, did it mean anything to you or was I just a hot one-night stand?"

"Eric! How could you say that? You know that's not true!"

"I thought it was perfect, Cameron. It obviously meant a lot more to me than it did to you. You know what, Cameron?"

Cameron sighed deeply and said, "Just let me explain, would you?"

"No. I wish for a better reality, because the dream was already perfect."

"Just let me explain..."

"You know what, Cameron, just go. If you haven't figured out what you wanted by now, you never will. I have to go."

Without saying another word Eric turned around and jogged back to his jock friends. His perfectly muscled butt bulged beneath his black shorts.

Cameron stared at Eric as he ran off, which made his entire body yearn for Eric's touch.

"Damn," Tamara said. "That was harsh of him."

Cameron turned around to face Tamara. "Hey," he said astounded. "What are you doing here, Tamara?"

"Oh, I, uh, was in the neighbourhood and saw you coming in. I thought I'd come say hi, you know, and check in on you."

Cameron grinned, but Tamara wasn't fooled by it. "How are you, Cam?"

Cameron scoffed and closed his eyes. "I've been a lot better, Tamara. Thanks for asking."

Cameron's cell phone vibrated in his jeans' pocket. He removed his cell phone and read the message.

It was from Ira, ordering him to go to the car after meeting with Eric. He didn't even realize that she was no longer there.

"I, uh, have to go, Tamara. Stop by Ira's later, would you?"

Tamara grinned and said, "Of course."

Tamara watched as Cameron started walking away. In no more than five minutes he had disappeared into the school building.

She turned her head the opposite direction and watched as Eric was tossing a football back and forth.

Oh, this is so not over she thought. She jogged over to where Eric and his jock friends were practicing.

Once she neared them, Eric said, "Hey, Tamara, how are you?"

"Listen up, you sad son of a bitch," she said whilst she was walking closer to him.

That immediately got his attention.

"You should have at least let Cameron explain himself, Eric. I mean, for God's sake, his mom was in the hospital. I'm sorry that you feel like your bruised ego is a big deal, but you really have to think about someone else before yourself."

Eric was left to stare at Tamara as she started walking away with that attitude he had become accustomed to.

CHAPTER 21

E ven though he always made fun of people that sat around feeling sorry for themself, he was doing exactly that. He was sulking too. He couldn't help but laugh at himself.

Cameron sat on his bed. The duvet cover beneath him was crumpled up into an absolute mess.

He didn't feel like doing anything at all. He was just sitting, staring at his cell phone, hoping that it would ring...Hoping that it would be Eric calling him.

Ira knocked on the door and without being invited inside, she walked in; it was her house after all.

She plonked herself down onto the bed and stared at Cameron. He didn't speak to her at all.

"Hey, Cam," she said softly. "How are you doing?"

Cameron chuckled and said, "I've been better, but I've also been a lot worse, so I can't really complain."

Ira nodded her head as if though she knew exactly what he was going through. In fact, she had known very well how he felt, because she was going through a similar situation.

"Can I tell you something, Cam?"

At last, she got his intention. He studied her face intently and sat up straight. Ira crawled all the way up to him and leaned against the headboard. She looked him in the eyes.

"Yeah, Ira, you can tell me anything."

"And you promise that you won't tell anyone?"

"I promise I won't tell a soul, Ira."

"I love her..."

Even though Cameron thought he knew exactly who she was referring to, he said, "Who is it?"

Ira punched him on the shoulder in a playful manner. "I'm sure you know exactly who I am talking about."

"It's Tamara, isn't it?"

Cameron sensed that if he didn't speak again soon that the conversation would go to a dead end.

"You really love her a lot, don't you?"

Ira sighed deeply and frowned. "Have you ever done something and wished every day that you could turn back time and undo it?"

When he spoke, he said it a little too sharply. "Yes."

"I really screwed up, Cam. I mean, I screwed up big time. I wish to God that I didn't, but yeah, it's too late now for any regrets."

"If you don't mind me asking, Ira, what happened between you two?"

Ira sighed and went silent for two minutes before she spoke again. When she spoke, her voice was strong and didn't sound weak at all.

"We were together a long time ago, Cam. I mean, we were more than that. We were in love, but I screwed up. Her little brother..."

"Wait," he interrupted. "Is it the same one that drowned by that spot down at the waterfall?"

"Yes," she said and felt as tears stung her eyes terribly. "In a way it was our fault that he died."

"What do you mean?"

"We were supposed to watch him, but he was sleeping, so we snuck out of the Jeep to make out. When we returned, he was gone. He had veered off by himself and must have fallen into the waterfall by accident. They found him later that day."

Cameron put his right arm around Ira's trembling body. In a way he could feel that she was reassured because she didn't tremble anymore.

"But it was an accident, Ira. You can't blame yourself and neither can she, okay?"

"Yeah," she said. "You're right, Cam, but that's not why we parted."

"Then what did happen?"

Ira had to close her eyes because she was seconds away from weeping her make-up off.

"I wasn't exactly out, you see. I didn't want to be seen with her in public, because it would have screwed up my reputation."

"Oh, no, Ira, you didn't..."

"What, Cam?"

"You didn't go to the funeral, did you?"

"No..."

"Ira!"

It was too late for her, because she had to defend herself. Her eyes shot open, and tears spurted from her eyes. The black eyeliner started dripping down her eyes down to her cheek bones.

"I wasn't ready for all of that, Cam. You of all people have to understand that. I mean, you are queer too. Cameron, I am not strong like you. It's different for me..."

"It's not different at all, Ira. So what if you are a lesbian? I mean, look at all the great people out there that are. There comes a time for you to own up to who you are. You can't continue to deny it, because you are only trying to fool yourself."

"It's like I said, Cam, there is not a day that goes by that I don't think about her. I love her more than I love myself."

Cameron nodded his head. He knew how that felt, loving someone else more than yourself. That was how he felt about Eric, or *did*, whatever.

Ira put her head on Cameron's chest and tried her best to stop crying.

When Cameron caressed her hair, she started to calm down a little.

"Why don't you just tell her that you screwed up big time and that you still love her?"

"Cam, it's different for me. I'm not as strong willed as you. If I tell people who and what I am I will never be the same again."

"Maybe that's exactly what you need to show her."

Ira looked at Cameron's face and frowned. "What do you mean?"

"Maybe if you show her that she is much more important to you than some stupid popular title at school, which, by the way, is also ending soon, she'll see that you love her and that nothing else matters but her."

"I can't," she said and rolled her head on his chest. "I can't give up my reputation and status."

Cameron nodded his head. Sometimes she could be so darned stubborn.

"Am I being a stupid bitch?"

Cameron didn't hesitate one moment. "Yes!"

She punched him in the stomach in a playful manner.

"That was so mean, Cam," she said in a mocking way. "You're supposed to be helping me through my rough patch, not criticising me all the way."

"What am I if not a critic?"

"A super intelligent queer young adult that anyone would be lucky to have in their lives."

Cameron chuckled anxiously and said, "Yeah, no, I wouldn't go that far, Ira, but thanks anyway."

"Why? I mean, it's true..."

There was a moment's worth of silence between the two of them before Ira broke it.

"You really think she'll see me in a different light if I did all that?"

Cameron couldn't help but feel relieved. Ira was finally being open minded and entertained the idea that perhaps she was wrong. He grinned victoriously.

"I think so."

"Yeah?"

"If she doesn't, she'll miss out on something great, Ira."

"Thanks."

It was at that exact moment that Miss Williamson walked into the room.

Is it a goddamn reunion or something? Cameron thought.

Ira got up as fast as she could and tried to hide her smudged and tear-streaked face, but she didn't succeed.

"You okay, Ira?" Miss Williamson asked as Ira went by her.

"Yes," she said and grinned. Cameron could tell that it was genuine by the way the corners of her lips moved slightly to the sides. "I have actually never been better, Auntie."

Without saying another word, she left the room. Miss Williamson walked over to the bed and sat down, neatly folding her dress behind her legs.

"So," she said. "When will I be meeting that boy?"

Cameron sighed deeply and said, "You won't be meeting him any time soon, Mom."

Miss Williamson frowned and put her right hand on Cameron's slouched shoulder.

"And why is that?"

"We kind of broke up today. Well, we weren't like exclusive or anything, or even dating, but it came down to that anyway."

"Oh, Cam," she said in that soothing motherly tone that he hadn't heard in a long time. "I'm so sorry to hear that. Just remember one thing, okay?"

Even though he didn't want to admit it at all, she was actually doing a pretty great job at making him smile again. A mother's wisdom was undeniable and unmatched.

"What would that be, Mom?"

She chuckled and said, "There's plenty of fish in the sea. Someday you'll find that fish and treasure it and maybe even hang it up on your wall as a trophy."

Even though it didn't come out the way she had meant it to, he fully understood what she had meant. He grinned.

"Thanks, Mom," he said.

"Well, I'm off to go to my new group therapy tonight, okay? So just be safe."

"Of course, Mom."

"And maybe we'll pack our bags and go home tomorrow, if you'd like that."

It was one of the best and worst summer breaks that he had experienced in his entire life. One part of his heart wanted him to stay in the hope of rekindling his 'relationship' with Eric. The other half of his heart ached and screamed at him to go home. Through all the craziness and emotional turmoil, he had gotten his *mother* back, and that was a blessing in itself.

"I guess I'll see you later then, Cam."

"Yes, Mom."

Both of them got off the bed. They hugged each other fiercely as if though it was going to be their last hug before the end of the world.

Cameron plonked down onto his bed again as Miss Williamson walked out of the room.

She stopped in the middle of the doorway and said, "Oh, cam, before I forget. There's someone downstairs for you. He said he needed to talk to you."

Cameron's eyes immediately shot up and looked intently at his mother. Without saying another word, she left. Her high heels clicked all the way down the stairs.

In that moment it hit him like a wave of saltwater at the sea: what if it was Eric waiting downstairs?

He gathered himself and looked at himself in the mirror of his cell phone. He wished he had time to get ready, to look perfect, but he didn't look that bad.

He exited his room and ran down the stairs like the Flash, wound up by the fact that his prince, a gay stud, was waiting for him.

Cameron was downstairs within two minutes. He ran into the living room and stopped dead in his tracks. His eyes were all over the place, searching for *his* Prince Charming.

"Hey," a voice from behind him said.

Cameron's heart must have skipped at least three beats as he suddenly jumped around.

When he looked intently at the person in front of him, a wave of disillusionment shot through his body and left him colder than ice.

"Jaleel?"

"Hey, Cameron," Jaleel said and grinned. His brown skin shined in the light of the living room. "Can we talk?"

It took Cameron's mind a couple of seconds to process the words. Meanwhile Jaleel looked at him as if though he was crazy.

"I, uh," Cameron said and shook his head. "Yeah, let's sit down. What do you want to talk about?"

The two of them sat on the same couch. Jaleel sat on the end and Cameron at the other end, leaving one space between the two of them.

"Amy broke up with me, Cameron..."

Cameron's eyes widened. The real reason for Jaleel's sudden and unexpected visit became all the clearer: he was there to beat the living shit out of Cameron.

"Oh, I, uh, that's not nice to hear."

"Yeah, it isn't, is it?"

"Look, I'm so sorry if I had anything to do with it, okay?"

Jaleel chuckled and grinned. Even though Cameron wasn't into Jaleel, that smile could make anyone fall in love with Jaleel.

"Why are you sorry, Cameron?"

"Nothing, I, uh, just..."

"I want to thank you, Cameron..."

Cameron wasn't always good at identifying whether someone was being sarcastic or not, so he frowned and said, "Oh? Why?"

"It's the best thing that ever happened to me. She told me everything you told her. I had an epiphany. I too deserve someone I love."

Cameron sensed that everything was going to be okay between them, so he grinned. "I am glad for you, Jaleel."

"We decided to still be friends and everything. You inspired me so much that I posted a picture of my boyfriend and I on Facebook. I haven't felt so exposed in my entire life, but I am enjoying every moment of this. I am finally able to be my authentic self, and there is nothing as braver than that."

"I am glad to hear that."

Cameron didn't really have the faintest idea what to say. In a way he felt green with envy, because everyone was getting their happy endings, except for him.

"Cameron, there are no words to explain how grateful I am."

"You have no need to find any," Cameron said. "I was just being a good friend."

Jaleel looked at his watch and said, "Oh, would you look at the time. I have to go now, because I am going on a beach party midnight date with my boyfriend."

Cameron grinned. "I guess I'll see you around then."

Jaleel chuckled and clutched his stomach. "I am never going to get used to saying that. Bye, Cameron."

Cameron got up from the couch and led him to the front door. Jaleel gave him a shy hug and disappeared into the night.

He turned around and kicked the door with his right foot. The door started closing at high speed.

The sound of something hitting the door made Cameron's arm hair rise up and stay upright. He turned around as swiftly as he could as to not lose his balance.

"Can I come in, or are you going to let me freeze out here?"

When Cameron spoke, he could almost not hear himself. He cleared his throat. He knew exactly who that voice belonged to. "Eric, what are you doing here?"

Eric's black hair was neatly combed. He wore a leather jacket and beneath it a red t-shirt. His black jeans and white sneakers completed the 'Stud Eric' look.

"It's freezing outside," Eric said. "Mind if I come in?"

YES! Cameron's mind screamed.

Before he could think he said, "Yeah, come on in."

Eric went into the house. Cameron closed the door and got right to the point.

"What are you doing here, Eric?"

Eric chuckled. "Jeez, what's with the third degree, officer?"

"I thought we were done..."

Eric's smile disappeared. "I thought I'd give you a chance to explain why you weren't here the other night, that's all."

"Why the sudden change of heart?"

"Why not?"

"Look, I'm sorry about the other night. I wanted to call you, Eric, but my phone's battery was dead."

"I saw the videos."

"What do you mean?"

"I saw the videos of you and your mother outside the Coffee Co., Cameron. I'm sorry that I didn't give you a chance to tell me what happened. I really am."

Cameron couldn't help but let go of his anger. All he could think of were Eric's perfectly soft pink lips.

Cameron walked closer to Eric and got a hold of his black hair. He pulled him towards him and landed the kiss on Eric's lips.

Eric kissed back with tongue and said, "I've been looking forward to that."

Cameron looked stunned. "You have?"

"Yeah," Eric said astounded. "What's the point of having a boyfriend if you can't do this," he said and kissed Cameron again.

Boyfriend? The word replayed around in Cameron's mind, like a record, over and over again. His heart hammered against his chest, but not because of anxiety. It was a warmth he had never experienced before.

"Want some coffee?"

Cameron didn't know where the hell that came from, because he was frazzled at Eric calling him his boyfriend.

"Uh, yeah," he said and kissed Cameron again. "That'd be great."

They walked hand in hand, side by side, into the kitchen. As they entered the kitchen, they kissed again.

A light bulb above their heads suddenly popped, scaring the heck out of them.

"So?" Eric said.

"So what?"

"Do you have any news to tell me?"

"I, uh," Cameron said. He couldn't really think of one thing to tell. Then it suddenly came to him. "I have been accepted to Harvard next year."

Eric's left hand covered his mouth in astonishment. "Oh my God, Cameron, that's excellent news! Congratulations, *my* young Einstein."

Cameron grinned shyly and said, "It's not that big a deal. I'm not going anyway..."

Eric's blue eyes nearly popped out of his skull. He frowned, but something about this frown wasn't appealing at all. "Why?"

Cameron grinned, revealing teeth. "I've got to stay here so that I can be with you."

Even though Cameron was one smart cookie, he didn't know anything about life or love. Perhaps he was only book smart.

"What?" Eric said.

"I love you, Eric. I want t stay here with you. If it means that I have to give up going to Harvard, then so be it."

Cameron expected, *wanted* Eric to say it back, but Eric's face suddenly became pale. Veins bulged on his forehead.

"I love you, Eric," he repeated.

Eric looked down at his hands and felt his heart ripping into two pieces and then four, eight, sixteen, until his heart was crumbled into dust.

Cameron could feel the tears stinging his eyes. He started cussing at himself for saying the 'L' word first. He wished that he hadn't said it in the first place.

It became obvious that Eric didn't feel the same way at all.

Eric shook his head and said, "I have to go. I, uh, just...I have to go, I'm sorry Cameron."

"Eric? What's going on? Are you okay? Are *we* okay?"

The first tear rolled down Cameron's left cheek and collected underneath his smooth chin.

Without saying another word, Eric started walking out of the kitchen, through the hallway and stopped at the front door.

He put his hand on the handle and turned his head to look at Cameron.

"I think it's best if we don't see each other anymore. I am so sorry. I can't do *this*, Cameron. I'm so sorry."

Without saying another word, he left though the front door and closed it.

Cameron stared at the door in utter disbelief and felt as more tears ran down his face. He tried his best to put an end to it, but he wasn't successful.

Where one door closes, another one opens, but another one also closes again...This wasn't a door he wanted to shut, but the choice wasn't his.

Chapter 22:

By the time Ira switched off the ignition it was completely dark out.

Ira took the last drag from her cigarette and shot it out of the window with her middle finger and thumb.

It was now or never. When she worked up enough courage to actually get out of the car, she did. She got out and slammed the door shut.

She was afraid that if she waited any longer that she wouldn't be brave enough to go through with it.

As she walked along the stone path to the front door she almost tripped twice because of her high heels. By the third time she impatiently pulled them off and continued to the front door.

As far she could see in the night nothing about the house changed. She looked at the house with new and wary eyes.

Once she stood in front of the front door she pushed the button. She could hear the sound of the ring camera inside.

Not a minute later the door swung open. Tamara stood there with her arms crossed over her chest to keep from getting cold.

"It's freezing," Tamara said. "Come on in."

Reluctantly Ira went into the house. She watched as Tamara closed the front door.

There goes my chance of not going through with this, she thought.

"Ira?" Tamara asked. "You look very pale. Do you want a cup of coffee?"

Ira rubbed her arms all over and said, "Yeah, thanks. That would be great. It's freezing outside."

Ira didn't need a written map to find the kitchen, since she had spent a lot of time there before.

Tamara opened the glass sliding door above her and removed two huge mugs. She went over to the station and waited for the kettle to boil.

She threw four sugars and two coffees into Ira's mug and three coffees into her own. She slowly poured in the boiled water and stirred.

She handed Ira the mug and folded her hands around her mug to warm them up.

For a minute neither of them spoke to each other. They were still inside the kitchen, sipping their coffee.

Then it suddenly came. "What are you doing here, Ira?"

Ira frowned and said, "Can't an old friend come visit an old friend?"

Tamara scoffed. She was sure as hell not going to let Ira be a complete bitch, not in her own house, not ever again.

"Why are you here?"

Ira went silent for a moment. When she spoke, she spoke loud and clear. "I should have been there for you, Tammy. I should have been there for his funeral."

Tamara's face became red with anger. "Don't call me that, Ira."

Ira looked at Tamara with eyes that looked like a puppy's. In them she could see sorrow and regret, but she didn't have the intention of freeing Ira from it.

"Look," Tamara said. "I think you should finish your coffee and go, please. I know we said that we'd pretend to be okay around each other for Cameron's sake, but he's not here right now."

Ira shook her head twice and said, "I didn't pretend, Tamara."

Those four words sent a wave of shock through Tamara. She clutched the mug as hard as she could to keep it from slipping out of her hands.

"What are you talking about?"

"I didn't pretend to be nice to you, Tamara. There hasn't been a day that I haven't thought of you, of *us*. I want us to go back to the way things were before, you know, everything."

Tamara snorted. "Yeah, you ruined any chances of that ever happening, Ira. You treated me like I was invisible, like I wasn't worthy of being in your presence."

Ira's eyes filled with tears. It felt to her as if though Tamara's green eyes bored holes in hers.

"I'm sorry, Tamara," she said and could no longer control herself. Tears and snot ran down her face in streams. "There are no words to describe how sorry I am."

"I think it's time for you to leave, Ira."

"Just, just let me explain. Please, just, listen to what I have to say, okay?"

Tamara put her mug down on the marble counter and sighed. "I don't really care what you have to say, okay? So, make it quick..."

"Falling for you confused the shit out of my pea brain. I didn't know what was happening to me. I was changing in all these tiny ways, and I couldn't control it at all."

Tamara's fingers ticked impatiently on the marble counter. "Time's up."

"No, just, please listen, okay?"

When Tamara picked up her mug again, she took another sip of coffee, but all she could taste was the bitterness in her heart.

"I didn't like not knowing who I was. I was so scared to come out of the closet and when your brother died, I thought you needed more help than I could give."

"What? I don't understand."

Slowly Tamara's protected heart started unwrapping itself.

"I am not a good girl, Tamara. I lie, cheat, drink and smoke. I didn't think that I was ever worthy of you..."

"How could you say that, Ira? I loved you for who you are, well, *were*. I can relate to the fact that you didn't like having an identity crisis, but we all go through it at least once in our life. It's called being human."

Ira wiped tears away with the back of her left hand. "I know it's selfish of me to say, but you and your mother may have lost a son, a brother, but I lost a close friend, a lover, *the love of my life*."

"It's not selfish at all, Ira. I lost you too, remember?"

"I was so buried beneath popularity and being normal that I never once looked back. And for that I'm sorry."

"Ira?"

"Yes?"

"I need to ask you something."

"What is it?"

"Do you still love me the way you did back then?"

Ira chuckled and nodded her head several times. "I still do, Tamara. You're the first thing I think of when I wake up and the last thing I think of before I go to sleep."

Tamara put her mug down again and walked over to where Ira was standing.

She plucked Ira's mug out of her hand and put it next to the microwave.

Ira studied her face intently.

"Me too," Tamara said. She moved closer to Ira's face. They were so close that both of them could smell coffee on each other.

"Really?"

"Yes."

Tamara leaned in and kissed Ira on the lips. Ira didn't hesitate for one moment. She kissed back. They became one organism with the primary objective to mend their broken relationship, but not with words, because there are no words to say what they felt for each other.

Neither of them seemed to mind the faint taste of coffee as their tongues entwined.

"Tamara?"

"Yes."

"I love you."

"I love you too."

They stood inside the kitchen and continued to make out. It seemed like the only right thing they could do.

Miss Williamson came in through the front door and locked it. She removed her high heels because they were a bit uncomfortable to wear considering that she hadn't worn any in years.

She walked into the living room and sighed when she saw Cameron on the couch, again in a fetal position.

It wasn't fun for her to see him so vulnerable at all. She walked closer to him and noticed that his eyes were open.

"Hey," she said in that comforting voice of hers. "Why the long face?"

Cameron scoffed. "I had my chance to get Eric back, Mom, but I blew it. I suck at this stuff."

"Why don't you tell me what happened?"

"Eric came by the house earlier. Everything was going great, but I think I scared him away when I said that I loved him."

"Oh, Hon," she said and sat down on the couch by his feet. She put her right hand on his leg. "Maybe he wasn't ready for that yet."

"I thought about what you said earlier, Mom."

"About what, Hon?"

"I think it's time for us to go *home*."

Miss Williamson grinned and said, "If that's what you want to do, Hon. I'll pack my suitcase tonight so that we can leave early. You know how I feel about the traffic."

"Okay, Mom. I packed mine already."

Miss Williamson got up and left Cameron alone.

He wanted to say goodbye to Tamara and Ira before he left. He filched his cell phone from his jeans' pocket and dialled Tamara's number.

Neither of them heard the cell phone vibrating on the nightstand.

Their breathing became all the more ragged, but they breathed as one.

Tamara kissed the nape of Ira's neck, which tickled so much that Ira giggled in high pitched sounds that were deafening to the ear.

Ira's hands were on Tamara's hips. A moment later Tamara pulled her short off and started removing Ira's.

Neither of them knew exactly what they were doing. They just went with the flow of things.

Ira pulled Tamara closer and closer until the two of them could feel and hear the faint whistling sound of their breathing.

Tamara's right hand moved down from Ira's neck until she reached her belly. Then her hand moved down a bit more until she got a hold of Ira's perfect booty.

She squeezed as hard as she could because the jeans would surely make it harder to feel it. A groan of pleasure escaped Ira's mouth.

They laughed anxiously.

He had reached Tamara's pre-recorded voice mail. "Yeah, uh, if you get this message, Tamara, I just wanted to thank you for everything. I mean, it was great meeting you and I had a great time. I hope we'll see each other soon."

He hung up the phone and put it back into his pocket. He got up from the couch and started climbing the stairs.

With each stair it felt to him as if he would plunge down at any minute, because his legs were weak.

He thought that if that was how it felt when you loved someone and they didn't love you back, he couldn't imagine how it would feel if the love of your life broke up with you.

It was his first flirtatious moment. His first crush. His first time. His first heartbreak. He wasn't very fond of it at all, and he never wanted to feel like that again.

Sometimes it took him much longer to learn things about life than others. But there comes a time in anyone's life that they learn something that didn't come out of a book.

Once he was inside his room he closed the door. He walked over to his bed and plonked down on it; the springs in the mattress croaked.

He lied down for two hours thinking about Eric: the way his nose wrinkled when he smiled; the way it made him look more adorable when he frowned; his perfectly tanned body; oh, that Greek godlike muscular body; those oceanic blue eyes that one could get lost in...

Slowly and unknowingly, he started to fall asleep with Eric on his mind, and surely he would dream about him too.

Cameron's eyes immediately shot open as his alarm blared in his ears. He filched his cell phone from his pocket and turned it off.

He lied down for another five minutes before finally getting up. When he got up, he ripped open the curtains.

It was going to be another morbid day, because the clouds were intertwined and looked almost black. A plastic bag flew past the window as the blustering wind took on full force.

"What a beautiful day," he said sarcastically.

There was a knock on the door.

"Come in, Mom."

Miss Williamson came into the room. She knew that Cameron was heartbroken and that the only reason why he wanted to get out of town was because of it.

"Hey, Hon," she said. "I made you some coffee."

She handed him the mug. He looked at her and said, "Thanks, Mom."

She cleared her throat. "I am afraid that I have got some bad news, Cam."

Cameron frowned and braced himself for God knew what. What else could go wrong?

"I am afraid that we won't be going anywhere today. The weather lady said that it isn't safe to be on the long road today."

"Yeah," he said. "I figured."

He took a sip of his coffee and looked out the window again.

"Oh, shit," Tamara said. She got a hold of her cell phone and studied the screen. "Cameron called last night. I hope he's okay."

She listened to his voice message and looked at Ira, who was still comfy and rolled up in the duvet.

She dialled his number and waited.

"Hello?" he said.

"Hey, Cameron," she said. "I'm sorry I didn't answer last night. I was, uh, a little occupied."

Ira giggled and threw a pillow at Tamara, who blocked it gracefully.

"Yeah, uh, it's okay. It's not like I am going anywhere today. The weather is not good. Looks like you're stuck with me a while longer."

"Oh, that's great, Cameron. So, I, uh, *we* were thinking of having a party at my house tonight. Tell me you'll be there..."

Cameron went silent on the other end of the line. He considered it and said, "Will there be lots of alcohol to get hammered?"

It was the first time since meeting him that she had heard him say something like. She didn't know whether to be stunned or amused by it.

"You got it!"

"Then I guess I'll see you tonight."

"Great."

"Can I stay over? I mean, I will be in no position to drive home tonight."

Tamara chuckled because the old responsible Cameron came through again. It was that one sentence that reassured her that they hadn't totally lost him *yet*.

"Yeah, of course you can, Cameron. See you tonight."

Cameron didn't know whether to ask or not, but he did anyway. "Have you seen Ira? I can't seem to find her here. I hope she didn't fall asleep somewhere."

"Uh, yeah," she said and handed Ira the phone.

Ira held it against her ear and watched Tamara walk out of the room. Tamara's perfect booty was total eye candy, especially because of the black laced panties.

"Ira?"

"Yes, Cameron, what is it?"

"What's going on?"

"I did it, Cam. I didn't think that I would be able to, but I did. I drove over here last night and explained everything. And boy, am I glad that I did."

Cameron grinned and said, "I am glad you two worked things out. Are you two, like, uh, girlfriends now?"

"Yeah," Ira said and bit her lower lip. "I think so. That's why we're having a party tonight, you know, to announce it, I guess."

"Okay," Cameron said. "I guess I'll see you girls later. Enjoy it..."

"Bye."

Ira hung up the phone and put it back on the nightstand.

Tamara came back into the room, still wearing a black bra and laced panties.

"Come back to bed," Ira nagged. "It's so cold in here. I am so lonely here, all by my lonesome."

Tamara chuckled. "I can't, Ira. I have stuff to do for tonight's party, you know. It's not going to organise itself and the guests won't smell a party."

"Yeah? How sure are you about that? I mean, I am going to have the wildest party yet. Oh, I have an idea for a theme."

Tamara frowned and said, "And that would be?"

"We can like, uh, have a pool party? We can turn the heating on for the pool, could be fun, *sexy* even."

Tamara nodded her head. "Yeah, and no one is allowed to come to the party with anything other than swimwear."

Tamara walked to the bed and bent over. She kissed Ira on the lips and said, "You're a sexy genius, you know."

"Yeah, I do."

"Get your lazy ass out of bed and come help me set up the party, why don't you?"

Ira sighed deeply and threw the duvet cover over her head. "NO! I want to sleep some more. Why don't you join me?"

Tamara knew Ira was being playful, but only to an extent. She got a hold of the duvet cover and pulled it back as fast as she could.

"NO! NO! NO!" Ira screeched, but she was grinning.

Her bare arms and legs were in a state of gooseflesh as the cold air rushed over her scorching skin.

"Do I really have to help you, Tammy? I mean, why don't you just hire someone to come and take care of the party?"

Tamara shrugged and said, "This is no ordinary party, Ira."

Ira took another pillow and threw it at Tamara. This time she didn't block it fast enough.

Ira cackled. "I got you! I got you!"

Sometimes Ira could be so immature, but seeing her like that made Tamara's heart fill up with even more love.

"I got you! What are you going to do about it?"

"This," Tamara said and picked up the pillow. She ran across the room and hit Ira eleven times with the pillow.

"HELP! HELP! I AM BEING ATTACKED!" Ira screeched.

She got a hold of the pillow and pulled it as hard as she could. She pulled Tamara back onto the bed.

They looked into one another's eyes and grinned.

Ira said, "What's so important about this party anyway? I mean, I have been to hundreds in my time."

Tamara looked intently at Ira. "It's going to be our first party being *together*, that's all."

CHAPTER 22

Tamara's chest heaved up and down as she ran from the kitchen to the pool and from the pool back to the kitchen.

"We are all set," Tamara said as she stopped in the kitchen to catch her breath.

Ira looked at her heaving chest. There was something to it that made it look comical, like something from an animation.

"It's great, Tammy," Ira said. "But I really don't see why there should be snacks inside the kitchen and by the pool. Actually, I don't see why we need to put out snacks at all."

Tamara scoffed. "You are a regular party goer, and you don't know the key to having a great party, do you?"

Ira shook her head. "No, not at all, but I have this growing feeling that you are going to tell me anyway."

"Yes," Tamara said. "It's like a rule to having a great time at parties, not that I would really know. You have to keep your body fuelled with nutrients when you have a heavy drinking night. It helps to keep you sober for a while longer."

Ira's hands shot up to her face so suddenly that she slapped herself. Tamara almost ripped in half with laughter.

"That's why I get as drunk as a skunk without drinking a lot. But hey, if I wanted to hear nerdy facts about parties, I would have asked Cameron."

Tamara was very anxious, because it was 6:39 pm and no one showed up for the party. She specifically said 6:00 pm sharp.

Tamara frowned and bit her lower lip. "Do you think people will actually come? I mean, they should have been here by now..."

Ira chuckled and said, "Oh, Tammy, you don't know how parties work at all, do you? The key is to never be on time, because it makes you look so, uh, overzealous and desperate."

"Wow, that's a big word you used right there."

"Hey now! There's no need to be mean, okay? I was just saying. People will arrive any time now."

"Yeah, you're probably right. I'm going to go check on Cameron."

"Wait for me."

Ira took Tamara's left hand in hers and started walking in front, pulling Tamara behind her like a little dog.

Finally, Tamara caught up and walked side by side with Ira.

The atmosphere outside was very party like. Streamers and balloons were strewn all over the place. In the background Taylor Swift went on and on about a Blank Space.

"Hey," Tamara said as she approached the swimming pool.

Cameron sat by the side of the pool with his feet in the water. He rolled up his jeans so that they wouldn't get wet.

"Hey," Cameron said softly.

He couldn't help but smile, because he really was ecstatic that they worked out their troubles.

"So," Cameron said. "I have a question."

"Yeah?" asked Ira.

"Are you two like together now? I mean, like girlfriends."

Neither of them hesitated one moment. Simultaneously they both said, "Yes!"

They looked at each other with those puppy eyes of love and kissed once. The sight was super revolting for Cameron. Perhaps it was because he was green-eyed towards their newfound relationship, or perhaps he desired to be close to someone with black hair. Eric.

"I am going back into the house," Ira said. "I was specifically ordered by me Queen to open the door for our guests."

Ira rolled her eyes and bowed as if though she were in the presence of royalty. Tamara sighed and shook her head.

Tamara sat down next to Cameron and grinned. She didn't put her feet into the water because she didn't want her red heels to get wet.

"Cameron?"

"Yes?"

"You love him, don't you?"

"Who are you talking about?"

Tamara clicked her tongue and sighed. "Oh, come on, Cam. You and I both know you are in love with Eric. What happened?"

"It was my fault," Cameron said as he looked at the crystal-clear water. "I think I scared him off when I said I loved him."

When Tamara spoke, she spoke in a soft manner, almost inaudibly. 'I have to tell you something. I hope you don't mind, Cam."

"What is it?" he asked without looking at her.

"Ira, uh, had to go to the front door to let Eric in."

She had his attention. He looked at her green eyes, dumbfounded at what she said.

"What? Why?"

"Well, I had a little talk with him. Let's face it, Cam, you are miserable."

Cameron didn't know what to say. Somewhere in the back of his mind he bawled at her for doing it, but...Somewhere in his heart he thanked her.

"Speaking of which," she said as she got up. "Some of my other guests have arrived."

Just before she was out of reach, he grabbed her hand. She turned around and faced him.

"Thank you," he said.

"You're very welcome."

Without saying another word, she left. He returned his focus to the crystal-clear water.

Somewhere behind him footsteps approached him. A shadow befell him from behind him. He turned his head and looked up at Eric, who looked even more striking than usual.

"Can I sit down?" Eric asked cautiously.

Cameron snorted and said, "It's a free country."

Eric sighed and sat down next to Cameron. He had worn black shorts, which was so familiar about him, and a red T-shirt. His feet were bare; he put them into the water.

"How are you, Cam?"

"I've been better, thanks for asking. How about you?"

"I'm fine, thanks for asking."

Cameron didn't know how long he would be able to control himself. It lasted and entire minute.

"You know what, Eric," Cameron said and turned his head to look at him. "I demand a reason for why you just left. And it better be darned good, okay?"

Eric sighed and frowned. "I don't want to talk about this, okay?"

"Well then, I am wasting my time here. No, let me rephrase that. *You* are wasting your time here. You can just go. I told you how I felt about you, and your first response was to leave and run away..." He was cut off by Eric.

"Cameron," Eric said. He put his left hand on Cameron's leg, which Cameron removed again. "I am so sorry for bailing on you like that without explaining myself."

"You have your chance to explain now. I mean, uh, did I scare you when I said I love you?"

"No, not at all, Cam."

"Then what the hell?"

"You scared me when you said that you wanted to stay here, with me, you know."

"What do you mean?"

"You said that you were going to Harvard next year, but that you weren't going to go because you wanted to be here with me."

"Are you telling me that you are afraid of commitment?"

Eric shook his head. "No, that's not what I am saying at all. You are so intelligent, and I mean, you got into Harvard."

"So you are threatened by my intelligence?"

"Just shut and let me talk, okay?"

Cameron felt a wave of cold air wash over him. He loved the way Eric took charge.

"I was afraid that I was going to hold you back from a great future that is ahead of you. I didn't want to be the one to stand between you and dreams and your future. If you went to Harvard next year you would probably meet someone terrific there. You will have a blast when you're there. I didn't want to stand between you and your epic future."

Cameron's throat was as dry as a desert. He didn't even know what to say.

"Even if it meant giving you up..."

"Eric?"

Eric looked at him with oceanic blue eyes that were filled with tears. "Yes?"

"Do you love me?"

"Yes."

Cameron's hand searched for Eric's and found it. He took it in his and squeezed it lightly.

"Do you want to be with me?"

"Yes, but..."

"No 'buts', okay?"

"Okay."

"I will make you a promise, Eric. I promise that I won't make a stupid mistake. I am going to Harvard, okay? I don't want to give up my dream of doing that, but I also don't want to give you up. Effort is a true reflection of interest. If we put in the time and effort, we will surely find a way to make it work."

"You will do that for me?"

"Of course I will, Eric. But you have to make me a promise too, okay?"

"Anything."

"Promise me that we'll see each other as much as possible, you know. That we will never be apart?"

"I promise."

"Eric?"

"Yes."

"I love you too."

Cameron kissed Eric on the lips. His entire body ached for more than just a kiss.

Eric continued to kiss Cameron, which was exactly what they needed. They had to kiss and make out, quite literally.

They made out by the pool, their tongues intertwining. Eric's hands cupped Cameron's face. Cameron's right hand went into Eric's pocket.

He removed Eric's cell phone and he pushed him with all the strength he had in his scrawny body.

Eric fell into the pool with a splash. Water gushed ferociously against the sides of the pool, making Cameron's rolled up jeans wet.

Somewhere behind them guests whooped and yelled. Dozens of guests jumped into the pool.

A minute later Eric came to the surface and looked at Cameron. He got a hold of Cameron's feet.

"Payback's a bitch, Cam," he said and started pulling him into the water.

"No!" Cameron protested. "Our phones are going to get wet."

Eric let go of his feet.

Cameron put their phones into each pocket and started unbuttoning his jeans' buttons.

"Yeah," Eric said. "Pull it off real slow and sexy."

Cameron was wearing something that he never thought he would be: a black and white jock-strap.

"Oh my God, Cam," Eric said. "Are you wearing a jockstrap?"

"Yeah," he said. "As requested."

Cameron jumped into the pool. The cold water against his already cold skin felt terrific. He came to the surface and looked at Eric.

Eric put his arms around Cameron and grinned. "You look pretty striking in that thing, you know."

"Thanks."

"Cameron?"

"Yes?"

"I'll be your Dark One if you'll be my Belle."

Cameron's mouth hung open in astonishment. He couldn't help it. To Eric, he looked like Jim Carry from the Mask.

Cameron's eyes nearly bulged out of his skull. "You watch Once Upon a Time?"

"I don't watch it, Cam, I *live* it."

They chuckled. Cameron put his head against Eric's cold chest. "Of course I'll be your Belle."

Eric kissed Cameron's forehead. They held each other like that for quite a while.

"Whoop," Ira yelled as she dived into the water. Tamara followed suit.

When both of them came to the surface, they put their arms around each other.

Tamara looked at Cameron and winked. Cameron grinned and winked back.

It all worked out for the best.

CHAPTER 23

There was something very satisfying about waking up next to Eric. He smelled faintly of sweat, but Cameron quickly became accustomed to it.

"Hey," Eric said.

"You're up?"

"Yeah, I like to look at you when you sleep. Not in a creepy way or anything. It's just, you look so peaceful when you sleep."

"We should probably get ready for church, huh."

"Yeah," Eric said and got out of bed. He quickly threw on a towel to go shower. Cameron followed him.

Whilst Eric was showering, and singing, even though he really didn't have a golden voice, Cameron stared at his reflection. It was the first time in his entire life that he accepted the person he saw staring back at him. He grinned and blew himself a kiss.

In the span of a few weeks, Cameron had grown to love himself in a way that he never thought possible. When he looked at himself in the mirror, he felt no negativity, no need to break himself down anymore. A sense of relief came to him when he realized that within imperfection was something that made everyone human. It was those imperfections that made someone unique.

In no more than an hour they were all ready for church. Cameron had arranged to meet his mother at the church.

The four of them got into Tamara's Jeep. Tamara and Ira were in the front. Cameron and Eric were in the back seat holding hands.

Tamara parked the Jeep in her allocated spot and switched off the ignition.

They got out of the Jeep and shut the doors, which nearly made their ears explode.

When they walked into church they were met by the reverend and Miss Williamson.

"Hey, Mom," Cameron said. "This is Eric."

She looked at Eric and said, "It's a pleasure to meet you, Eric."

She led the way to their seats. Eric and Cameron were in the lead and the girls trailed behind them.

The reverend walked up to his podium and commenced the ceremony.

"Welcome to church, members of the community. It is with great pleasure that I stand here before you today. Today's ceremony will be different from what you are used to. I will ask a couple of volunteers to come up and say a little something they learned since the previous week. Please be seated."

The members of the community sat down.

The reverend's eyes scanned the entire church. He pointed his finger to the first row where Cameron and his friends were seated.

"You," the reverend said. He pointed a long and bony finger at Tamara.

Tamara reluctantly stood up and went to the podium.

Ira and Cameron cheered her on. Tamara's cheeks started burning red.

"Uh, my name is Tamara Kellerman. I learned that life is a bitch, so learn how to tumble and toil with it!"

Some of the members of the community burst out laughing whilst others murmured comments to one another.

The reverend took the microphone from her and said, "Uh, thank you very much for sharing, Tamara."

His eyes continued to scan the church. Once again, his long and bony finger pointed to someone in the first row. This time it was Cameron.

He got up and went to the podium. He didn't even feel anxious at all even though all eyes were on him. Public speaking was something he had feared, in the past perhaps, but with his mother and boyfriend there, he didn't feel an ounce of anxiety.

"Good morning, members of the community," he said and was startled by his own voice, because it was deep and resonant.

Some of the members greeted him and others only stared at him.

"Sometimes when you look at yourself in the mirror, you ask yourself what you see, what you want to see, but somehow you know that you will never be able to be that person. Many questions arise in your mind about who you are, but you are unable to answer them.

This is something every teenager has to deal with, whether they want to or not. It's just one of those things, like the air we breathe, the food we eat or the people we have to deal with every day of our lives.

I learned that the road to self-acceptance is not just your average route. It's an expedition that some people take their entire lives to complete.

I have had a journey of my own and have yet to find the end of it. Every time you think you know yourself, you start to change again.

Sometimes change can be good, sometimes not. It's what you make with it that matters. Much like a moth in its cocoon, we have to go through various stages of change and evolve emotionally.

The road to self-acceptance has nothing to do with your friends, parents, family, popularity, appearance or money status. It has got to do with *you* and *only* you. It's up to you to know who and what you are. Having supportive people that are there for you can certainly make this task easier.

If you can wake up in the morning, whether you wake up next to someone or alone, and say that you like the person you see and know, you are off to a good start.

I would like to conclude with one thing: in the end everything is just one big illusion of what the heart desires the most and a never-ending battle of what the mind believes. We are all just victims of the heart's desire and the mind's belief, leaving our souls to drown in the pool of our emotions.

Thank you."

The members of the community applauded and whistled. Some of them were wiping tears away with their handkerchiefs.

Ira, Tamara, Eric and Miss Williamson gave him a standing ovation.

There was something satisfying about the way he felt. He felt secure, confident and most of all, he loved every moment of it.

The reverend took the microphone from Cameron and gave him a strong handshake.

"Have you ever thought of becoming a political speaker or motivational speaker, young man?"

Cameron shook his head. The reverend gave him a pat on the back as he walked away.

Cameron joined the rest of his little gang. Miss Williamson wiped away tears that still spurted out of her eyes.

"That was so beautiful, Cam," she said. "It was so sophisticated and heartfelt. I am so proud of you, my son."

Cameron grinned shyly and said, "Thanks, Mom."

Eric put his arms around Cameron and hugged him fiercely. Tamara and Ira joined in.

The community was still applauding him.

The road to self-acceptance will never be straight forward. It's a never-ending battle that one must fight in order to know your identity. The road to acceptance by society is a whole different ballgame...

Acknowledgements

Many thanks to my mom who has always been there for me and in many ways helped to shape this novel by giving me her feedback as she read it. Many thanks to my parents for always supporting me with everything I do, without them there would be something incredible missing from my life. Much love goes to them.

I also want to thank author Becky Albertalli, the author of Simon vs. the Homo Sapiens Agenda, who has in many ways inspired me to write this coming-of-age novel. The aforementioned novel was the first time I read a novel with a gay protagonist, and I will forever be grateful for the experience as it helped me through my very own coming out story. Rock on queen!

ABOUT THE AUTHOR

Renier Nienaber is the author of The Road to Self-Acceptance, his first coming of age novel with strong queer centered voices. He is a passionate pastry chef by day and likes to use his creativity in everything he creates. He has an incredible sweet tooth. He is father to 2 furry friends, Riley and Gemma. His obsession with Chihuahuas burns bright.